They both froze, faces inches apart. She could feel his warm breath on her skin, and her gaze was caught by his compelling gray eyes.

"What are you thinking? Right now!" he demanded.

"I wish he would kiss me!" she responded guilelessly.

An instant later, his lips were on hers. Her eyes fluttered closed as the kiss she had been dreaming of for a lifetime finally happened. They both fumbled a little, but then—then his lips aligned with hers, slanting to fit perfectly. The sensation sent warmth pooling within her, and, without thinking, she opened her lips to allow his tongue to access the warm depths of her mouth. After a moment, tentatively, she touched her tongue to his, and a flame of passion fired through her. He groaned, the sound heightening her desire further.

His hands were gentle on her face, stroking both cheeks, while his tongue danced with hers in an intimate waltz of longing. Jane lost all sense of time, or place or propriety. Robert was everything, her only reality.

Author Note

Jane's story was something of a surprise to me. I had intended this set of books to feature a trio of governesses, all seeking employment through the same agency. Instead, Jane Bailey, Marianne's maid from *The Earl's Runaway Governess*, called out for her own story.

Jane's journey is the reverse of Marianne's. Marianne was a lady who had to seek paid work for the first time in her life. Jane, on the other hand, is a maid who suddenly and unexpectedly finds herself wearing silk dresses and dining with the family. With some challenges on the way, she will of course find her way to her happy-ever-after with the gorgeous Robert.

One quick factual note: in this book I've used a piece of music by Mozart called "Ruhe sanft." Although written in 1780, it is in fact unlikely that the piece would have been well-known in England at the time of Jane and Robert's story, but it was so perfect for Jane's tale that I've included it anyway!

I do hope you enjoy *Rags-to-Riches Wife*. Next, I think I might turn my attention to Lady Cecily, who is now of age and itching for adventure.

CATHERINE TINLEY

—

Rags-to-Riches Wife

Recycling programs
for this product may
not exist in your area.

ISBN-13: 978-1-335-50530-9

Rags-to-Riches Wife

Copyright © 2020 by Catherine Tinley

This edition published by arrangement with Harlequin Books S.A.

For questions and comments about the quality of this book,
please contact us at CustomerService@Harlequin.com.

Harlequin Enterprises ULC
22 Adelaide St. West, 40th Floor
Toronto, Ontario M5H 4E3, Canada
www.Harlequin.com

Printed in U.S.A.

Catherine Tinley has loved reading and writing since childhood, and has a particular fondness for love, romance and happy endings. She lives in Ireland with her husband, children, dog and kitten, and can be reached at catherinetinley.com, as well as through Facebook and on Twitter, @catherinetinley.

Books by Catherine Tinley

Harlequin Historical

The Earl's Runaway Governess
Rags-to-Riches Wife

The Chadcombe Marriages

Waltzing with the Earl
The Captain's Disgraced Lady
The Makings of a Lady

Visit the Author Profile page
at Harlequin.com.

For my sisters,
Donna and Aisling,
with love

Prologue

'Your papa has passed away.'

'What? I do not understand.' Even as she spoke, the impact of the doctor's words swept through Jane. It was as though they were a dark cloud, seeping through her ears to contaminate every part of her. 'Passed away?'

The doctor looked pained. 'I am very sorry, little one. I tried very hard to save Mr Bailey, but the fever was too strong.'

Behind him, his assistant, a middle-aged woman, emerged from the bedchamber with a dish filled with blood. *They bled him, yet still he died?* Her own internal words sank in. *He is dead. Papa is dead.*

'Impossible!' Her voice sounded strange, as if it was not her own. 'I want Mama!'

Before the doctor could stop her she dashed forward, then stopped abruptly in the doorway. This was her parents' bedchamber—the place that had always been her haven, her refuge. When she was upset, or had a nightmare, they sometimes allowed her to share their bed. Snuggling up to Mama and Papa had always been her moment of perfect happiness—even though she had recently celebrated her eighth birthday and had a tiny chamber of her own.

Her eyes were drawn immediately to the bed. There he was, looking white and strange and still and most unlike himself. 'Papa?'

'Oh, my darling Jane!' Mama rose from a hard chair beside the bed. Her eyes were red with endless tears and lack of sleep. 'He is gone. Papa is gone.'

They held each other, crying together for an eternity. The doctor quietly closed the door.

In the days that followed Jane gradually understood that losing Papa had more implications than simply being the cause of untold grief. Without Papa's earnings as clerk to Mr Simmons—the best lawyer in Duxford—they would no longer be able to stay in Rose Cottage, their little rented home.

Jane was old enough to understand a little of how things worked.

'But Mama, where shall we live? And how shall we get money for food?'

'Hush, child. We shall manage.'

Yet Mama looked worried, as if she was not entirely sure just *how* they would manage.

Jane thought about it carefully. 'What of Papa's family? He spoke to me of my grandfather and told me they had become estranged. Could we not write to him? Perhaps—'

'Out of the question!' Mama's tone was sharp. 'Your father's family wanted nothing to do with him. That has not changed—in fact it is even less likely now Papa is gone. Your grandfather's cruelty towards my Ned was implacable. There is no way back. Do not speak of it again!'

Jane gulped. 'Yes, Mama.'

Mama's face softened. 'When I met your papa I was a servant—and a very good one. I shall find us a situation and we will both work hard so we can be comfortable.'

Without Papa? Jane thought. *I shall never be comfortable again.*

Chapter One

January 1815, Beechmount Hall, Yorkshire

Robert strode along the hallway to his uncle's library. He entered without knocking, his mind still half-lost in the ledgers he had been reviewing with the steward. The estate's finances were in good shape, so perhaps this would be a good year to build a few new cottages in the lane beside the east field…

'What kept you?'

His uncle's barking tone immediately made Robert's hackles rise. Biting back the retort that came to mind, instead he said simply, 'I was with the steward.'

'When I send for you I expect you to come immediately!'

His uncle was sitting ramrod-stiff in his armchair, the fire in his eyes contrasting sharply with the signs of his advanced age. His walking stick rested by the fireplace, just within reach, and his valet had provided plump cushions at his uncle's back. The old man's morning brandy rested on the table beside him, along with his hand bell. It was no longer easy for him to walk to the bell-pull, so his valet had come up with this solution. The valet would be working within earshot, ready to attend to his master's needs instantly.

Good.

Robert sat in the facing armchair, stretching his long legs out in front of him. 'And here I am.' Robert took a deep breath and reminded himself that nothing was achieved by arguing with his uncle.

'Pah! Do not indulge me! I am no child!'

Robert ignored this, instead asking mildly, 'Why did you send for me?'

'I have an errand for you.' His uncle picked up the sheaf of papers that had been resting in his lap. 'I have just received an interesting intelligence and I must… But no, it would not do to speak of it… The report is well written and yet I cannot be certain— No, not until I see her…'

Robert waited patiently. In recent months his elderly uncle had become increasingly introspective, without losing any of his fire and cantankerousness.

Refocusing, his uncle looked at him directly. 'Last autumn I hired a Bow Street Runner.'

Robert lifted an astonished eyebrow.

A Runner? What on earth is he up to?

'I paid him in coin, so you and that officious new steward would not find me out.' His uncle cackled with glee at his own ingenuity.

'But, Uncle, you may spend your money on anything you wish. You are master here.' He forbore to point out that the 'new' steward had been there almost ten years.

For this impertinence he received a glare. 'Your saying so is the surest proof that I am no longer any such thing!'

Robert frowned. 'Now, that is unfair. I have taken some of the burdens from your shoulders these past years only to assist you, never to undermine you.'

His uncle waved this away. 'Make no mistake, I would not wish to have them back again. What care I now about the concerns of the steward or the tenants or my fortune? My days are ending and I have other fish to fry.'

'Nonsense! Why, you will outlive us all—just to spite us!'

This earned a brief guffaw. 'Nevertheless, there are things I must do.' His eyes dropped to the papers in his lap, then back to meet Robert's gaze. 'I need you to fetch someone. A visitor.'

Robert's senses were suddenly fully awake. 'What visitor?'

'Her name is Miss Bailey—Jane Bailey—and she may be found at or near...' He consulted the report, 'Ledbury House, near the village of Netherton in Bedfordshire.'

'Bedfordshire! Wait—you wish for me to travel all the way to Bedfordshire and back again? Can't you send a servant?'

He nodded. 'That's it. And, no, it must be you.' A sly look flitted briefly across his face.

'Who is she?'

'Good question. In truth, I do not know for certain...the Bow Street Runner has hit upon her as a possibility, but I cannot be sure until I see her, assess her...'

What is he talking about?

'What can you tell me? Why did you commission a Bow Street Runner?' Robert was struggling to comprehend the situation.

Has he finally run mad?

The old man pondered for a moment, then nodded to himself. 'I can tell you I mean her no harm. As for the rest,—it is best if you do not know. You might say something to her that may complicate the situation.'

Unacceptable.

'Then I cannot go. You are not asking me to travel a few miles, to Knaresborough or Harrogate. You are asking me to go all the way to Bedfordshire and back—four or five days each way. Before I agree to such a thing I need to understand the reasons behind it.'

'You seek to bargain with me, boy? How dare you!' His ire raised, the old man's eyes flashed fire at Robert. 'You shall do this because I *order* you to!'

'Indeed?' Robert sat back, adopting a languid pose. 'It

seems to me that it will be my decision, not yours.' Just occasionally, Robert felt the need to stand up to his uncle.

His uncle half rose from his chair, his face mottled with anger. 'You—' The papers slid from his lap and dispersed onto the richly coloured carpet. His hands gripped the arms of his chair tightly, the knuckles white. Then he sank down again.

After a brief pause, Robert bent to pick up the papers. Resisting the temptation to read, his eye nevertheless caught sight of a name—Lord Kingswood. As far as he knew, there was no connection between his uncle and Lord Kingswood. His curiosity increased further.

He glanced at his uncle as he handed him back the papers. The old man looked smaller, defeated.

I should not have pushed him so far.

'Robert.' A claw-like hand gripped his. 'This is important to me. I cannot tell you why—not yet, leastways.' He swallowed. 'I am making a request. Please grant me this.'

Five days there. Five days back. In winter. Inns and a jolting carriage and endless inconvenience.

'Very well,' he heard himself say. 'I shall fetch her for you.'

Two weeks later, Ledbury House, Netherton, Bedfordshire

The day Jane's life changed began just like any other. It was one of those early February mornings that could not decide whether to wallow in winter or look forward to spring. The pale blue sky teased with the promise of sunshine, but the blustery wind argued in favour of warm shawls and smoking chimneys.

As personal maid to Marianne Ashington, Lady Kingswood, it was Jane's responsibility to anticipate her mistress's needs, and weather predicting was part of it. Miss Marianne might wish to walk in the garden today, or visit friends, or she might be content to read or embroider inside the house. Jane, therefore, needed to prepare both a fine silk day dress and a stouter wool walking gown.

Normally the Countess spent much of her time with her young son, John, and Jane's life was complicated by the impact of grubby hand marks and food spills on her mistress's fine gowns. Still, one could forgive little John almost anything, she thought, picturing the child's angelic smile.

'Good morning, my lady,' she said cheerfully, entering the Countess's room a little after nine, as usual.

She pulled back the heavy curtains, allowing the pale winter sunshine to spill into the chamber. One of the scullery maids came behind her, immediately beginning to clean out the fireplace. Jane eyed her mistress closely. The Countess yawned and stretched, mumbling a sleepy greeting.

'I hope you have slept well, my lady.' Jane picked up the chamber pot and passed it to Aggie, the scullery maid, who disappeared with it. Everyone in the household knew their place and their tasks.

'I slept very well, thank you.' The Countess eased herself into a sitting position. 'Even though I had company.' She indicated the small tousled head beside her.

The Earl was in London, dealing with matters of business, so Master John had, it seemed, undertaken to keep his mama company in his papa's absence.

Jane smiled. 'Good morning, Master John.'

The child was awake, eyeing her with solemnity. Within minutes, Jane knew, he would be up and running around like a spinning top. At nearly two years of age he was the undoubted darling of Ledbury House. His parents adored him, as did all the servants, yet he was in no danger of being spoiled. His mama was not over-indulgent, and neither was—

'There you are, my lambkin!' Nurse bustled into the room, all starched white cotton and kind efficiency. She scooped little John up into her arms and he nestled into her ample bosom. 'I shall change those damp linens immediately, my lamb!'

The Countess, smiling indulgently at her offspring as he disappeared, accepted a cup of tea from Jane with a murmur of thanks.

'Would you like a bath today?' asked Jane. Miss Marianne had talked of it yesterday.

The Countess shivered. 'Perhaps later, when the chamber is warm. For now—' she threw back the covers '—I shall get up.'

After her mistress had washed, Jane helped her dress in a clean shift and, following some debate, a stout walking dress of fine russet merino. Lady Kingswood's favourite nightgown was in need of a wash, so she folded it to take downstairs.

Aggie had returned, and lit a fire in the Countess's fireplace. As the morning chill began slowly to ease a little the Countess took her seat before the mirror, sipping a dish of tea and allowing Jane to dress her hair.

Jane smiled inwardly. She loved this part of the day. The Countess's hair was long, dark and lustrous, and Jane adored brushing and styling it. She had cared for Lady Kingswood for almost ten years—since she was plain Miss Marianne Grant and Jane, then thirteen, had been assigned to serve her. Inwardly, and sometimes aloud, she still called her Miss Marianne.

After Papa had died, Jane had had to adapt quickly from the carefree life she had lived while he was alive to one where she earned her keep. The first year after Papa's death had been particularly harrowing. Once their meagre savings had run out, Mama and Jane had left their little cottage and sought temporary work in a series of taverns. They had frequently gone hungry that winter, and their clothes had become decidedly ragged. Thankfully Mama had secured a position in Miss Marianne's home the following summer, and had risen eventually to the exalted position of housekeeper.

Jane, too, had done well for herself. After starting as a scullery maid in the same household she had, given her gentle manners, been promoted to the role of upstairs housemaid. At thirteen she had been offered the opportunity to train as Miss Marianne's personal servant, and had been devoted to her mistress ever since.

More recently, in the year Miss Marianne had married, Jane and her mama had followed their mistress to Ledbury House, where Jane's mother was now housekeeper. Apart from a dark few months spent apart, Miss Marianne had been the centre of Jane's life since she was thirteen.

'Now, Jane. Some French today, I think.'

'Yes, Miss M— I mean, my lady.'

Miss Marianne, discovering that Jane had, until the age of eight, been raised as a gentleman's daughter, had decided to continue her education. Over the years Jane had developed a creditable knowledge of French, German and Italian, along with an appreciation of history and philosophy. The Countess was a born tutor, and had used her skills as a governess when she had had to leave her home following the deaths of her parents.

Jane frowned, remembering that dark time. Miss Marianne's stepbrother, Henry Grant, had importuned her, causing Miss Marianne to leave her home in the dead of night. Two months later Jane and her mother had been forced to follow, after Master Henry had attempted to violate Jane herself.

She shuddered. *Do not think of it!*

Thankfully Henry had died four years ago, leaving Miss Marianne free to marry the man she loved, and Jane and her mother safe in her employ.

He no longer has the power to hurt us, she reminded herself as she responded to Miss Marianne's French conversation.

And yet Henry was always with her, lurking in the shadows of her heart. Laughing at her.

We are safe here in Ledbury House.

But for how long? Ever since that day when the fever had taken Papa, Jane had felt as though the ground beneath her was soft, uncertain. Hunger and insecurity had worked its way into her bones during that year of mourning, of scarcity, of homelessness. Much more had vanished along with her papa—Rose Cottage, a regular income, food, warm clothes…

But Mama and Jane had worked hard—harder than most of their colleagues—and their industry had been rewarded with long-term positions. Jane had just begun to settle after a few years, begun to believe they had found a new home, when all had shifted again. The master and mistress they had been serving had died in a terrible carriage accident, leaving Miss Marianne orphaned and under the care of her stepbrother.

Once again the home Jane had come to love had been taken from her, when Master Henry's evil intent had meant it was not a safe place to live. Once again she and Mama had found themselves homeless and needing to start again.

But then they had followed Miss Marianne here, to Ledbury House, where they had now been living for almost five years.

In her heart, though, Jane could not feel fully at ease. Always it seemed to her that some disaster would surely occur, causing her once again to lose her home. She felt as though her life would be ever thus—that she would always be at the whim of others, never the mistress of her own fate. Memories of hunger, of poverty, of homelessness lay buried within her, rising at times to flood her with anxiety.

When she had voiced her worries to Mama, her mother had not understood. 'But we are secure here with Lady Kingswood! So long as she remains pleased with us we need not worry.'

'But what if she becomes ill, or—or dies? What if some disaster occurs and Lord Kingswood loses his riches? What if—?'

'Oh, Jane! Do not allow your mind to run away with you. Why, you are lost to all common sense! Why should such things occur? Now, stop thinking of things that are not real and focus on what you can do to keep in favour with Miss Marianne!'

Mama's words made sense. Jane knew how close she was to her mistress, and she could not in truth imagine displeasing the Countess so much that she would be let go, but there were so many other possibilities that might lead to them once again being homeless. That fear had never left her.

For now, though, she would do as she always did: she would work hard and hope to stay as long as possible.

Having directed the housemaids to make up Miss Marianne's bed, Jane picked up the Countess's nightgown and tripped lightly downstairs. No one but her, she had decreed, must deal with milady's clothing. She washed, ironed and mended everything herself, ensuring Miss Marianne's personal needs were met.

She also advised the Countess on fashion—poring over the fashion plates in Miss Marianne's magazines and periodicals and never once wishing for such finery for herself. She and Miss Marianne had an unusual relationship—if it had not been for the differences in their station Jane might even have called her a friend. Miss Marianne was all kindness, and treated Jane with much more warmth and flexibility than she ought.

Sometimes the Countess gave her an old dress she no longer wanted—but, despite her mistress's protests, Jane would remove the lace and flounces before wearing it. Jane suspected that Miss Marianne looked for ways to be kind, but she herself still heeded Mama's warnings.

'You are a servant now, Jane. Never forget it.'

And, as a maid, she should always wear plain, simple clothing and dress her hair neatly.

But she had the pleasure of seeing Lady Kingswood well turned out, and the joy of caring for embroidered silks, delicate lace-trimmed gowns and delightful bonnets.

In those early years in the servants' quarters of Miss Marianne's childhood home she would never have dreamed of reaching the great heights of becoming a lady's maid. And yet here she was. The other servants treated her with respect, she shared a comfortable chamber and private sitting room with her own mama, she had a secure wage and her very own tea allowance, and she had the sweetest, kindest mistress any servant could wish for. It made her secret fears seem even more preposterous.

My situation is a good one, she reminded herself for the hundredth time. *How many servants have the opportunities Miss Marianne has given me?*

Miss Marianne's parents, like Jane's own papa, had not subscribed to the popular view that a lady's brain was not strong enough for book learning, and Miss Marianne had had an excellent education—much of which she had passed to her maid.

Jane made her way to the scullery with Miss Marianne's nightgown and spent the next half-hour washing and scrubbing it, along with two shifts and some stockings. The lye was sharp on her hands, which were perpetually red and chapped from her work. Oh, she knew the laundry maid would happily do this task, if asked, but Jane had no notion of surrendering Miss Marianne's nightgown to anyone else.

She sang softly as she worked, conscious of a strong sense of purpose in her life. Today her deepest fears seemed far away, and the anxious voice inside her quiet. For now.

'I declare, Jane, you have the sweetest singing voice I ever heard.' Jane's mama bent to kiss her on the cheek.

Jane laughed. 'You always say so, Mama, and I always repeat that your ear is attuned to my voice simply because

I am your daughter. Now, I see you are dressed to go out. Do you need me to do anything while you are gone?'

'Nothing in particular,' Mrs Bailey replied, tying her plain bonnet under her chin. 'Thomas will take me to the village, where I must speak with the butcher. All is quiet upstairs, and Mrs Cullen is content, so now is my chance to slip out for an hour. I have told them all that you speak for me in my absence.'

'Yes, Mama.' As housekeeper, Mrs Bailey rarely left Ledbury House, but when she did Jane was an able deputy. 'Though I am sure nothing untoward will happen.'

Jane returned to her laundry work and Mr Handel's aria.

Once satisfied, she stepped outside with the wet night-gown and spread it on a bush near the kitchen door. There it would remain for a couple of hours, until it was nearly dry, at which point Jane would bring it indoors to air in front of the kitchen fire. If it did not rain the nightgown would be dry and pressed long before Miss Marianne's bedtime.

She paused for a moment, enjoying the sensation of the pale winter sunshine on her face.

I am content here, at Ledbury House, she realised.

Then the wind whipped up again and sent her scurrying inside to her mending.

Chapter Two

Bang! Bang! The persistent knocking at the door finally penetrated Robert's slumber. He grunted, gritting his teeth. His chamber at the inn was positioned directly over the taproom, and he had, he believed, just suffered the worst night's sleep of his life.

Until near dawn he had tossed and turned in the narrow bed, listening to the collective voices of what had seemed like hundreds of local farmers and tradesmen talking, laughing and occasionally singing. Finally the sounds had dwindled, but now, what seemed like only moments later, the landlord had returned to torture him anew.

'Mr Kendal? Mr Kendal, sir? You asked me to wake you up in the morning, sir.'

'Very well,' Robert managed. 'I am awake.'

Thankfully this was enough to get rid of the man. Robert lay there, contemplating his fate. Having left home five days ago, his bones felt as if they were still rattling with the trundling carriage. Five days of endless roads, of feeling trapped within the coach. Five nights of inns of various quality. Five long days of his own unalleviated company.

Today—finally—he would reach his destination, for it lay only a few miles from here. The name of it, as with every other aspect of this unexpected and unlooked-for assignment, was by this point permanently etched into his brain: Ledbury House.

Disorder had erupted in the scullery. One of the parlour maids had bumped her head, causing a small wound to bleed profusely. The other two were clucking around her like distressed hens, making a tragedy out of what seemed to Jane to be a commonplace injury.

'No need to fuss,' she told them, with a hint of her mother's sternness in her tone. 'Just let me see to it.'

They continued to exclaim loudly, while trying to mop blood from their friend's face with towels and wet rags, splashing the bloodstained water far and wide.

Jane, notoriously calm in such situations, pressed a rag to the wound to slow the bleeding. 'Hold this in place.'

'Lord, what's amiss?' It was Mrs Cullen, the cook, a tray in her hands.

The injured party and her two friends tried to explain, simultaneously and with a cacophonous lack of clarity.

'Never mind! Who will bring the tea to Miss Marianne and her guest?'

Everyone knew the Countess had welcomed an unexpected visitor, and tea and refreshments had been ordered.

'Me!'

'I shall!'

Jane frowned in puzzlement. These girls were not normally so dedicated to their work.

Something is wrong here.

She decided to intervene. 'Neither of you can do it, for you both have Mary's blood on your clothing.'

It was true. They looked at the stains with dismay.

Jane's own gown had thankfully been spared. 'I shall take it myself.' She took the tray from Cook, wondering at the parlour maids' evident disappointment.

'But—' Sarah, the more impudent of the two, looked as though she would defy Jane.

'Yes, Sarah? There is something you wish to say?' Jane made a fair approximation of her mother's steely glaze. It had the desired effect. Sarah subsided, looking rather mutinous, and ceased her protest.

'Come back for the sweetmeats, Jane,' Cook advised.

'I shall.'

Keeping an eye on the tray, which was laden with everything Miss Marianne would need for tea for herself and her guest, Jane walked carefully up the back stairs and pushed the door open. The second footman opened the door to the drawing room for her and Jane stepped inside.

Robert appraised the setting. The drawing room at Ledbury House was a comfortable, nicely presented room, with luxurious wall hangings and a well-maintained air. His hostess, Lady Kingswood, had welcomed him inside, bidding him sit and ordering refreshments. She was an elegant, good-looking young woman who looked to be a few years younger than he. She still held his card in her delicate hand and there was an air of puzzlement about her.

As well there might be when Robert himself did not even know why he was here!

'Your husband, Lord Kingswood, is not at home?'

'He is not.'

'I see.' His discomfort increased. He had hoped to speak to the Earl directly. 'Might I ask, Lady Kingswood, if you are acquainted with my uncle—?' He corrected himself. 'With Mr Millthorpe of Arkendale, in the West Riding of Yorkshire?'

She frowned. 'I am not familiar with the name, no. My own family is from Cambridgeshire.'

'Does your husband, perhaps, have links to Yorkshire?'

'None that I am aware of.'

'Curious…' He shook his head. 'Beyond curious.'

She was waiting patiently.

'I apologise, Lady Kingswood. No doubt you are wondering why I am here.' Her puzzled expression confirmed it. 'Let me explain. I—'

The door opened, admitting a serving maid. Robert bit back his words in frustration. He tapped his fingers on the edge of the chair as the maid set the tray down on a small table beside her mistress, then proceeded to move the items from the tray to the table-top. It seemed to take an age.

'Have you come far today, Mr Kendal?' asked Lady Kingswood, filling the silence with an innocuous question.

'I stayed last night at the inn at Netherton,' he confirmed.

'A most excellent establishment, don't you think?'

'Indeed,' he lied, pushing away the memories of last night's raucous farmers' choir. To be fair, the place had been clean, and his mood had been somewhat assuaged by a hearty breakfast less than an hour ago.

He accepted tea in a delicate china cup. Thankfully the maid had finally left, murmuring to her mistress about sweetmeats.

Lady Kingswood eyed him keenly. 'You were about to tell me what brings you to Ledbury House.'

He set the cup down. 'I was.'

How to begin? She clearly has no inkling what this is about either.

'If you will indulge me, I should wish to tell you a little of the background,' he said.

She lifted her own cup. 'I am all curiosity, Mr Kendal, I can assure you.'

Jane chuckled to herself as she tripped lightly back downstairs. Well, *that* mystery was now solved. Whoever Miss Marianne's visitor was, he was the most handsome young man Jane had seen in a very long time. It was no wonder the parlour maids were all of a giggle. They must have seen him arrive.

Lord Kingswood was held to be good-looking, and Jane had been delighted when her beloved mistress had chosen to marry a man of looks as well as character. But this man, whoever he was, quite cast His Lordship into the shade. Piercing grey eyes under arching brows, a perfectly formed jawline, high cheekbones and luxuriant dark hair combined to create a visage the Great Masters would surely have wished to capture on canvas.

And he was every inch the gentleman, Jane had noted with a sweeping glance, with long, muscular legs encased in pale buckskins and glossy boots. His lean frame and broad shoulders were shown to advantage in his fine coat made by Weston, Jane surmised, her connoisseur's eye having recognised the cut and style of the master tailor. Yes, a fine-looking man indeed—and one who had clearly caught the eye of the parlour maids.

Jane idly wondered who he was and what business he had at Ledbury House. Perhaps he was a suitor for Lady Cecily? The Earl's ward was now seventeen and was possibly thinking of marriage.

Jane tutted at herself. A servant should never speculate about such matters. It might, as Mama had so frequently warned her, lead to an urge for gossip and tittle-tattle. That would never do. And nor should she, a servant, allow herself to feel drawn to a gentleman visitor.

But drawn to him was exactly what she felt. He had not noticed her, of course—and why should he? Yet Jane's senses had been momentarily rather disordered by the sight of the mysterious young man. Master Henry's treatment of her meant she avoided men wherever possible. But she was no nun, and could appreciate a fine face and firm male body as much as any other girl.

Settle, she told herself. *He is not for you.*

Five minutes later she was on her way back to the drawing room, this time bearing a selection of tempting sweetmeats and pastries. When she stepped inside she felt immediately the changed atmosphere in the room. Miss Marianne was leaning forward, her eyes huge and her attention completely gripped by whatever her guest was saying. Neither of them seemed even to notice Jane's arrival.

Quietly, and as unobtrusively as possible, Jane walked across the room towards Miss Marianne's table, intending to deposit the refreshments and leave without disturbing their attention. It was one of the greatest skills of a good servant.

'And he gave you no notion of why you were sent to fetch her?' The Countess looked astounded.

The gentleman spread his hands. 'None whatsoever. I was hoping you might enlighten me.'

She shook her head. 'It all sounds most peculiar, Mr Kendal. But can you tell me the name of the woman you are sent in search of?'

'I can. Her name is Jane Bailey.'

Chapter Three

*C*rash! Tray, dishes, pastries and sweetmeats tumbled to the floor in a clatter of china, cutlery and food, the debris spreading far and wide. Jane could not understand why the visitor had said her name, but her attention had been completely diverted to the horror now adorning Miss Marianne's best carpet.

It was a servant's role to be unnoticed, unobtrusive. A shadow. Never to be seen unless the quality chose to interact with you. Since beginning her training as a scullery maid at the age of eight Jane had understood that to do what she had just done was the worst possible error she could ever make.

'I am so sorry, my lady,' she muttered, bending to gather some of the debris.

One of Miss Marianne's prized Chamberlain Worcester plates was broken in two. Jane could not even begin to think how much the delicate china was worth. If any of the other girls had caused this calamity they would get a rare telling-off, and possibly even a warm ear from Mrs Bailey.

Just because the housekeeper happened to be her mother it did not excuse Jane from this culpability. What would this gentleman think of her? Of Ledbury House?

Lady Kingswood, issuing soothing reassurances, had already rung the bell for another maid, and shortly afterwards Sarah arrived—still with faint bloodstains on her sleeve.

Jane groaned inwardly. Of course it would have to be Sarah.

Together they swiftly gathered up the tumbled food, cutlery and crockery, while Lady Kingswood and her guest engaged in stilted empty conversation.

Oh, please, let us be done here, for I cannot bear to be in this room a moment longer!

Miss Marianne would think her stupid and clumsy. And what if she was so displeased she consigned Jane to work below-stairs?

Part of Jane's mind was aware this was neither rational, nor likely, but the other part—the part currently overcome by fear and anxiety—could not at that moment be logical.

Thankfully, before long they were done. Jane would return later, to sweep the crumbs, but for now at least all the noticeable debris had been scooped up into her and Sarah's aprons. Jane stood, bobbed a curtsey, and left alongside Sarah without a backward glance.

As they descended below-stairs in silence she could sense Sarah's glee at her misfortune.

Oh, Jane was well aware the other servants thought she saw herself as better than them, but it was not true—not really. Being highly educated, and being a lady's maid as well as daughter to the housekeeper, meant she had never been able to form friendships with any of the maids near her own age. But it was not that she saw herself as above them. Why, she had even served tea today in order to be helpful.

It was more that she could not be comfortable with their conversation—which focused mainly on village scandals, family gossip—and their fixation on flirting with any eligible lads in the district.

And moments like this is when I pay for it.

Sarah was clearly delighted that, having deprived the other housemaids of the pleasure of serving the handsome gentleman, Jane should have suffered such a spectacular calamity.

Jane maintained a stony silence and walked on.

Robert's sense of disquiet was growing by the moment. Already uneasy about being sent on this wild mission by his uncle, he had felt his discomfort increase when he had realised Lord Kingswood was absent.

Apart from his mama and his aunt—and the occasional society of a courtesan or ladybird—Robert did not often find himself in the company of women, and had no idea how to respond to the archness, flirtation and simpering often displayed by the young ladies of his acquaintance.

Thankfully, Lady Kingswood had so far displayed none of these tendencies, and he had dared to hope he could communicate his delicate tale without sounding like an utter fool.

Until the maid had decided to trip over nothing and fling pastries and plates across the room.

He had glanced down at her, absently noting her pink cheeks and mortified expression. Strangely, it had made him feel a little easier, knowing that someone in the room was even more agitated than he.

She is very pretty, he had noted, surprising himself with the thought.

Another maid had arrived to help, and this one had immediately sent him a sideways bold glance.

Robert had looked away.

'I do hope your postilion is being looked after,' Lady Kingswood had offered politely, after murmuring reassuring words to the two maids.

'Your groom came out to meet us,' he had confirmed. 'I have no doubt they are even now discussing horseflesh and poultices and whatnot.'

She had smiled. 'Grooms and coachmen share a common language. Do you ride?'

'I do.' Wistfully, he had pictured the green hills around Beechmount Hall. 'I am fortunate to live close to some of England's finest countryside.'

'My husband is a fine horseman.' Lady Kingswood had not disguised her pride. 'Such a pity he is not here today.'

'Indeed.'

There had been a short silence.

Thankfully the maids had now completed their task and departed, the second one once again trying to catch his eye.

Robert kept his gaze firmly and politely on Lady Kingswood.

The door closed behind them and Lady Kingswood's demeanour instantly changed. Bringing her hands together, she narrowed her eyes. 'I must tell you, Mr Kendal,' she asserted, 'Miss Bailey is very dear to me, and I should not wish her to become embroiled in anything unsavoury or anything that might bring her harm.'

'Then she exists and you know her!' Seeing her startled expression, he made haste to explain. 'My uncle—that is to say, Mr Millthorpe—was very clear that he wished to speak to Miss Bailey and that she would come to no harm by it. I think,' he added reflectively, 'that he sent me in order to reassure Miss Bailey and those close to her on that very point.'

'And do you know why he wishes to speak with her?' There was a decided crease on Lady Kingswood's brow.

'I do not—not for certain, at least. I confess until this moment I was not convinced Miss Bailey even existed, or that I would find her here. My uncle is elderly and in poor health. While this was decidedly *not* a deathbed request— for he enjoys reasonably good health—he made it clear he wishes to meet Miss Bailey before he leaves this earth.'

This elicited a response—a flicker of something in the Countess's eyes. Recognition? Memory? Then it was gone, and so quickly he might have imagined it.

He coughed politely. 'Mr Millthorpe is aged, and somewhat eccentric, and likes to try to make me do his bidding.' He grimaced. 'That sounds wrong. I have great affection for him. But I confess that although we have lived in the same house for most of my life, he still manages to surprise me on occasions.'

Lady Kingswood nodded politely, clearly believing it would be indelicate for her to comment on this.

'So,' he offered, leaning forward. 'Might I enquire a little about Miss Jane Bailey? Does she live nearby? Might you be able to give me her direction? I confess I am curious about her. Is she a woman in her middle years, perhaps?'

The Countess tilted her head to one side. 'I shall consider the matter, Mr Kendal. But tell me: what led you to believe you might find news of her here, at Ledbury House?'

A decided rebuff. He had travelled all this way and might yet fail. He would have to tread carefully with Lady Kingswood. If she denied him, Robert would be obliged to return to Yorkshire empty-handed.

'Ah! That I do know. My uncle indicated that he had commissioned a Bow Street Runner to investigate the whereabouts of Miss Bailey. While he would tell me nothing of his motives, he was most proud of his methods.'

'A Bow Street Runner!' She shook her head in bemusement. 'Mr Kendal, I shall be frank with you. I have never met you before, and I am unsure whether I should trust you with the information you seek. You have made it clear your undertaking is not simply to *speak* with J— with Miss Bailey, or to pass on information. Instead you wish to take her hundreds of miles away to the wilds of Yorkshire, with only yourself to accompany her.'

The wilds of Yorkshire? It was hardly deepest Africa! But Robert noted she seemed genuinely concerned for Miss Bailey's safety.

He nodded. 'I see that. But I know not what further reassurance I can provide, save my word as a gentleman.'

Her lip curled. 'Both Miss Bailey and I are aware that supposed "gentlemen" do not always behave honourably.'

Robert blinked, noting this for future reference. Politeness prevented him from asking the Countess for more details.

He cast around his mind, but no further strategy came

to him save honesty. 'Then we are at a standstill. I know not what I can say or do to convince you. Certainly on a practical level I can undertake to hire a maid to travel with her—perhaps one of your own maids?'

For some reason, an image of the pretty pink-cheeked maid suddenly filled his inner vision. *Cease!* he told himself sternly. *Now is certainly not the time for dalliance.*

For some reason this seemed to amuse her.

She thought for a moment, then nodded. 'Mr Kendal, I shall make you an offer. Come back tonight for dinner, at half past six, and we can discuss this further. I hope you understand I need time for consideration?'

'Indeed, and I am grateful that you have not sent me away with a flea in my ear.' He rose. 'I thank you for your time, and I shall indeed return.'

He bowed, smiled, and departed.

'Oh, Lord!' Jane cradled her head in her hands. 'I am so sorry, Mama!'

Miss Marianne might understand, but Mama had such high standards for both of them Jane felt she had let them both down.

Mrs Bailey was still removing her bonnet and shawl. 'What on earth happened, Jane? Sarah could not wait to tell me that one of the Worcester plates had broken and that it was not her fault!'

'It is true.' Jane's tone was rueful.

She gave her mama a brief summary of the disaster in the drawing room.

'The gentleman has not yet left, but when he does I shall be sure to go directly to my mistress and apologise.'

'I should think so! But why were you there? And what on earth made you do it? You are not normally clumsy.'

'Ah, that I must tell you... Mary cut her head, so I decided to take the tea. Then the gentleman said my name, and it was so unexpected that I dropped the tray.'

Jane, still lost in mortification, could not even describe the disaster properly.

'He said your name? What on earth are you talking about? Honestly, Jane, sometimes you baffle me with your incoherence.'

'Sorry, Mama. There is truly little more to tell. I was not particularly listening to their conversation—you have always encouraged me to develop the skill of not attending to business that does not concern me. Then suddenly he said, *"Her name is Jane Bailey".*' She nodded furiously. 'Yes, I know! I am puzzled too. I have been racking my brains, but I cannot think of why he might be here, or why any gentleman might be seeking me.'

As she spoke, a bell on the wall rang—Jane's bell—swiftly followed by the housekeeper's bell. Miss Marianne wanted them both!

They glanced at each other, then wordlessly rose, making for the drawing room.

The gentleman had gone—Jane ascertained as much from the second footman as they went through the hall. Strangely, Jane felt a pang of—*something*—at this news. But of course he was gone—which was why they were now summoned to their mistress.

'Enter!'

The Countess's voice rang out in response to Mrs Bailey's gentle scratching on the door. Jane was conscious that her heart was beating rather quickly. Despite all her years of service to Miss Marianne, and knowing of her kindness and her loyalty, a servant's greatest worry was always that of being dismissed.

Lady Kingswood was seated in her favourite armchair, looking pensive.

Jane glanced automatically towards the carpet, instantly spotting various crumbs and tiny shards of china—clear evidence of the recent mishap.

'Oh, my lady, I apologise! I do not know what came over me, for I am not normally so clumsy.'

Miss Marianne snorted. 'Well, if *you* do not know, Jane, I most certainly do. Lord, when he said the name of the woman he was seeking I almost collapsed in shock. If I had been holding a tray I have no doubt I, too, would have dropped it. No—' she waved a hand '—I do not wish to hear any further apologies. It is forgotten!'

Jane smiled weakly.

See? You need not have worried, the rational part of her brain offered complacently.

Her still racing heart and moist palms could not agree.

Mrs Bailey was frowning. 'Might I ask, my lady, who is this gentleman? And what is his interest in my daughter?'

'I confess I do not fully understand it myself.' She picked up a card. 'His name is Mr Robert Kendal and, in essence, he says he has been sent here by an elderly relative of his to fetch Jane to visit the old man in Yorkshire before he dies. Although his death is not imminent. The old man's, I mean.'

She was looking closely at Mama, as if waiting for her to say something.

Mama remained silent.

'But why?' Jane was mystified. 'I know no Mr Kendal, nor *anyone* with the name Kendal, and I have never seen this gentleman before.'

That I am sure of, for I would not have forgotten a gentleman so handsome!

'Mr Kendal himself seems not to know why you are sought, Jane. In fact, he hoped I could enlighten him.' Lady Kingswood's eyes danced. 'I suspect he thinks you may be the result of a youthful adventure on his relative's part. He pictures you as middle-aged.'

'Youthful adventure? What—? *Oh!*' Jane gaped.

Mrs Bailey was bristling with indignation. 'Well, I shall tell him straight! My Jane is no man's by-blow, for me and my Ned were married fair and square! And my own parents were as respectable as they come! Youthful adventure, indeed!'

'Of course, Mrs Bailey!' Lady Kingswood's tone was soothing. 'I suspect Mr Kendal knows very little about either of you, and so he has reached his own conclusions.'

'Well, if he thinks I shall allow my Jane to go off with him to visit some unknown elderly gentleman—' Mama broke off, as if an idea had just come to her. 'Did you say Yorkshire?'

'I did. Does that mean something to you?'

'Did Mr Kendal specify which part of Yorkshire?'

'Er—the West Riding. A place called Ardendale or something.'

Mrs Bailey gasped. 'Ardendale...or Arkendale, perhaps?'

'Yes—Arkendale!'

'And his relative's name?'

'Mullinthorpe? Melkinthorpe?' Lady Kingswood was frowning with the effort of trying to remember.

'Millthorpe?'

'That's it! Millthorpe!'

Mrs Bailey put a hand to her chest. 'Mr Millthorpe! Never again did I think to hear that name!'

Jane rose, touching her mother's arm. 'Who is he, Mama?'

'If it is him, and not some other relative—' she looked directly at Jane '—he is Ned's father. Your grandfather!'

'My *grandfather*?' Jane almost squeaked in shock. 'But why is his name not Bailey? And I thought he would have nothing to do with Papa—with any of us—after Papa married you?'

'So Ned always said. As a servant, I was not good enough for the Millthorpe name, apparently. Ned defied him by changing his name to Bailey—which was from his mother's side.'

Jane's mind was reeling. 'Then—my grandfather may be still alive and wishing to meet me?'

'So it would seem.'

Jane's knees felt strangely soft, as if the bones were melting. She had not thought of Papa's family in years.

My grandfather! What is he like? Do I look like him? Has he, perhaps, forgiven Papa?

An image of a tender deathbed reunion filled her mind. She shook it away—there was nothing to suggest what Mr Millthorpe's motives might be in trying to find her.

'And who, then, is this Mr Kendal? A servant?' Mama's tone was sharp.

'No, definitely a gentleman.' The Countess tilted her head on one side, remembering. 'He referred to Mr Millthorpe as "Uncle", yet clarified that he is not truly his uncle but a distant relative. I did wonder if there was some connection with your husband's family...'

'Hmph! The whole thing smacks of Mr Millthorpe's desire to manage everyone around him. That was Ned's abiding memory of his father. Even now, with my poor Ned long gone, his domineering father seeks to control him through my Jane!' Mama wiped a tear away with the corner of her apron.

'Mama!' Jane touched her arm. 'Of course I shall not go, if you do not wish it.'

Mama *never* cried. After that day—the day of Papa's death—Mama had been careful to keep her grief to herself. Jane had come upon her suddenly on a couple of occasions, and seen her mother wipe away tears, but never had she allowed herself to cry in front of Jane. For her to do so today was shocking, and Jane felt the force of it.

Mama continued, her voice tight with pain and anger. 'Mr Millthorpe was cold and cruel. He pushed away his only child—and why? Because Ned had the misfortune to fall in love with me: a servant. I have never met the man, but my impression is that he thinks of me—of *all* servants—as vermin, to be used and discarded. He has no heart, no conscience. He must have known Ned would struggle, yet he never made any attempt to reconcile with him.'

Jane, her mind too disordered to operate clearly, nevertheless felt the force of Mama's pain. And Papa's.

Lady Kingswood's brow creased. 'How awful! I remember, of course, that your husband had died not long before you came to us, and that he was a gentleman, but I do not recall hearing any more about his family.'

'I did not speak much of it.' Mama pressed her lips together. 'Again, I should like to know, who is Mr Kendal and what is his role in all of this?' She eyed her mistress. 'What have you told him about Jane?'

'Not a word,' Lady Kingswood assured her. 'He knows I am acquainted with Jane, but has no notion that he himself has already met her!'

Jane, still in something like shock, voiced her bemusement. 'My grandfather is alive! Why would he wish to see me? What if he is still angry with Papa, and wishes to punish him—or me…?' She shuddered. 'I cannot put myself in any man's power.' Cold fear trickled through her belly as Master Henry threatened to resurface in her memory. 'What is to happen next?'

'Well,' said Lady Kingswood diffidently, 'I thought you both might like to meet him yourself before he knows who Jane Bailey is.'

'Thank you, Miss Marianne. I declare that is sensible.' Mama was all gratitude. 'But how shall we contrive it?'

'I have invited him to dinner. Lady Cecily is returning later—please prepare her room, Mrs Bailey—and I have sent a note to Reverend Burns to make up the numbers. It is only right that we should attempt to discover more of his character, and of Mr Millthorpe, before you decide whether Jane should go with him.'

Mrs Bailey shook her head. 'I am not sure she should go anywhere near the old man, no matter how personable this Mr Kendal may be.'

Jane listened with trepidation, and more than a little confusion. At this moment she had no notion of what she wanted, beyond a sneaking suspicion that she would very much like to see Mr Kendal again…

Chapter Four

Strange... thought Robert idly, glancing at the few remaining russet, gold and yellow leaves still clinging to the trees as his carriage rumbled through the country lanes towards Ledbury House. *Even in February some of their trees still hold a few autumn leaves, while in Yorkshire winter has been with us for nigh on four months already. Winter comes later and kinder this far south.*

He felt a pang of nostalgia for his home. He was often gone from Beechmount Hall on matters of business, but after a few days away he always ached to return. Not long now. If Lady Kingswood would only tell him where he could find this Jane Bailey, then...

Then his next task would be to convince her to come with him—but what method of persuasion Robert was to use he honestly did not know.

He sighed as the carriage pulled up outside the front door. The postilion dismounted from the lead horse and let down the step. Robert descended, glancing around instinctively. Ledbury House was a fine dwelling, comfortable and cosy without being imposing. The contrast with Beechmount Hall, where he had lived for the past twenty years, was stark.

His hostess was there to greet him and introduce him to her guests—the local vicar and a young relative whom she addressed as Lady Cecily. Apparently she was Lord Kingswood's ward and lived at Ledbury House. She had been away visiting relatives and had just returned.

How could he discover more about the identity and whereabouts of Jane Bailey when there were four of them for dinner?

Shortly after his arrival, dinner was served. Robert accompanied Lady Kingswood to the dining room, with the Reverend Burns and Lady Cecily following. Naturally rather reticent, he had learned over the years to endure social gatherings with an appearance of equanimity. Afterwards, he always found himself drained by the effort of being in company.

I do believe, he thought now, *my aversion to empty social intercourse goes back to my circumstances at the time when I first moved to Beechmount Hall.*

Tonight, however, Robert had a purpose, and he intended to make the most of the opportunity.

He had the honour of being placed on Lady Kingswood's right, and as the first course was served she politely drew him out, asking if Yorkshire had always been his home.

'It has,' he confirmed. 'I was born in Harrogate and lived there with my parents until my father died, after which my mother and I moved to Beechmount Hall. I was eight, so that was exactly twenty years ago.'

The vicar and Lady Cecily were conversing politely at the other side of the table. Robert absentmindedly thanked the footman who was serving the first course—soup, along with a squab pie and some leeks. He tried a forkful, which tasted delicious.

'Your mother is related to the family there?' Lady Kingswood continued.

'Distantly,' he confirmed, as a middle-aged female servant entered, carrying further dishes. She was followed by a maid—the pretty one who had dropped the tray earlier.

Females waiting at table? Unusual. A deliberate informality, Robert suspected.

Lady Kingswood was politely waiting for him to say more.

'My mother's aunt is Mr Millthorpe's second wife—his first having died many years previously. Aunt Eugenia is my mama's only living relation, so it made sense for us to move there.' He shrugged. 'I was too young to fully understand the reasons, but I believe my mother and her aunt provide female company for each other, so it suits both of them.'

'Wait. Mrs Millthorpe is your great-aunt, and yet you also address her as "aunt"?'

'Yes—at Mrs Millthorpe's request. I should explain I call her husband my uncle, although he is in fact only my great-uncle by marriage. Mrs Millthorpe desires me to call them simply "aunt" and "uncle", as my mother does, declaring she would not suffer the indignity of being anyone's *great*-aunt!'

Lady Kingswood smiled at this. 'And are they both still there at Beechmount Hall?'

The servants, having placed all the dishes on the table and removed the covers, now stood back impassively, waiting for them to eat. Normally Robert would barely notice, but the maid with rosy cheeks continually drew his attention. Not that she was doing anything in particular.

It is just that she is remarkably pretty.

A footman served Robert a slice of pie. 'Er—yes, they are. My Aunt Eugenia swears she could not manage without my mother.' He frowned.

Lady Kingswood glanced briefly across the table, to where the vicar and Lady Cecily seemed entirely focused on their own conversation. 'And it is your uncle who has sent you here?'

Robert nodded. 'It is.'

'Tell me more of Mr Millthorpe.'

For the next two hours Robert attempted to reassure Lady Kingswood of his honourable intentions. He could not be dishonest about his uncle, but carefully used words such as 'eccentric' and 'strong-willed' to signal something of the old man's character without, he hoped, frightening the Countess.

At times Lady Kingswood conversed politely with the vicar, while Robert chatted about botany and books with

Lady Cecily. However, each time the table turned he and Lady Kingswood returned to their discussions of Beechmount Hall and those who lived there.

The name Jane Bailey was not mentioned.

All in all it had been a most pleasant evening, if tiring, he concluded, climbing into his coach while the coachman held up a lantern for him. And hopefully a useful one. Lady Kingswood had asked him to return on the morrow, which he took as a positive sign.

As the post chaise made its way down the lanes by moonlight towards the inn at Netherton his thoughts turned again to the pretty housemaid. It had been a long time since a woman had caught his eye. He had had his share of discreet liaisons—most recently with a London courtesan, and until just two months ago a flirtatious widow in York. He had no thought of marriage, so restricted himself to encounters where the woman involved would understand what he could and could not give.

Respectable servants, no matter how beautiful, had never been of interest to him. *Until now.*

I wonder what her name is, he thought idly. *She should be Diana, goddess of the woods. The huntress, the wild one...*

He chuckled at his own flight of fancy.

Ah, but she is a goddess, hiding in a servant's livery.

'My fair Diana!' he muttered aloud, imagining himself offering her a sweeping bow, before kissing her hand. 'Lord!' he told himself. 'You are drunk, Robert. Do not let a flirtation distract you from your obligation.'

Yet as the carriage trundled on he lost himself in imaginings which would have shocked the ladies of Ledbury House.

Jane awoke early, before the first light of dawn began seeping into the basement window of the chamber she shared with her mother. Serving at table—not something she or her mama normally did—had been challenging, and she had needed all her years of training to remain impassive as Mr Kendal had talked of her grandfather, his second wife and her father's family home.

Until yesterday she had known very little about such things. Sensitive to her mother's pain—and to her decree that they must not speak of Papa's family—Jane had kept her curiosity to herself, where it had burned in a glowing ember, deep within her.

Once her mother had frowned at her, and she had, with effort, torn her eyes away from Mr Kendal's handsome profile. He had been entirely focused on his conversation with Miss Marianne, but Lady Cecily had been eyeing her with puzzlement.

Jane had diverted her gaze from the good-looking visitor, instead staring fixedly into the middle distance, over the heads of all the diners, with, she hoped, no interest. Lady Cecily, who knew full well that the housekeeper and Lady Kingswood's personal maid should not be serving, had, after a moment, returned to her conversation with the vicar.

After that Jane had been careful not to look directly at Mr Kendal, though in truth she had remained entirely conscious of him throughout the evening. At times she had struggled to hear his words over Lady Cecily's conversation with the vicar and the scrape and clang of cutlery on china. But she believed she had the essentials.

I find him interesting.

The thought made her heart flutter in a strange and novel way. If he had been, like her, a servant, she might have sought to get to know him. The realisation was disturbing. Ever since Master Henry had attacked her four years ago she had been wary of men of all classes, but particularly gentlemen, some of whom seemed to believe they could use their power however they wished.

She turned over on to her side, watching the light slowly grow on the unadorned wall in front of her.

Will Mama permit me to travel to Yorkshire?

Looking into her heart, she was unsurprised to find her own wishes were now clear. She wanted to meet her grandfather and spend time in the place where Papa had grown up.

And, she admitted to herself, *I wish to see Mr Kendal again.*

Mr Kendal would return today, she knew, hoping to have an answer to his request for information.

Ten minutes later Mama awoke, and they both rose and prepared for the day. Conscious that her hands were shaking a little, Jane donned a plain grey gown with a lace fichu and buttoned herself into stout boots. She brushed her hair and tied it up, then added the crisp white cap denoting her status, along with a clean apron.

Mama did not mention Mr Kendal, and nor did Jane, yet there was an air of expectancy about everything. It tingled just out of Jane's reach. Something different. Interesting. Exciting.

In only a few hours all would be resolved one way or another.

'There you go, my lady,' said Jane, adding one final pin to her mistress's coiffure. 'You look beautiful.'

Lady Kingswood patted her hand. 'Thank you, Jane. Now…' She turned as she spoke, away from the mirror, to look at Jane directly. 'What did you make of Mr Kendal?'

Jane felt a slow blush build in her cheeks. 'He seems a true gentleman.'

Miss Marianne's eyes narrowed. 'I believe he is.'

Unspoken between them were their experiences at the hands of Master Henry.

'I know,' said Lady Kingswood after a moment, 'that you will heed your mother's advice, but if it were up to you, would you wish to travel to Yorkshire?'

Jane nodded firmly. 'I would. I have never met my

grandfather, and it sounds as though this may be my only opportunity. I assume my grandfather will pay the costs of my travel, and as a serving maid I need no chaperone. In that sense my going will inconvenience only myself and you, Miss Marianne!' She bit her lip. 'How should you manage if I am not here to assist you? I could not leave you for so long. Why, it will take nigh on a week to get there, and another to come back, plus whatever time I spend there…'

Lady Kingswood seemed to be considering her words carefully. 'Jane, you have been my maid since we were but children ourselves, and I shall, of course, miss you dreadfully. But I believe it is important you take this opportunity, should your mama permit. I shall ask Mary to assist me while you are gone.'

'Mary!' A spasm of anxiety coursed through Jane.

What if Miss Marianne prefers Mary? What if I am ousted from my place on my return?

She frowned at her own fears. Miss Marianne would not do such a thing!

'Yes, Mary,' Lady Kingswood repeated firmly. 'She can at least dress hair, though I am not hopeful of her mending skills being anywhere near yours.' She smiled. 'Do not fret, Jane. There is much more between us than mistress and servant. Your place in my heart makes it impossible you could be forgotten.'

'Thank you, my lady,' Jane replied gruffly.

'Mr Kendal is expected in the next hour. Ring the bell for Mrs Bailey and we shall see what is to happen.'

'Lady Kingswood!' Robert gave a smart bow, conscious that the moment of truth had finally arrived.

Was he going to be obliged to return to Yorkshire having failed in his task? He could just imagine his uncle's biting reaction if that were the case.

The old man could go from mild-mannered and easy to severe and sharp in an instant—particularly when his demands were thwarted. As a child, Robert had quaked in his boots at such moments. Now, remembering his uncle's wistful expression as he had contemplated the report on Miss Bailey, Robert felt a burning need to succeed in the task set for him.

Do I still seek my uncle's approval, even after all this time?

'Good day, Mr Kendal. Please be seated.'

Her expression gave nothing away. They exchanged niceties—he being careful to thank her once again for her hospitality and for the excellent dinner the night before. Then there was a pause.

'Lady Kingswood,' he ventured. 'You understand I have come here in the hope that I may finally be informed about the whereabouts of Jane Bailey. I have been away from home now for a week, and must soon either speak to her or return to Yorkshire.'

She nodded decisively. 'I am aware.' She tapped her fingers lightly on the arm of her chair. 'Let me be frank with you, Mr Kendal. You have given me information about your uncle, and about your home. You have also indicated that you are unclear about why Jane Bailey is being sought in Yorkshire.'

'That is correct.'

'Miss Bailey has never been away from her family before, and is not well-travelled. Can you guarantee no harm or upset shall come to her should she go with you?'

He was conscious of a thrill of victory—which might be premature. 'Whatever is in my power to influence I shall do so in order to protect her, I assure you.'

Her eyes narrowed. 'Your phrasing does not inspire me with confidence, Mr Kendal.'

He spread his hands. 'I only meant to say I am not in control of the roads, the weather, disease, or unexpected events such as accidents. But I can assure you, my lady, her happiness and comfort will be my priority. I have brought my own post-chaise, and intend to hire horses and postilions at the posting inns. We shall travel by easy stages, and no more than forty or fifty miles per day.'

In his head he was imagining Jane Bailey as a fearful, vulnerable, middle-aged lady, anxious about travel and nervous about being gone from her home.

How am I to endure five days with such a person?

'And what of her personal safety? She will travel without a chaperone.'

Ah, so she is not a gentlewoman. Perhaps, then, my notion is correct and she is a by-blow of my uncle.

Lady Kingswood was regarding him evenly. With a start, he realised the Countess was checking to see if he might have designs on a vulnerable female in his care. His temper rose.

'You have my word,' he said coldly. 'She will suffer no harm from me.'

This seemed to please her. 'Good. In that case, I am happy to inform you that I have…er…been in discussion with Miss Bailey and her mother, and she has agreed to travel to Yorkshire for a short visit.'

His heart leapt. But he was puzzled. Miss Bailey's mother yet lived? Why didn't his uncle wish to see the mother of his child?

'How short?'

'No more than two weeks. Given the distance, that would require her to be gone from home for nigh on a month. She must return by early March.'

'Very well,' he returned, with the air of a man conceding a point.

Inwardly, he was delighted. Even a few days would have been enough. To have her at Beechmount Hall for an entire fortnight was more than he had hoped to offer his uncle.

'I shall write to my uncle to make him aware of Miss Bailey's impending arrival. Will she be free to leave tomorrow morning?'

'She will.'

'And might I meet her before then?'

She glanced away, frowning slightly, then seemed to come to a decision. 'Unfortunately, as I am sure you understand, she will be busy today, packing for her journey. It is no little undertaking for someone unused to travel.'

'Of course.' He had no wish to press the point, content with his achievement in convincing Lady Kingswood of his respectability and trustworthiness.

It was only afterwards, back in the inn for one final night, that he realised Lady Kingswood had told him exactly nothing of Jane Bailey herself, nor of their relationship with each other.

'Now, Jane, you be careful.' Mama hugged her tightly. 'I shall.'

Tears sprang into Jane's eyes. Never had she and her mama been apart. Even after the incident with Master Henry, when they had left his employ, they had done so together, following Lady Kingswood to London and then on to Ledbury House. Those were the only long journeys Jane had ever undertaken in her life. The thought of travelling all the way to Yorkshire was daunting, yet strangely exciting.

Standing in the hallway, awaiting the arrival of Mr Kendal, Jane suddenly shivered. Change had come to her and, while it was exciting, it was also more than a little frightening.

At her feet was a large trunk, stuffed to the brim with clothing that Miss Marianne had suddenly and inexplicably decided she no longer needed, and which 'would do Jane very well'.

Jane had protested to no avail as dresses, stockings and slippers had been thrown in a heap onto Miss Marianne's bed. She and Jane were of a similar size, which had always assisted Jane when mending Miss Marianne's dresses, or making new ones. And Jane had stood frozen in stunned silence as she tried to understand that all these beautiful things were now hers.

This morning, though, she had resolutely donned her maid's grey gown and white fichu as usual, unwilling to wear finery in front of Miss Marianne, Mama and the other servants.

I should not wish them to believe I am acting above my station.

As well as her trunk she had a battered bandbox, containing the essentials for her journey—the main items being a spare grey dress, her hairbrush and some wool stockings. Miss Marianne had also given her a reticule as a present, embroidered with a trail of blue flowers and with a blue silk drawstring ribbon. Inside was a handkerchief, some coins, and a small scrap of paper on which Mama had written a note.

Go well, my Jane, and never forget who you are.

Never! Jane had vowed, tucking it back into the reticule and hugging Mama again.

Mama had warned her to be wary of all—and particularly Mr Kendal. 'He will no doubt attempt to influence you to be forgiving towards Ned's father, but you must resist. If Mr Millthorpe has genuinely repented you may discover that for yourself. Until then I advise you to keep your own counsel.'

Jane had nodded thoughtfully. 'That is wise advice, Mama. Indeed, I shall endeavour to avoid speaking of anything to do with Papa or Mr Millthorpe.' She had frowned. 'Mr Kendal may think it odd, yet it seems to me to be the wisest course of action.'

Miss Marianne had agreed. 'Mr Kendal seems perfectly amicable, and yet we know nothing of his motives, nor of Mr Millthorpe's. I think it best to keep your views on Mr Millthorpe's treatment of his son to yourself. And the easiest way in which to achieve that is to avoid being drawn into conversation about either of them.'

'Promise me, Jane, you will tell him only what you must. Keep your own counsel until you meet the old man yourself,' her mama had begged.

Jane had promised, shivering a little with apprehension.

Miss Marianne, whose generosity knew no bounds, had then passed her three more coins, equivalent to a full two months' salary. When she had quailed, Lady Kingswood had hushed her.

'Remember, Jane, that while I was a governess, before my marriage, we were fully friends for a time. This is my gift to you in memory of that friendship.'

'Thank you, my lady.'

Jane's words had been choked with emotion as the money had been stowed safely deep within Jane's trunk. And that feeling was strengthened now, as the carriage drew up and Mr Kendal stepped out.

Jane had been trying, with little success, to ignore how handsome he was in face and form, and how thoughts of him had disturbed her sleep these past two nights. Today he wore fine buckskins, gleaming boots, and a shoulder-hugging claret jacket.

He would be considered a fine-looking man by anyone who encountered him, Jane knew. And the thought of being alone with him in a carriage for much of the next week sent a shiver through her. Anxiety? Anticipation? Delight? She could not be sure. Nigh on a week travelling, then two weeks in Yorkshire, followed by the journey back…

The housemaids were agog with interest and envy at Jane's good fortune.

'Why could it not be me?' Sarah had wondered aloud. 'I should love to spend five days locked in a carriage with the delightful Mr Kendal!'

There had been something earthy and raw in her laugh

that had left Jane feeling both uncomfortable and yet strangely in harmony with the sentiment.

Miss Marianne arrived in the hall to greet her guest. The footmen picked up Jane's trunk and carried it out to the carriage, where Mr Kendal's postilion strapped it on. Jane took a breath, then donned her cloak and bonnet.

Her action caught Mr Kendal's eye. He looked from Lady Kingswood to Jane, and for an instant his gaze blazed into hers.

'Are we to take a maid with us to accompany Miss Bailey after all?' he asked Lady Kingswood.

Miss Marianne did not respond directly. Instead she looked at Jane.

The moment had arrived. She must speak.

She stepped forward, looking him in the eye. 'I am Jane Bailey.'

Chapter Five

'*I am Jane Bailey.*'

For a moment, Robert could not take it in. Already distracted by the sight of the beautiful maid putting on a cloak, he had felt his spirits raised at the prospect of her accompanying them. To discover that she was, in fact, Jane Bailey herself, seemed impossible.

'Pardon me?' he managed.

Lady Kingswood intervened. 'Now, Jane, I trust you will enjoy your time in Yorkshire and return to me safe and sound. I shall be lost without my personal maid for an entire month.' She turned to Robert. 'I do hope, Mr Kendal, you realise just how much of a sacrifice we are making. Jane will be greatly missed here at Ledbury House.'

She is personal maid to the Countess!

Robert, conscious of the interested gaze of his hired postilion, two footmen, and a disapproving older servant, decided his best option was to take the situation as he found it.

'Indeed. In that case I shall be sure to return her to you as soon as I may.' He addressed the maid directly. 'I am pleased to make your acquaintance, Miss Bailey.'

He bowed politely, feeling deeply uncomfortable. He never liked public attention at the best of times. The pressure of saying the right thing in such a delicate situation was even more fraught.

'And I you,' she replied.

Her voice was soft and pleasant, and sent an unexpected jolt through him.

The older servant embraced her, as did Lady Kingswood, and a few moments later he handed her up into the carriage.

She wore no gloves, and the warmth of her hand in his discomposed him somewhat.

Lord! This is a complication I had not counted on.

He sat opposite her, in the small backwards-facing seat. His post-chaise was larger than many, and fairly comfortable, yet after his long journey down he had come to hate it. Now five more days on the road lay ahead. Five days backwards-facing. Five days in the company of—he stole a glance at her—truly one of the most beautiful women he had ever seen.

She kept on waving at the Ledbury House ladies until they were out of view, so he took the chance to study her. Her dark hair was just visible under the simple straw bonnet which framed quite the prettiest face he had seen in a long, long time. Her eyes were blue, and trimmed with long dark lashes. A straight little nose, tempting pink lips and a rosy complexion completed the vision.

He tried to assemble his disordered thoughts. The mysterious Jane Bailey was a young woman—a lady's maid working as a servant in Ledbury House. Surely too young to be his uncle's by-blow. Who, then, was she?

They had turned out of the Ledbury House drive now, and he was disconcerted to see that Miss Bailey was a little emotional. Wordlessly, he offered her a clean lawn handkerchief.

'Oh! Thank you, but I have…' She rummaged in her reticule, pulled out her own rather dainty handkerchief, then blew her nose with a no-nonsense air that impressed him a little.

'Forgive me, but you have not been away from home before?'

The fact that she was a servant made it easier for him to converse with her. Particularly when the servant was as beautiful and as intriguing as this one!

Social gatherings generally bored him. He still remembered the ordeal of having to perform like an actor on a stage any time he was brought into his aunt and uncle's presence. He had suffered it many times as a child, and echoes of it still sometimes came to him in empty gatherings.

She shook her head. 'Never! Well, that is to say I have never before left my mother behind.'

It only took him a moment to work it out. 'The other lady you embraced just now?'

She nodded. 'My mama is housekeeper at Ledbury House.'

The pride in her tone was unmistakable.

'Indeed? I should tell you I was impressed by Ledbury House. A well-run household, I think.'

He was rewarded with a slight smile for this.

'My mother is an excellent housekeeper, and we are fortunate to serve at Ledbury House.'

'Have you always lived there?'

'No.' Her brow creased slightly. 'I grew up in Cambridgeshire, in service to Miss Marianne's—Lady Kingswood's—own family. After Miss Marianne's marriage my mother and I—er—we followed her here.'

Abruptly, she closed her mouth, as if reluctant to say more.

There is some story there. Too soon to press for more information now, though.

'And have you ever been to Yorkshire, Miss Bailey?'

'Never.'

Her face closed. She clearly did not wish to discuss her connections with the north, whatever they were.

Too many questions too soon, Robert. You have five full days to discover whatever she might tell you.

'Today we shall travel as far as Market Harborough. I have written to the King's Head to reserve rooms for us there. I trust that is satisfactory?'

She nodded, and then sat back to look out of the window. He took the opportunity to watch her surreptitiously and to review what he knew about her. A servant…the daughter of a servant. Already lady's maid to a countess at a young age—which indicated both capability and dedication. Lady Kingswood thought highly of her…that much was also clear.

What had she to do with his uncle? From what he had seen Miss Bailey's mother had been a good-looking girl in her youth. Could his uncle have had a liaison with the mother only twenty or twenty-five years ago?

Robert tried to calculate Miss Bailey's age and his uncle's likely age when she had been born. He frowned. It was possible, though unlikely.

He glanced at her again.

My, she is beautiful!

He shifted slightly in his seat. As a servant, she needed no chaperone to accompany her. Not that she should need one. As a gentleman he had vowed to protect her and he would do so. He must. Honour required it.

He frowned. He had not brought a footman on the journey, preferring to make his own travel arrangements, so they would be alone apart from the various postilions who would steer the horses as they journeyed.

In blithely assuring Lady Kingswood of his good behaviour he had not known the temptation which was to follow. The temptation currently sitting opposite him, wearing a fine grey dress that hugged her form.

Some gentlemen, he knew, entered into liaisons with willing servants and ensured they did not suffer afterwards. This generally amounted to ensuring they gained another suitable post and that any children resulting from the association were brought up in suitable safety and comfort.

He squirmed uncomfortably in his seat. Viewing Miss Bailey's innocent face—currently she was gazing at the passing landscape—he could not imagine anyone being so lacking in principle as to pursue her for an irregular relationship. Despite her possible origins she had clearly been raised by good people with strong moral values. Everything about her—her demeanour, her demure clothing, her reserved conversation and the complete absence of anything resembling flirtation—confirmed it.

Shockingly, he found himself wishing she was otherwise…

'I am sorry, sir. Nuthin' I can do about it.'

The innkeeper's face was twisted with concern—as well it might be. Mr Kendal's expression was thunderous.

This is all about me.

Jane, used to remaining unseen and unnoticed, was deeply uncomfortable at this unwarranted attention.

'I specifically requested *two* bedchambers,' Mr Kendal repeated.

'That you did, sir,' the landlord acknowledged. 'But I got your letter just this afternoon and I only have the one room free.' He glanced at Jane's servant garb. 'Your servant may share a room with our chambermaids, if you like. We have three of them in the one room, with a spare bed free.'

A perfectly suitable arrangement! Jane breathed a sigh of relief.

Mr Kendal, however, was not to be diverted so easily.

'Or Miss Bailey could have the bedchamber and I could sleep somewhere else.'

Jane gasped. 'I am quite content with the innkeeper's suggestion, sir. I am well used to sharing a bedchamber with other female servants.'

His gaze swivelled towards her, grey eyes meeting blue. 'But…' He frowned. 'It does not seem right.'

Has he forgotten I am a serving maid?

'It is entirely reasonable, sir.'

He looked confused, then nodded slowly. 'I suppose you have the right of it.' He turned back to the landlord. 'Very well. I should also like a private parlour for dinner.'

'Yes, sir. That I *have* got.'

The innkeeper's relief was palpable. Taking a key from a cupboard behind him, and a lighted candlestick from the table, he led Mr Kendal up a twisting narrow staircase to the upper floor. Jane trailed behind, hovering on the narrow landing as Mr Kendal followed the innkeeper into his allocated bedchamber.

The landlord lit a branch of tall wax candles from his single one, casting warm light around the room. Moving to the fireplace, he lit the fire that had been set there. From her position in the dark corridor Jane glanced around. The chamber looked spacious, comfortable and clean.

'Would it please you to dine in one hour, sir?' The innkeeper paused, awaiting his guest's response.

Mr Kendal consulted his pocket watch. 'Very well. Er… Miss Bailey?'

Jane started. She moved to the doorway. 'Yes, sir?'

'I shall expect you to dine with me.'

'Yes, Mr Kendal.'

He frowned. 'That is to say I should like to *request* that you dine with me.'

Jane's brow creased in bewilderment. What was the difference? 'Yes, sir.'

'But, no, I…' He glanced at the landlord, whose puzzled expression mirrored Jane's own. 'Never mind.'

Jane considered the matter as she followed the landlord to the servants' quarters, but was unable to fathom Mr Kendal's meaning.

'Here you go, miss.' The innkeeper opened the door at the top of the attic stairs and stepped inside.

Jane followed, shivering as a blast of icy air hit her.

'A bit draughty in here, mind, but once all the others are in here with you it will soon warm up. They are all busy below, and shall be until around ten o'clock.' He lit a small tallow candle, which sputtered in the draught. 'This bed is free.' He pointed to a slightly stained pallet—the second in a row of four to Jane's left. 'I shall send up a sheet and a blanket for you later.'

'Thank you.'

The door closed behind him and Jane sank down onto the thin pallet. Oh, how she ached from being stuck in the jolting carriage for most of the day! The pallet was nothing to her comfortable bed at Ledbury House, but was typical of servants' accommodation in less wholesome establishments.

Reaching for the tallow candle, she carefully inspected the pallet for lice and fleas. There were none visible, which gave her some hope. They might not survive in a room this cold.

She shivered again. *Nor might I!*

Carefully she searched in her bandbox for her woollen stockings and put them on, on top of the thin pair she was already wearing. Keeping her cloak on, she wrapped it tightly about her, but decided to remove her bonnet as the straw was beginning to scratch at her scalp.

Drawing the hood of her cloak up, she concentrated on watching her breath fog the air in front of her and, despite the cold, on enjoying *not* being in a moving carriage.

Finally—thankfully—she judged that almost an hour had passed, based on the tallow candle having shrunk to half its length. She unfolded her legs and stood up slowly. Since sunset the temperature had kept on dropping. There would be a sharp frost in the morning.

With some regret, she removed her cloak, folded it, and left it on the pallet.

The thought of seeing Mr Kendal again made her heart skip momentarily. She could not quite divine why it was behaving so erratically.

As she descended she could feel the air getting warmer. By the time she had reached the ground floor there was a welcome warmth which danced on her skin and heated the air in her lungs.

One of the chambermaids showed her to Mr Kendal's private parlour. He had not yet arrived. Jane made straight for the fireplace, which boasted a small but cheerful fire.

Hurrying across the room, she held her frozen hands out towards it. It surely was the most beautiful thing she had ever seen!

The door opened and closed behind her, sending a puff of smoke billowing out into the room. It must be him! Briefly, the heat reached all the way to her elbows, then subsided again.

She turned. 'Good evening, sir.' Her voice sounded normal. Good. At least her stuttering heart had not revealed itself in her tone.

Mr Kendal had changed his clothing for dinner. She could not resist running her eyes over his fine figure.

'Good evening, Miss Bailey.'

He frowned, causing her to run a nervous hand over her hair, wondering if she were untidy. There had been, of course, no looking glass in the attic. At her back, slight heat from the fire began to penetrate through her dress and thin shift. Strangely, and most inconveniently, she now began to shiver. But she was warming up. It made no sense.

He strode towards her, peering into her face. He was still frowning. 'Miss Bailey,' he announced. 'Your lips are blue.'

She brought a hand up to touch her mouth. 'Th-they are?'

He nodded grimly. 'Give me your hand.'

She obeyed instinctively. He took her right hand, then the left, but she could barely feel his touch. With a muffled exclamation he wrapped both his hands around hers, rubbing gently.

'You foolish girl! You are half-frozen!'

'Oh, n-no!' she lied. 'I am j-just a little chilled.'

'Your teeth are chattering, your hands are like ice, and your lips are as blue as—as your eyes,' he muttered. 'How on earth did you get so cold? Have you been outside?'

'No! Of course not!' His eyes bored into hers. 'I have been in my chamber.'

His lips pressed into a single angry line. Releasing her hands, he walked to the table and drew forward a stout wooden chair. The stiffness in his spine and the set of his shoulders displayed his irritation. Arranging the chair directly in front of the fire, he bade her sit.

She did so, anxiously aware that she had displeased him. Schooled her entire life to be complaisant, obedient, and most of all unobtrusive, she was aware that right now she was being much too visible.

Without a word, he left the room, closing the door gently and carefully behind him. She shuddered at this evidence of his carefully banked anger.

Oh, no, he meant to speak to the landlord!

Unhelpfully, at that precise moment her mind decided to entertain her with the memory of a previous occasion on which she had caused trouble for those around her. It had been four years ago, when Lady Kingswood—then living under a false name—had been working as governess to Lady Cecily, Lord Kingswood's ward. Jane had inadvertently revealed that the governess was not, as His Lordship had believed, Anne Bolton, but Miss Marianne. This had led to Miss Marianne leaving in great distress and no one seeing her for weeks afterwards.

Overcome by shame, Jane held her head in her hands. From what she knew of Mr Kendal he seemed generally mild-mannered and calm. Her instinct told her he was not the type of gentleman who customarily challenged innkeepers or expressed displeasure with their services. Yet, because of her, he was forced to leave his warm parlour to take issue with his host. She felt terrible to have caused this much inconvenience.

The door opened, admitting a different serving maid. 'Good evening, miss. Dinner is almost ready, so I am here to prepare the table, if you will permit?'

'Of course! Mr Kendal has asked me to dine with him. I am honoured, but I am used to dining with the other servants.'

'Ah! So you are the maid who will sleep in our attic tonight?' The maid began setting out crockery, cutlery and carving knives on the clean table cloth.

'I am.' Jane paused. 'I was upstairs earlier. It was very cold.'

'That'll be the gap in the eaves. When the stuffing falls out it gets powerful cold up there.'

'The stuffing?'

'Aye, me and the other girls have stuffed an old mattress into the hole. It works a treat, but now and again it falls out, and the wind whistles through like the very devil!'

'That explains it! I did wonder how you managed to survive, sleeping in such a cold room.'

The maid laughed. 'It's not perfect, but we are glad to have a roof over our heads and an honest day's work. Though I shan't get the chance to nip upstairs and stuff the mattress back in place until after dinner, and even then we might be busy in the taproom.'

She moved around the table competently, arranging everything in neat formation. Watching her, Jane was struck by the similarities in their station—and the differences. They were both servants, but Jane was used to rather more luxury than a cold attic bedroom with holes in its walls.

'Is that your master in the taproom?'

Jane raised an eyebrow at the maid's question.

'The good-looking gentleman as is giving my uncle an earful about something?'

Jane closed her eyes briefly. 'Er…yes.'

The maid departed, satisfied with her work, giving way to Mr Kendal in the doorway. 'Sorry, sir.'

'Not at all.'

He is considerate towards servants, Jane noted.

He moved towards her and she searched his face for hints as to his mood. The earlier irritation had gone. What she saw now was— Was that an air of *satisfaction*?

'How do you now, Miss Bailey?'

'I am perfectly well, thank you, sir.'

He threw her a sceptical look. 'You are still shivering. And yet—' he leaned forward to inspect her more closely '—your lips are returning to their normal rosy hue.'

He paused for a moment, his gaze lingering on her mouth, then he seemed to shake himself out of it.

He took a step back, stating in quite a different tone, 'I wonder what delights our landlord will offer us for dinner?'

Food was not uppermost in Jane's thoughts. She was freezing, exhausted, and still stiff from a full day stuck in the carriage. Yet, strangely, her heart was fluttering foolishly and her insides were melting with a curious warmth. It was, she recognised, to do with Mr Kendal's proximity and the way he had looked at her mouth just now.

What is happening to me?

Since Henry Grant's assault upon her person she had never felt this way. Of course she had encountered attractive men on occasion, but her appreciation of them had been impersonal, almost scholarly. Never visceral.

Never like this.

Before she could gather her thoughts the innkeeper appeared in the doorway, leading a procession of three maids and a manservant, all bearing dishes.

In the ensuing fuss, she found her equilibrium again, and not long afterwards her appetite.

Chapter Six

The innkeeper had provided a tasty and filling meal, with capons, turnips and potatoes, as well as some sort of stew flavoured with herbs, and there was even cake and cream.

Jane had found herself conversing lightly with Mr Kendal—the polite equilibrium of their discourse during today's travel reasserting itself and making her question whether anything had actually happened in that moment before the fireplace, when her pulse had raced and her knees had felt peculiarly soft.

Soft in the head, more like, she admonished herself as she finished her meal.

'That was an excellent dinner,' she said.

Mr Kendal shrugged. 'It was perfectly adequate.'

Of course. A splendid dinner such as this—which seemed both extravagant and grand to her, as a servant— was probably commonplace for a gentleman like Mr Kendal.

She eyed him through her lashes. He was contemplating the port wine in his glass. His handsome face was open and relaxed, and he was ignoring the servants who had now swooped in to clear the table.

The room had warmed up nicely, as had Jane herself. The warm food had helped too. But the thought of returning to that freezing attic was daunting.

'What are you thinking about?'

His voice was soft, and sent a peculiar tingle dancing through her.

'Your face is so expressive, yet it speaks a language I do not understand. Not yet, at least.'

She flushed. *He is watching me!*

'In truth, sir, I was wondering what time it is. The other maids will retire at ten o'clock and I should do likewise.'

He consulted his pocket watch. 'It is not yet nine, so there is yet time to enjoy a pleasant after-dinner hour.' He paused. 'I have taken the liberty of amending the arrangements for tonight. The attic the landlord offered you to sleep in is clearly inadequate.'

She gaped. 'You have been to the attic?'

'I have. I was almost frozen in the brief time I was standing there. I told the innkeeper that no one should be expected to sleep in it—not least a female under my care.'

'The maid has told me there is a gap in the eaves. I was going to stuff a mattress into it—'

He held up a hand. 'Neither you nor the other maids shall sleep there tonight. The maids are to bring their pallets to the kitchen and you will have my chamber.'

'Oh, no, sir! I cannot!'

'You can, and you shall!'

'But where will you sleep?'

He smiled slightly. 'I shall sleep here. The landlord is arranging for a mattress to be installed.' He smiled again at her gasp of shock. 'I shall be perfectly comfortable, I assure you.'

Despite all her protestations he would not be persuaded. He moved the conversation on to an outline of their journey on the morrow, and she agreed to be ready to be on the road soon after sunrise, so as to make the most of the daylight.

Afterwards they moved their chairs to the fireplace and sat in comfortable silence, watching the dancing flames. She could see out of the corner of her eye his long legs, stretched out towards the hearth. Most of her life she had been surrounded by women—mainly servants, but also her beloved mistress. Men had always been there, of course, but as a lady's maid she'd normally had only the briefest contact with them.

Wistfully, she recalled dim memories of her father. He

had used to tell her tales of magic and far-off lands, and had sung to her and read her poetry.

Not since those long-gone days had she sat in congenial harmony with a man.

I like it, she decided. *I must remember this night.*

As expected, a strong frost greeted them the next morning as the carriage pulled away from the inn. Jane delighted in observing the delicate filigree of white on trees and hedgerows, and the dainty outlines of frosted silken webs on gates and fences. After a good night's sleep and a hearty breakfast she felt alert and ready for the day's journey.

She had insisted all three serving maids move their pallets into what had been Mr Kendal's chamber. If she was to sleep in luxury, then so would they, she had declared.

Some judicious questioning had revealed that one of the older maids had a bad back, so Jane had offered her the large bed. Sleeping on a pallet in a warm, comfortable room had been a welcome relief after her hour in the cold attic earlier in the evening.

One of the chambermaids had snored during the night, but once she had worked out what the sound was she had gone back to sleep with little difficulty.

The landlord had assured Mr Kendal he would mend the hole in the eaves that very day. The maids had confidentially confirmed to Jane that their master did truly mean to do so, as he was concerned Mr Kendal had the power to harm his reputation among the aristocracy and gentry by spreading what the landlord labelled 'false rumours' regarding his treatment of the inn's servants.

Feeling a warm sense of satisfaction at this outcome, and increased confidence that she was, despite her worries, managing quite well without Mama by her side, Jane settled back in her seat. The scratchy straw bonnet was firmly in place, and her feet were already cold, but these things were to be expected.

Mr Kendal looked across at her and Jane could not help smiling at him. He looked a little startled, then smiled back and all was well.

As the hours passed they amused themselves with light conversation, exploring each other's opinions, likes and dislikes on a range of topics including the seasons—both loved spring—food—Jane had tasted most of the dishes he mentioned, though had rarely had more than a few bites of the delicacies returned to the kitchen once the family had finished—and pastimes.

Here Jane was at a clear disadvantage, for when one's day was filled with attending to one's mistress, her clothes and her possessions, it left almost no time for leisure. However, they *were* able to agree on the delights of walking through pleasant countryside.

Mr Kendal described the lands around Beechmount Hall, which sounded both extensive and pretty.

'The Hall itself,' he admitted, 'seems rather dour on first glance, but its situation is delightful. I learned to ride in the fields and hills surrounding it. Do you ride, Miss Bailey?'

Jane laughed. 'I think,' she said with a twinkle, 'that you are in danger of forgetting I am a servant, sir. Of course I do not ride!'

His eyes widened. 'Do you know you are right? We are having such a comfortable conversation that it had, in truth, slipped my mind.' His eyes gleamed with humour. 'In future I shall cultivate the acquaintance of *all* the servants I meet. If they are even half as diverting and witty as you are I shall be well pleased.'

She flushed. 'Oh, well, I dare say you would be surprised at the conversations we share in the servants' hall.'

'Indeed? Now I am intrigued!' He leaned forward. 'Do tell me more.'

'Oh…' She waved her hands airily. 'We discuss the Royals, and the French—and the war, of course.'

'Tell me more. Now Napoleon is defeated, what is your opinion on peace in Europe?'

She shuddered. 'That Napoleon! Why, we were all terrified he would cross the sea and kill us all! It was such a relief when he was defeated and sent to Elba. I do hope he remains there.'

'As do I.'

From there, they discussed the burning of Washington by General Ross—which Jane could not agree with, although she knew she was in a minority.

Surprisingly, Mr Kendal felt the same. 'There was no need for it,' he declared.

Jane beamed at him, delighted to find an ally. 'Oh, how I wish you had been there when we discussed it at Ledbury House, for I was the only one who said so! Both Mama and the steward believed it was justified in the circumstances. But I could not agree.'

He raised an eyebrow. 'Now it is you who forgets the difference in our station. Had I walked into the servants' hall it would have instantly ended all conversation.'

'Oh, but most of the servants would not have been discussing such matters. Only those of us who—'

'Who what?'

She flushed. 'As lady's maid I have had some education—such that I am more informed than most of the staff. I often sit with Mama and the steward in Mama's sitting room.'

'I see.'

And on their discussion went.

They were so occupied that it was a surprise to both of them when the carriage pulled into an inn yard for a change of horses. Mr Kendal, who had agreed the plan earlier, with today's postilion, declared the time had passed so quickly he could scarce believe it was already noon.

His words gave Jane a warm glow inside.

Half an hour later, following refreshments and the use

of the retiring rooms, they climbed back into the carriage. The new horses were fresh and they sped along through the countryside. Jane and Mr Kendal alternated conversation with periods of companionable silence as on their left the sun began to sink towards the horizon and the day began to get colder.

'We must be almost at Grantham,' murmured Mr Kendal. 'A pity there is no blanket in the carriage for you. It is growing colder by the minute.'

Jane was about to protest that she was fine, and needed no blanket, when suddenly the carriage slowed, then stopped altogether.

'What's amiss?'

Mr Kendal's brow was creased. He opened the door and jumped down lightly. Her curiosity getting the better of her, Jane leaned out to discover what was happening.

She could make out a cart ahead, its rear wheel stuck in a ditch. The cart was angled in such a way that it was blocking the road. Biting her lip, and ignoring the voice in her head that told her to stay put, she jumped down and made her way to the accident. The cart was tethered to a single horse, which was currently nibbling on some short winter grass at the side of the road.

Mr Kendal and the postilion were walking towards a person lying in the road. Someone was hurt.

Instinct drove her forward. She had always been fearless when tending the wounded. It went right back to her admiration of the doctor and his assistant who had tried so hard to save Papa. She had made it her business to learn to tend such minor ailments and injuries as were commonplace at home. There was a bone-setter in the village, as well as a midwife, and she had pestered them until they had agreed to pass on to her what wisdom they had.

The injured man must have been thrown from the cart when it went into the ditch. Jane could tell at a glance that his leg was broken. He was moaning in pain, and Jane immediately bent to speak to him.

'Sir,' she said in a firm, clear voice, 'you have broken your leg. Do you have any other hurts?' She was running her eyes over him as she spoke and could see no other injuries.

'No,' he grunted. 'My horse…?'

'Your horse is sound,' confirmed Mr Kendal. 'The cart also looks undamaged. It appears the only casualty is you.'

'Thank God!' the man said, then moaned more loudly as Jane touched his damaged leg.

'I am sorry.' She grimaced. Turning to Mr Kendal, she muttered, 'I shall need something to splint it with.'

'Of course!' He nodded to the postilion and they disappeared together towards a nearby stand of trees.

Jane stayed with the injured man, keeping him occupied with conversation until they returned. The men had found some thin dead wood of a decent length, and the postilion had produced some twine from the carriage.

As gently as they could, Jane and Mr Kendal lined up the splints either side of the man's leg, then fixed them with twine. They worked well together, and Jane was grateful for Mr Kendal's acceptance of her skill. He obeyed her instructions without question, and before long they were done.

'Now then—Mr Lingard,' said Jane briskly—for she had established the injured man's name. 'How far are we from your farmhouse?'

'Not more than half a mile,' he replied. 'First lane on the left. My missus will be worriting, for I should have been home an hour since.'

Mr Kendal, following a hurried conversation with the coachman, returned with a plan. 'We shall attempt to pull your cart out of the ditch,' he said.

'I am exceedingly grateful to you, sir,' the man managed. He was clearly in pain, and needed to be in his own bed.

The sun had finally slipped below the horizon, and it was becoming colder and darker by the minute.

The men lifted the injured farmer out of the way and Jane stayed with him while they heaved at the cart. Eventually, and in a sudden rush, they managed to get the left wheel out of the ditch.

'Now, Mr Lingard,' she said calmly, 'they shall lift you into the back of the cart.'

He groaned at this, knowing any movement would hurt. Mr Kendal and the coachman were as careful as possible, but poor Mr Lingard could not help but cry out. As soon as they had settled him in the flat bed of the cart Jane immediately climbed up beside him. There were beads of sweat on the man's forehead, and his hands were bunched into tight fists.

'Now, then...' She spoke soothingly, dabbing his brow with a handkerchief. 'We shall have you home in no time.'

A still figure was hovering at the edge of her vision. She lifted her head from her charge to observe Mr Kendal, eyeing her with a raised eyebrow and a gleam of humour in his eye.

'Miss Bailey.'

'Yes, Mr Kendal?'

'Are you expecting me to drive this cart?'

'Well,' she replied tartly, 'you can hardly expect *me* to do it!'

'And yet...' he spoke slowly '... I somehow think if the need required you to do so you would be equal to it.'

She snorted. 'A plain cart and a placid horse? Of course I would! But my place is here, with Mr Lingard. The postilion shall follow with the carriage.' She held up her hands. 'Is it not plain that is what we must do?'

He closed his eyes briefly. 'Miss Bailey, you are an extremely managing female!'

'Thank you, Mr Kendal.' Her eyes danced.

'That was no compliment.'

'Oh, I know.'

She threw him a dazzling smile and he shook his head and climbed into the driver's seat, gathering the reins. She could tell he was amused even by observing the back of his head and the shape of his shoulders.

She grinned, conscious of a strange feeling of delight. Then the cart moved off, the injured farmer groaned, and she returned to her task.

Chapter Seven

'Another day in this blasted carriage!' Mr Kendal looked cross. 'Apologies, Miss Bailey, but I felt all night as though I were still moving.'

Once again they were travelling, and today would mark the midpoint of their journey. It had been late when they had left the Lingard farmhouse, and the day had, in truth, felt interminable.

This morning Mr Kendal had ensured there were blankets for both of them in the carriage. And Jane was grateful for the extra warmth as they travelled through the cold February countryside.

'There is no need to apologise, for I know exactly what you mean. In a way, I am becoming hardened to the jolts and the bumps and the cold, yet in another sense I shall never become accustomed to it.' She paused for a second, then offered diffidently, 'Do you wish to sit beside me, in the facing seat? There is plenty of room, and it is so much more comfortable than travelling back-facing.'

He frowned and she held her breath. His proximity now seemed a way of life for her, yet meeting his gaze so frequently was disconcerting. On occasions when their eyes met a delicious shiver would go through her—an effect as disturbing as it was delightful. Perhaps if he was beside her, rather than opposite, she might avoid it and be calm.

'Very well—if you are certain you do not mind?'

She confirmed it, and he shifted across to sit next to her. He kept to the far corner and immediately his eyes were drawn outwards, to the passing fields and hedgerows.

She glanced across at the empty facing seat and a pang went through her at the absence of the view she had become accustomed to. She closed her eyes, recalling every detail. Long legs, stretched out in front and to her right, solid body—torso, shoulders, arms, hands... His face— yes, she could see it in her mind...every detail. The strong jaw, straight nose, clear skin and those stormy grey eyes.

'Are you planning to rest a while?'

His voice penetrated her reverie and she jumped.

I should not have been thinking of such things!

'Apologies, I did not mean to startle you.'

She turned her head—to be met with that very face, those eyes, alongside her and much closer than before.

What on earth was I thinking? Of course I cannot avoid his effect on me!

'Oh, no! I— That is to say, I am not fatigued.'

'Good,' he said simply, 'for I have an idea to pass the time on today's journey.'

She eyed him quizzically.

'I thought we could share some riddles.'

'Oh, yes! What an excellent notion!'

She knew her face was flushed, but hoped he would think it due to excitement at his suggestion rather than a racing heart from the effect of having him seated so close.

'We often share riddles in the servants' hall at Yuletide and on other festival days.'

'Excellent. I shall begin, if you will permit?'

She nodded and clasped her hands tightly together. For the next while they tested and challenged each other. She was able to appreciate his quick wit, and the harmony between them could not be denied.

Have I found a friend?

The thought sent a warm glow flowing slowly through her. She had never before had a friend who was a man.

Following the interruption of their journey for refreshments, and a brief walk around a village to shake the stiffness from their limbs, they returned to the carriage. This time Mr Kendal made no complaints. He took his place beside her as if it were the most natural thing in the world, and she welcomed it despite the effect of his proximity on her body.

Or perhaps because of it.

Thankfully she felt no danger from him, and her old memories remained dormant. This she was glad about, for there had been frequent occasions in the past years when she had been completely overcome by powerful memories of Master Henry's attack.

During the long, slow afternoon they passed the time in sharing stories of childhood. Although from different stations in life, both had lost their fathers at a similar age. While being wary of where the conversation might lead—for Mama's warning was still at the front of her mind—Jane nevertheless decided to trust him with some memories of her papa, and the tale of his death from fever.

Mr Kendal listened with great sympathy, and asked her some warm questions about her father's character and strength. She had a little cry and he gave her his handkerchief.

Afterwards he told her of his own father, and the sense of loss he had felt when his papa had passed away.

'Not only did we lose him,' he offered, his gaze distant as he focused on those long-ago days, 'we lost our home, too.' His gaze swung towards her. 'Although he was a gentleman, his wealth was modest. We had some land outside the town, and he had invested all his savings in buying a herd of merino sheep.'

She barely heard this last part, instead focusing on his first sentence. She gasped. He, too, had lost his home. Immediately treasured memories of Rose Cottage flashed through her mind, lightning-quick, stabbing at her heart. *Home.* The one true home she had ever known.

He was looking at her. She swallowed, then managed, 'Merino! It is a fine wool. I love to work with it.'

'Indeed. My business now still involves merino wool.

However, our English weather was too harsh for those sheep. They did not thrive and my mother eventually sold them, and the land, to create a small fund for us. Eventually she had no choice but to call upon the charity of her aunt. We moved there less than a year after Papa died.'

'It must have been hard for you, moving to Beechmount Hall so soon,' she offered, picturing him as a lost little boy clinging to his mother's hand. Or was that her? A lost little girl clinging to her mama?

'It was terrifying,' he said simply. 'I was used to living in a modest house in Harrogate, on the main street, with all the sounds and busyness of the town as the background of my life.'

Jane spoke quietly. 'Mama and I moved from a simple cottage to work in a large country house, so I understand a little of what you must have experienced.'

She declined to mention their year of hunger.

His eyes met hers and there was a silence. Dimly, Jane felt something shift between them.

Mr Kendal sat up straighter, and adjusted his waistcoat. 'Beechmount Hall was a decided contrast to my previous home. It was huge, remote—and decidedly Gothic!'

She nodded furiously. 'I feel daunted by going there and I am three-and-twenty!'

'There is no need.' His expression was entirely serious. 'I shall stand with you.'

Her eyes widened. *What ordeal does he expect me to face?*

Yet her heart could only be distracted by his declaration of support, so she subsided into confused silence.

There was a pause. 'I wonder how Mr Lingard is faring,' he offered, in a lighter tone.

She smiled, relieved. 'It was a clean break, I think. A few weeks of rest and loving care and he will be back driving his cart again. I am glad we came upon him. He might have lain there for hours as the road was so quiet.'

'He was fortunate indeed—doubly so.'

She eyed him questioningly.

'You do not understand my meaning? Very well. He was fortunate we found him and fortunate that you, Miss Bailey, were at hand to care for him.'

She flushed. 'I only did what anyone might have done.'

He shook his head. 'We both know that is not true. Why, your skills were evident, and you prevailed like—like an army commander, sweeping me and the postilion aside and—'

'I did not!' she declared hotly. 'I only wished to establish how serious his injuries were and to offer him some reassurance.' She spoke earnestly. 'It is always important, I find, to quieten and comfort the injured person immediately. If they are anxious it becomes much more difficult to assist them. I certainly did not intend to *command* anyone, or— You are laughing at me.' She shook her head. 'But truly I did not—I mean I have never sought to act above my station or to interfere...'

He was still smiling. 'I suspect both Mr Lingard and his wife are entirely grateful for your interference, my dear.'

He lifted his hand and ran a light finger down her cheek, his touch leaving a trail of fire in its wake. She caught her breath then looked away, flushing. She stared unseeing at the passing countryside, conscious of the charged atmosphere in the carriage.

Why did he do that? No man has dared touch me since... And why am I suddenly incapable of speech?

The easy companionship they had built over these past days seemed suddenly lost, replaced by something chaotic, and wonderful, and entirely dangerous.

Jane had no idea how she was supposed to behave towards him. He was a gentleman and she a servant. Their familiarity was simply because they had been forced into travelling together.

For a moment she allowed herself to imagine him a servant, like her. Or she a lady.

Perhaps my grandfather is motivated by kindness and means to elevate me?

She rejected the possibility immediately. A man so determined to be cruel to his own son would hardly welcome a granddaughter who had a servant for her mother. No, she must not allow herself to hope for such things. Even if it would make friendship possible between herself and a gentleman. Make him someone she would be permitted to get to know. Someone who might even…

A pang of wishful regret stabbed through her.

It is not to be.

Inwardly, she shook her head. She had been too much at ease with him. It would be better for both of them if she remembered from now on that he was a gentleman and she was a lady's maid—not a lady.

Chapter Eight

Robert was furious with himself.

You foolish idiot! he raged internally. *Why did you touch her?*

For days they had spent almost every waking moment in each other's company. And to his great surprise, this journey had been immeasurably more pleasant than the trip down from Yorkshire. Far from tiring of Miss Bailey's company, he had found himself ever more at ease with her—and, he'd thought, she with him.

He had delighted in her companionship, enjoying her alert mind and invigorating conversation. Watching the true Jane Bailey emerge from beneath layers of reserved propriety had been a delight. He believed he now knew something of her true self, and learning about her had become a fascination.

Even so she had been remarkably reticent when it came to her parentage and her links to Beechmount Hall. Despite his best efforts he had been politely dissuaded and diverted. Yet through it all he had believed she was beginning to trust him. And now one imprudent action might have undone the work of days.

Oh, but how he had wanted to do it!

Finally he had admitted it to himself. Miss Bailey was more than a riddle to be solved. In his madder moments he thought himself quite bewitched. Of course when he returned to sanity he saw immediately that she was simply an attractive woman. A beautiful, charming, intelligent, kind-hearted and witty young woman.

Apart from that, she was nothing out of the ordinary.

It is only because we are being forced to spend so much time alone together. Alone, yet with intimacy forbidden.

Indeed, it was hard to believe he had met her less than one week ago. Naturally he would never seek to persuade an unwilling woman, but he sensed that she, too, had become more at ease with him. Perhaps not quite in the way he wished—she did not yet trust him enough to tell him of her history, and she might well see him simply as a companion rather than harbour any stronger passion.

She was perfectly amiable towards him but, he conceded ruefully, had given him no sign of anything warmer.

This was rather disconcerting. He was used to women liking him. Flirting, even. Yet there was nothing of flirtation in Miss Bailey's manner towards him. She gazed at him with an open, direct look and, he believed, would have shown just as much interest in him had he been seventeen or seventy.

It matters not! he reminded himself.

She was a servant, and therefore forbidden to him. Any attachment between them could never be. He was a gentleman, prevented from marrying a servant, and she was too respectable, too pure, to agree to be any man's mistress.

Even if she *was* related to his uncle, Robert knew he would be much too proud to elevate a servant. Robert himself did not set much store by such things, but Mr Millthorpe was rigidly traditional in such matters. No, he could not see any way for his station and Miss Bailey's to become level.

So why, then, had he, in a fit of madness, dared to touch her?

He groaned inwardly, recalling her instant distress, her withdrawal. Yes, the sensation of her soft cheek had thrilled him, but he had been foolish to succumb to his baser impulse.

She is alone with you in a carriage! he berated himself inwardly. *A servant in your care.*

She had trusted him to behave properly and he had betrayed that trust. He felt both ashamed and strangely uncertain. Neither feeling was welcome.

In truth, nothing in his life had prepared him for this. As a child he had coped with his new surroundings in Beechmount Hall by becoming quiet, watchful and reserved. After two years he had been sent away to school, where loneliness had etched itself into his bones. He had been a dutiful scholar, son and nephew, at first terrorised by his uncle's disapproval and his teachers' discipline.

But he had grown into himself and found his own strength, and he no longer felt the same quaking fear. Yet still, somewhere deep inside, lurked the loneliness that had somehow become part of him.

He was his own man, sure of himself and of his place in the world. Yet now, having torn at the fragile sense of trust he had been building with Miss Bailey, he must chastise himself.

He glanced towards her, felt an unexpected uncertainty vexing him as he regarded her pretty face, turned outwards towards the passing trees and hedgerows. The feeling that she was not in charity with him bothered him much more than it should.

Eventually he did the only thing he could think of. He spoke to her of trivialities.

'We shall be arriving in Lincoln soon, I think.'

She turned her head and looked at him, her face expressionless.

He continued with seeming equanimity. 'I have reserved rooms at the White Hart, which is a well-known and comfortable posting inn there.'

She inclined her head, replying, 'We shall be early, then?'

'We have made good time today—for the roads, I think, have been particularly smooth. It makes sense to stop here, for the next decent inn is many miles further on. Tomorrow will be our last full day of travel.'

'Good,' she said simply.

Good? He could interpret that in a hundred ways—very few of them flattering.

Her forehead creased. 'So what shall we do? For it is too early to dine...'

'There are seemingly ramparts at Lincoln Castle, which is apparently an interesting and pleasant place to visit. I thought we might go there for an hour or so, to divine if the reports of its beauty and antiquity are accurate. There is also a market which I would like to visit. You may accompany me if it pleases you.' He was deliberately offhand.

She inclined her head, matching his coolness. 'It is not for me to say what we shall do, sir. Nor must you feel any responsibility to ensure I am entertained. I am, after all, a serving maid.'

He felt the sting of her rebuke and the force of the unseen wall now standing between them.

So be it. Miss Jane Bailey, for all her gifts, would be gone from his life in a matter of weeks. No one but the two of them would ever know what had passed between them.

He stared out at the passing hedgerows, unseeing.

Her opinion of me will not affect the course of my life, nor my reputation. It matters not a jot.

'Oh, how wonderful!'

Jane could not stop herself from giving voice to her enthusiastic response. The views were stunning. From their vantage point on the medieval walls Jane could see all of Lincoln spread out below them. The day was bright and cold, but her cloak was wrapped tightly around her and her bonnet gave some small protection from the biting wind. They had already seen the cathedral, and the remains of the Bishop's Palace, and had now climbed up onto the walls.

She had stumbled slightly on the way up, and Mr Kendal had instinctively reached out to steady her. The grasp of his hand on her elbow had been brief, and at the time welcome, yet it had left a now familiar tingling awareness in its wake.

Since that moment earlier in the carriage, when he had touched her cheek, she had been intensely aware of him. Her senses seemed attuned to his presence, tracking his whereabouts and his distance from her. She was entirely consumed by this new consciousness, and at the same time mystified by it.

After enjoying the prospect they walked together to the Below Hill side of the city, towards Cornhill. The market was a busy press of people, goods and livestock.

Jane and Mr Kendal ambled together among the traders and stallholders, Mr Kendal stopping to converse with a wool merchant. Jane listened with interest as they spoke together. Mr Kendal displayed great knowledge on wool quality, the dyeing process, and eventually asked the man about his sources for imported wool, including merino.

Ah! she thought. *That has been his purpose all along!*

Watching his handsome features become so animated was strangely diverting. Absentmindedly she eyed some beautiful shawls, trying to disguise the fact that all her attention was on Mr Kendal.

At this moment he was to her right. There was less than a foot of space between them, and out of the corner of her eye she could see his arm and the front of his coat. Unfortunately her bonnet prevented her from seeing more. She was becoming quite adept at keeping her head respectably straight ahead while her eyes glanced sideways for any glimpse she could manage.

She opened her reticule without looking, as if checking what coins she had. Yet her mind was entirely focused on Mr Kendal.

Robert. His name is Robert.

A thrill went through her.

Stop! she told herself.

Yet she could not. Would not. It was as though his touch on her cheek earlier had awakened within her an entirely new self.

He likes me. Or does he?

She had thought so, but then he had become distant.

Am I flattered? Is that it? He is such a fine gentleman, and so handsome. For him to notice a simple serving maid is a compliment. But I should not be conceited!

She frowned. Mama would warn her to be on her guard against flummery and coaxing.

She considered this.

His touching my face was an impulse of the moment, nothing more.

Even at the time, although withdrawing in confusion, she had instinctively known there was no ill intent behind it. Having served in the Grant household, she had seen for herself what evil looked like. Mr Kendal was a man of honour, unlike Master Henry. Mr Kendal, she knew, was not the sort of man to press unwanted attentions on a woman, or to seduce an honest maid with flattery and charm. She need not worry on that account.

Daringly, she tried to imagine what it would be like to be intimate with Mr Kendal. Her heart began to race and her breath to quicken as she imagined his strong arms enfolding her, his mouth approaching hers, the weight of his body pressing on her…

Oh, Lord, no!

In her mind Mr Kendal's face was abruptly replaced by that of her former employer. Henry Grant had continually seduced, attacked and abused women—including some of the maids. She shuddered.

It is happening again!

Suddenly, and for the first time in at least a year, she found herself back there again, in that awful moment…

She sits sewing quietly in the housekeeper's parlour and Master Henry appears out of nowhere. At first she is simply confused. Why is the master below-stairs? Then she sees the intent in his eyes and tries to run. Hampered by her skirts, she is not swift enough. He catches her and over-powers her, despite her screams of fear.

Who would save her? Who would stop him?

He inches her backwards until she feels the table be-hind her. His hand is grabbing her breast. It hurts. Now he presses her down, using his weight to pin her while he fumbles with his breeches. She has seen enough animals mating to dimly understand what will happen next.

'No!' she screams, still fighting and struggling to get away. 'Master Henry, please, no!'

But he is bigger and heavier and immensely stronger. He laughs. He throws his head up and laughs.

She feels physically sick. Fear has made its way through every part of her. Soon he will have his way, and she is powerless to stop him.

Then somewhere far, far away she hears Mama's voice. 'You disgusting animal!'

There is a sound—the slap of liquid on solid—then a foul stench.

With an enraged roar he levers himself upright, momen-tarily abandoning his assault on Jane. Free of his weight on her chest and hips, she takes a quick breath before rising swiftly. Her limbs are weak, but escape is her first priority.

Mama is standing before him, white-faced yet defiant, a now empty chamber pot hanging loosely from her hand.

'How dare you?' He lifts his right hand and punches Mama hard, in the stomach. She doubles over, retching.

'Mama!'

Fear for her mother propels Jane forward. Her entire body is shaking, yet somehow she reaches Mama. They cling to each other, yet Jane is numb. She cannot feel the warmth of Mama's body against hers.

Master Henry lifts his hand again and Jane swerves in-stinctively to avoid the blow.

'I want a bath. Immediately!'

Jane stares at him blankly.

'I said, I want a bath now!' His words sound like the roar of a wild animal.

Jane nods, still overwhelmed by terror.

He leans forward. *'I shall finish with you later.'* His voice oozes menace.

Jane is completely frozen with fear. She cannot move, think, or speak. As he stomps away, the world turns black...

Chapter Nine

$\mathcal{Robert}$ reached for her, managing to catch her as she fell. He could barely think, all his attention sharpened on Jane.

'Over here, sir!'

The trader he had been talking to pointed to a small chair at the back of his stall. The ground was muddy, so he could not lay Jane down there. He carried her to the chair and sat, still supporting her in his arms.

How pale she looks!

Her beautiful skin was ashen, her body limp. He felt helpless. Gently he straightened her bonnet, in case it should cause her discomfort. As he did so her eyes fluttered open. His heart lurched as he beheld the dazed fear in her eyes. She struggled to be free and he loosened his embrace.

'You are safe,' he muttered hoarsely as she rose to a sitting position. 'You are safe.'

Her breathing was rapid and he could tell her pulse would be tumultuous. She swayed slightly, dizzy with her sudden change in position. Immediately he steadied her with a firm hand on her arm.

'Slowly,' he advised. 'You will faint again if you rise too quickly.'

Part of him was aware that he was holding Jane Bailey in his lap, but he could not think of that now.

'Here is your reticule, miss.'

The trader was brushing mud off her silken purse, which had fallen to the ground open. Some coins fell from it as he picked it up and he scrambled to collect them and return them to their rightful place.

'Thank you.'

Her voice was tremulous, and her hand shook as she

accepted the reticule. Robert could feel that she had begun to tremble all over. Instinctively, gently, he wrapped his arms around her. This seemed to be her undoing for she began to cry, great sobs heaving through her delicate frame.

Robert felt as though his heart must break.

The trader averted his eyes as Robert simply sat there, holding her close. She turned towards him, hiding herself from the interested eyes of the traders and their customers who had come to gape at the spectacle.

Without thinking about it Robert rested his chin on the top of her head as she cried into his chest. Closing his eyes, he directed his mind and his senses entirely towards Jane.

The warmth of her body flowed through him, and he knew he was also sharing his heat with her. Her hands were fisted against his breastbone, her elbows tight by her sides. Great sobs racked her body, and each sound she made pierced him with pain. This was the self-possessed, steady, serene Miss Bailey, momentarily broken by some evil act that he could only guess at.

Her cry had been telling: *'Master Henry, please, no!'*

She had gone rigid beside him, her reticule falling unnoticed from her hand. He had tried to speak to her but she had simply stared at him, her eyes huge and sightless. She had called out once, then a moment later had collapsed in a dead faint.

Eventually she quietened, her sobs turning to hiccups and then ceasing entirely. She muttered something to his chest.

'I cannot understand you,' he said gently. 'What did you say?'

She pulled back a little, but did not look up. 'Handkerchief.'

Unlocking his arms from about her, he fished for his handkerchief and handed it to her.

She blew her nose and dried her face before looking at

him. His hands now rested uselessly in his lap, though he wished he could embrace her again.

Finally her eyes met his, inches apart. The intimacy was unbearably wonderful. Perhaps she felt it too, for she flushed and quickly stood, resting her right hand briefly on his knee in order to lever herself upright. Immediately she swayed and her pallor increased.

Leaping to his feet, he gently took her elbow and stepped to one side. 'Be seated, Miss Bailey.'

She all but collapsed on to the chair.

Bending down, so he was at her level, he spoke softly to her. 'You have sustained a shock. It is best to rest here until you are feeling better.'

She nodded, seemingly unable to speak. She was shivering and her hand was cold.

'I have brandy, sir, if the young lady wishes?' The trader was back with a stoneware flask.

'That might be just the thing!' He offered it to Jane, who hesitated, then took it.

She spluttered a little, then sat back in the chair and closed her eyes. 'Please tell them to stop looking at me,' she murmured.

Robert nodded to the trader, who went to scatter the spectators with a few polite words.

'They are gone,' he confirmed.

She nodded and opened her eyes.

Robert asked the trader for one of his cashmere shawls. The man reached for the nearest one, but Robert stopped him. 'No, not that one. The blue.'

He passed it across and Robert draped it over Miss Bailey's shoulders.

I was right—that blue is exactly the same shade as her eyes.

He paid the trader and waited. Gradually some colour returned to her cheeks.

He could tell when her self-awareness started to return.

Her hands began to twist the handkerchief in her lap, and after a time she looked at him.

'Mr Kendal, what an idiot you must think me! To become vapourish for no reason... I—'

'Do not be distressed, Miss Bailey. It is clear to me that you had reason. Someone, at some time, hurt you, and I believe the memory of it assailed you again just now.' His voice was thick with emotion.

Who the hell is 'Master Henry' and what evil did he commit?

She nodded, her expression bleak. 'It has been many years—I was seventeen. I thought I had recovered, but very occasionally the memory takes me over. It has never before occurred in a public place, however. When I think of my behaviour just now—fainting and crying like a child—I can say only that I am mortified, and truly sorry for subjecting you to such an ordeal.'

He waved this away. 'In truth, Miss Bailey, it is not I who has suffered any ordeal. I count it an honour to be able to assist you today.'

Seventeen. She was just seventeen? Hell and damnation!

She shook her head, but did not argue the point. 'Shall we return to the inn now? I feel quite recovered.'

His eyes narrowed. 'Are you certain? Very well. If you will stand...?'

Gently he took her arm, although she seemed fairly composed. After a brief argument over the shawl, which she tried to reject, they bade farewell to the trader. They moved slowly through the market, conscious of the interest of some people around them.

As they walked back towards the Above Hill part of the town, where the gentry and the clergy resided, he kept a close eye on her and was encouraged to see that she maintained a reasonably healthy colour. Still, he was relieved when finally they reached the inn and went inside.

Pleading tiredness, Jane ascended to her chamber for

a lie-down before dinner, while Robert stayed in the tap-room, enjoying a home-brewed beer and considering the day's events.

Helpless rage boiled within him as he recalled that moment when he had heard her cry and realised she was living through the memory of a foul attack.

But what had brought it on today?

There could be only one thing. His mild advance earlier, touching her cheek without her say-so, must have…

Lord!

He allowed himself to feel the full force of his guilty conscience. He had not had permission to touch her earlier, and it surely was no coincidence that memories of a harsher event had taken her over soon afterwards.

He must be resolute from now on and maintain a distant friendship with Miss Bailey rather than anything more intimate—for both their sakes.

Draining his mug, he stalked outside and stomped his way to the walls, attempting to purge himself of the restlessness that consumed him. If only he could gallop it off on his stallion! But, no, Blacklock was at home in the stables at Beechmount Hall.

Returning in time for dinner, he was surprised to find he remained anxious about Miss Bailey's wellbeing even after two hours of frustrated walking around the streets and parks of Lincoln.

She joined him late, flustered. 'I am so sorry, Mr Kendal. So rude of me to keep you waiting!'

'Not at all.'

Despite his earlier determination, he could not prevent his heart from dancing a little on seeing her again. Her cheeks were flushed, and she seemed a little distracted, although thankfully otherwise calm.

He resisted asking after her health, knowing she would not want to be reminded of the incident earlier. Instead, smilingly, he enquired, 'Did you, by any chance, go to sleep?'

Her colour deepened. 'I did. The landlady had to shout to wake me up.' She patted her hair. 'I must look shabby...'

Her hair was, in fact, a little out of place, but it served only to increase her beauty.

He avoided saying so, commenting only, 'Indeed you do not! Now, please be seated and I shall help you to whatever dishes you fancy.'

In the event she ate very little. Her hand shook slightly as she sipped her wine, spilling a couple of drops as she did so. His lips tightened as he witnessed this evidence of her ongoing distress.

Seeing him looking at her, she flushed and reached for her reticule. Her handkerchief was not there.

'Oh! My handkerchief must have fallen out when it— when I—' She broke off, dipping her fingers into the deepest crevices of the silk reticule. 'Oh, no! It is lost too!'

He handed her a napkin. 'What have you lost? Something important?'

She looked crestfallen. 'No—at least only important to me.'

He raised an eyebrow.

'My mother wrote me a note on the morning I left Ledbury House. I put it in my reticule for safe-keeping. It must have been lost at the market.'

'I am sorry for your distress. Shall I go and search for it?'

'Of course not! Why, it is full dark and we leave at daybreak. No, it is gone.' She gave a small smile. 'Besides, I know what it said.'

He did not argue further, and tried to divert her with talk of his wool business. To his surprise she engaged readily, having many opinions—and sound judgements—on the best fabrics for dressmaking.

It proved an excellent way of soothing the uneasiness between them and restoring a more distant equilibrium than that which had been building before today.

'I should look into cotton, too, if I were in such a business,' she declared. 'Why, the variation in quality is truly shocking! If you could source good-quality cotton in the latest fashions every dressmaker from here to London would be seeking it!'

'Strangely, I have actually been looking at cotton recently. Now, tell me, just what are the current fashions for cottons?'

Two hours passed, then three... It was only when the clock struck eleven that she started, rose, and announced that she must retire.

'I cannot understand how it came to be so late!'

'It is late indeed,' he said. 'I hope you shall not oversleep again in the morning!'

She laughed, and wished him goodnight.

He, knowing matters were once again easy between them, mounted the stairs with a lightness he could not have imagined earlier. He felt strangely connected to her. As though... As though he were not alone.

Chapter Ten

'I apologise for my tardiness!' Mr Kendal wore a wry smile, and was clearly anticipating Jane's response.

Jane was equal to it. 'Did you oversleep, Mr Kendal?' She could not help but give him a teasing, arch look.

He grinned in appreciation. 'In truth, I did not!'

He walked with her towards the waiting carriage, offering no further explanation.

This was puzzling. They did not normally breakfast together, as most of the inns sent food directly to their chambers, but on every other day he had been ready at the appointed time. Just now she had been waiting for him downstairs for a full half-hour.

'What is our destination today?'

He handed her into the carriage, then took his customary seat beside her. The familiar presence of his long-legged solidity soothed her soul, while at the same time disordering her senses.

'I have reserved rooms for us at the famous Red Lion in Doncaster.'

She frowned in puzzlement. 'Famous? For what reason?'

He grinned. 'Because of a race called the St Leger Stakes. It was devised there some years back.'

'Horse racing?' She wrinkled her nose.

'You do not approve?'

'I do not see the point of it. Why should people get so excited about which horse is the fastest? And why do they push the poor creatures to run at breakneck speed, even if it kills them?'

'I confess I have not thought of it that way before. It is

always unfortunate when a healthy animal has to be destroyed, but it happens off the racecourse too.'

On they went, and something almost like their usual amity was restored.

Neither mentioned yesterday's incident.

Unlike the cold, clear weather they had been used to, today was grey and overcast, with occasional showers. Jane felt sorry for the poor postilion, riding the lead horse, and said so.

'I know,' Mr Kendal agreed. 'I wonder if we should dally longer during our rest break?'

'An excellent notion!' She smiled shyly at him. 'Not every gentleman is so considerate of the needs of servants.'

He snorted. 'Do not think me so virtuous! I am certain I have frequently been blind to the needs of many people around me.' He fixed her with an intent gaze. 'Tell me, does Lady Kingswood appreciate you?'

She nodded instantly. 'Oh, yes. I enjoy being busy and purposeful, and I have spent years building my knowledge of my mistress's needs and wishes.' She frowned. 'I do hope she is managing without me.'

'Who will look after her during your absence?'

'Mary, one of the other maids.' She bit her lip. 'I shall tell you something now—and I hope you do not think me uncharitable.'

'I am all ears.'

'I must confess to a wish that Mary looks after Miss Marianne well, but not *too* well!'

He laughed. 'My impression is that Lady Kingswood places great emphasis on your unique abilities.'

She smiled nervously at this, hoping he was right.

'I confess I am enjoying a few days without washing clothes. My hands are still red and chapped, but much less so than is usual.'

She held them up for inspection. Sure enough, there were patches of healed white skin among the red.

'I shall be mistaken for a gentlewoman if I am away from my work for too long!'

He shook his head. 'I have never had to think of such things.' His gaze became unfocused. 'There are many people who work for me—spinning, dyeing, knitting and weaving. I confess their welfare has never crossed my mind.'

'That we are even having this conversation means you are more considerate than most masters.'

'But that is the point I am trying to make. I am not considerate at all, for I have no idea what their lives are like, or whether they earn enough for the work they do.'

'It is true that some servants and workers are not well-treated. Remember the maids in that first inn, who were sleeping in the cold attic? I was conscious of how lucky I am to have such a beneficent mistress as Lady Kingswood.'

'I believe,' he replied slowly, 'that servants and tenants may in general be better looked after than the weavers and spinners paid for piece-work. Certainly the tenants at Beechmount Hall estate are reasonably well cared for.' He looked directly at her. 'I was raised to believe it was the family's duty and responsibility to see to their needs.'

'That is true, and yet the weavers and spinners have an independence that they highly value.'

She spent the next hour drawing him out about the number of tenants and servants at Beechmount Hall, their roles, and the various assistance they had been given over the years. She could not but be impressed.

'I think,' she said, tilting her head to one side, 'you are a good master, Mr Kendal. They are lucky to have you.'

A slight flush appeared along his cheekbones. 'Oh, well, it is my uncle who is their master.'

'And yet it is you who are overseeing the repairs to the cottages, and it is your mother who visits the tenants when they are sick or when there is a new baby.'

'My mother is as kind-hearted a woman as you could

ever hope to meet, and she raised me with a strong sense of duty.'

Noting the warmth in his voice as he spoke of his mother, she pointed out the evident truth contained in his words. 'You feel a sense of connection to the estate, and to those who live there.'

He shrugged. 'I suppose it was inevitable. I gradually took on more responsibilities as my uncle became older. He is much less interested in estate matters now, preferring to leave everything to me and to his steward.'

'He trusts you.'

He gave a short laugh. 'Now, that is overstating the case. He allows me to perform tasks which hold no interest for him.'

'And you do them.'

He eyed her ruefully. 'I have been blessed—or cursed—with a strong sense of duty. I sometimes think my uncle uses this more than he ought—but I should not be critical of him.'

'I do not take it as criticism, merely as an observation. Do you…?' She stopped and frowned.

'What were you about to say?'

'It was an impertinent question. Thankfully I caught myself before I asked it.'

Do you expect to inherit the estate?

Thankfully she had not voiced such an impudent question aloud! Thinking of it, she realised they had still not discussed her grandfather, nor Mr Kendal's notions about why he had suddenly invited Jane to visit him.

She frowned inwardly. *I must not forget Mama's warnings.*

The fact that Mr Kendal was so good and so noble did not change what her grandfather had done. Mr Kendal apparently did not know why Jane had been summoned—though he must suspect she was a relative. He was not responsible for her grandfather's actions, but neither did she wish to burden him with the need to be partisan.

The dispute was between Jane and her grandfather; there was no need to draw Mr Kendal into it. Particularly as he must have a deep loyalty to his home and those who lived there.

She felt the usual pang at the thought of a proper home.

Mr Kendal is blessed, though perhaps he does not realise it. He found a true home after losing his father. I did not. Also, she admitted, *I do not wish to speak of my grandfather.*

The thought of him generated anxiety and uncertainty in her. Far better simply to enjoy her continuing journey with Mr Kendal.

And enjoying it she was—most of the time. He was gentleman enough not to refer to her collapse yesterday, for which she was grateful. And the awkwardness she had felt when he had touched her cheek was forgotten. His kindness towards her in the market had profoundly affected her. His strong arms around her as she had cried had felt safe, comforting, and not in the least threatening.

All night she had been restless, yet there had been none of the nightmares that normally followed a memory attack.

Perhaps my spirit is finally recovering.

The thought was exciting in many ways. For over five years—long after his death—Henry Grant still haunted her, shaping the way she saw herself and preventing her from considering marriage or even friendship with a man. Was she finally changing?

There was silence between them now. Somehow, during the hours they had spent together today, her posture had slackened, as had his, and now her right leg was touching his left one. His arm, too, was in contact with hers. She liked it and did not move away.

After what happened yesterday I should be wary of this feeling of warmth towards Mr Kendal, she told herself.

She did not wish to disgrace herself again. Yet she did not move away.

Yes, I am changing. I could not have done this even two days ago. I believe I trust him. That is what is different.

'I have something for you.' Dipping his fingers into his watch pocket, he withdrew something and pressed it into her hand.

She unfolded it in wonder. 'Mama's note! But—how?' Her eyes stung with emotion. 'You went to the market this morning at first light, didn't you?'

'I knew it was important to you.' His voice was gruff.

The paper was creased, and there was dried mud on it, but it was undoubtedly Mama's note. Emotion surged within her. 'Thank you, Mr Kendal, thank you!'

Overcome, she leaned towards him and briefly pressed her lips to his cheek. He caught his breath and turned his head towards her.

They both froze, faces inches apart. She could feel his warm breath on her skin and her gaze was caught by his compelling grey eyes.

'What are you thinking? Right now!' he demanded.

'I am thinking *I wish he would kiss me!*' she responded guilelessly.

Somewhere deep inside part of her mind was screaming a warning.

No! He will remind you of Henry!

She ignored it.

I am changed now! she told herself defiantly.

An instant later his lips were on hers. Her eyes fluttered closed as the kiss she had been dreaming of for a lifetime finally happened.

A wanted kiss.

They both fumbled a little, but then—then his lips aligned with hers, slanting to fit them perfectly. The sensation sent warmth pooling within her, and without thinking she opened her lips to allow his tongue to access the warm depths of her mouth. After a moment, tentatively, she touched her tongue to his and a flame of passion fired through her. He groaned, the sound heightening her desire further.

His hands were gentle on her face, stroking both cheeks, while his tongue danced with hers in an intimate waltz of longing. Jane lost all sense of time or place or propriety. Robert was everything…her only reality.

'Whoa!'

The postilion's exclamation sounded loudly between them as the lead horse slipped in the mud—it had done so a few times that day—and the carriage briefly lurched, jolting them apart.

Jane's eyes shot open as she was propelled forward. Instinctively Mr Kendal reached out to prevent her from colliding with the wooden frame of the carriage. He was successful in this endeavour, but his hand accidentally connected with her right breast.

In great confusion Jane murmured a thank-you, then straightened her bonnet.

'Sorry, sir!' The postilion turned briefly to shout an apology to Mr Kendal.

'Well, drive more carefully, then!'

He sounds decidedly cross. That is strangely satisfying.

Jane stifled an inner smile. Despite the confusion she was feeling, some deeper part of herself was spiralling, singing, soaring. She felt more alive than she had ever felt.

I kissed a man and I enjoyed it!

'Yes, sir!'

The postilion sounded chastened—as well he might. But Jane's instinctive sympathy for a fellow servant falling foul of his master's displeasure was tempered by the heady realisation that she had kissed Mr Kendal.

When he had asked her what she was thinking she had replied instantly, without consideration of propriety, morality, fear or consequence. Even now, when all the thoughts of what she *should* have done were crowding into her mind, she could not regret it.

Yesterday's turmoil was forgotten. Mr Kendal had kissed her. She had kissed him back. She had not felt sickened or frightened.

Desire continued to flood through her and fear seemed far, far away.

Something has truly changed inside me. In my heart I am beginning to understand what my head already knows—that all men are not beasts like Henry Grant.

She reflected on the difference between yesterday and today.

Mr Kendal's care of me yesterday was so gentle, so respectful, that the usual panic has not overcome me. It is to do with trust.

Daringly, she relived the moment just now, when his hand had touched her breast through the fine fabric of her gown. This proved to be a blunder, as instantly a mix of emotions rose within her—desire, yes, but also the sickening memory of Henry Grant's rough cruelty.

With great effort she pushed the terror away, focusing on keeping her breathing measured and distracting herself by counting trees and gates as the carriage moved through the countryside.

Eventually she was calm again.

Very well, she told herself. *So I am not able for a full mating. Not yet, leastways. But I have shared a full adult kiss with a man and not felt frightened even for an instant.*

And there was something else. It was significant that the man she had kissed was Mr Kendal. When she had first laid eyes on him she had responded to his male beauty, yet been wary of his strength. Her appreciation of him had been largely theoretical—as if he were a sculpture or a painting. Seeing him as a man—as someone she might kiss and lie with and do nameless things with—had been impossible. Henry had made it so.

Now all was changed. He had touched her cheek and she had welcomed it. While it was true that afterwards her confusion had stirred up old fears, today she felt strengthened, powerful, as though there was steel inside her.

Like a highwayman hidden within her, memories of Henry's foul actions had attacked her—yet she refused to continue to live in fear of him. It had been she who had initiated the kissing just now, with her entirely spontaneous act of gratitude.

That is important, she realised.

It had been her choice. It had not been forced on her, or expected of her. She had wanted to feel the warmth of his skin on her lips, to take in his scent, to break the barrier of propriety between them. And she had had the courage to execute it!

There was more. Mr Kendal had kissed her back, and for the rest of her life she would have a memory to treasure.

Chapter Eleven

'How much further to Beechmount Hall?'

Robert glanced at Jane, sensing the anxiety behind her question. 'Not more than an hour.' He hesitated. 'How do you, Miss Bailey?'

Since that kiss in the carriage yesterday morning Robert had been relieved to find no coldness between them, no withdrawal on her part.

Following her collapse in the market, and his understanding that something foul had been done to her when she was seventeen, the last thing he had expected was her spontaneous salute when he had given her the note from her mama. He, sensing her desire, had responded by asking her the question that had been uppermost in his mind. When she confirmed that she desired his kiss, he had not hesitated.

The kiss had been all he might have hoped for, and yet afterwards he had been filled with regrets, not dissimilar to those following the previous incident.

He reviewed the litany of objections.

She is in your care. There is no future with her. She will be gone from your life soon. She experienced a foul attack when she was little more than a child.

And yet nothing could depress the strange jubilation within him. He had been her companion for five long days, and could only wish the journey had been twice as long.

Knowing it would be their last evening together, Robert had ordered dinner early and they had stayed in their private parlour until nearly midnight, talking, laughing and enjoying each other's company. The Red Lion had been warm, clean and comfortable, and the fire in the parlour had warmed their bodies even as the company had warmed their hearts.

He had awoken this morning with a sense of foreboding. Today it would all end. Normally he delighted in returning home after being away. Not this time. This time arriving at Beechmount Hall would mean the end of his journey with Miss Bailey.

After almost five days of her endless presence he had to acknowledge that she had not irritated him nor disturbed his comfort. At least not by being difficult in any way. On the other hand she had completely destroyed his sense of equanimity through being so beautiful and witty and— *Damn it.* Through simply being *Jane*.

Dimly, he remembered feeling a *tendre* for one of the Harrogate debutantes when he had first started attending the assemblies there. Miss Weatherhead had been pretty, and vivacious, and he had thought himself in love with her for all of three weeks.

He recognised some similarities to what he was now feeling for Miss Bailey—a preoccupation with her to the exclusion of all else being the predominant symptom. Yet there were differences, too. He had not actually *known* Miss Weatherhead very well, and had occasionally been irritated by her and by her lack of opinion on matters he found important. Miss Bailey was not short of opinions, nor the ability to express them, and yet she did so in ways that were stimulating and interesting rather than dogmatic, arc, or coy. He liked her straightforwardness. It was one of the many, many things he liked about her.

Right now it was clear she was worrying over their imminent arrival at Beechmount Hall. During their five days alone both had avoided the topic, as if speaking of it would somehow break the spell. His curiosity about her link to his uncle remained. He fully expected to discover she was in some way related to the old man—or perhaps to someone important to him—but was determined not to try to whee-dle the truth from Miss Bailey if she did not wish to share it.

At this point he was content to wait to learn what his uncle's reasons were for summoning her; he was simply grateful to have enjoyed one of the best weeks of his life.

'I am well,' she replied now.

He knew she was wearing a brave mask over her wor-ries, yet her manner indicated that she was not open to di-rect questions about them. Instead, he would attempt to reassure her indirectly.

'We enjoy the society of many good neighbours near Arkendale. We see them at assemblies, musical evenings and dinners—and, of course, at church.'

They had attended the Sunday service in Doncaster that morning, before leaving the town, and Robert had felt an unexpected pride in accompanying her to church. Almost as if they were—

'Oh, but I shall not be involved in those,' she declared. She thought for a second. 'No, I do not expect to be involved in social engagements with the family.'

He opened his mouth to issue a strong denial, then re-alised he could not. He simply had no idea why she was being brought to his home or what his uncle's expectations were. And once again he had forgotten she was a servant.

'I have no notion why you are invited by my uncle nor what his intentions are,' he said carefully.

She looked at him for a long moment before nodding decisively. 'I believe I shall speak of it.' She took a breath. 'My mama has told me we are related. But if it is true that he sent a Bow Street Runner to find me he must know I am a servant.'

His eyes widened. 'You *are* related! That, then, con-firms my musings—and explains why my uncle is so de-termined to meet you. In what way are you related, if you do not mind the question?'

She shrugged. 'At this point I believe you know almost

everything there is to know about me, so I do not mind at all. He is, apparently, my grandfather.'

Her grandfather! Well, the sly old devil, fathering children on servants! I wonder if Jane's mother or father was his child...

'I see.'

At least I believe I do.

'My mama would have nothing to do with him all those years. Indeed, she feels most strongly about it.' She grimaced. 'She is angry with him. Justifiably so, in my opinion.'

He frowned. Such situations were notoriously complicated. 'Then—my uncle has not supported either of you?'

'He has not.'

A grandchild and not a penny of support!

He shook his head.

'So what does it mean, do you think, his sending for me?' she asked.

He shook his head. 'I cannot say for certain. He is elderly, so perhaps meeting you is something he wants to do before he...' His voice tailed away.

'Before he dies?' she offered gently.

Strangely, her words sent a pang through him. The old man might be a difficult, cantankerous old Caesar, but somewhere inside Robert felt a spark of warm affection for him. Although that spark was, of course, being severely tested by the knowledge Jane and her mother had had no support from him.

'That was my thought, and it is why I agreed to travel to visit him,' she continued. 'But now we are almost there I confess I am quaking in my boots!'

What to say to this? He would not offer her false assurances. Even if his uncle had sent for her out of sentimentality, which he could not assume, it did not mean he would treat her with kindness.

'My uncle,' he offered carefully, 'can be strong-willed

and opinionated. He is not a man much given to softness or tenderness.'

She nodded. 'That is the impression I have already sensed from my mama and from your earlier reference to him.' She swallowed. 'Still, I have chosen to meet him—and it will only be for a fortnight or so.'

'Indeed…'

His throat closed as he was immediately transported to the moment when her visit would end and he would have to bid her farewell for ever.

Stop! Today is not that day. And besides, it should not matter.

She gave a shy smile. 'Having avoided speaking of this for five days, I now find endless questions tripping off my tongue.'

He could not help but remember that tongue, playing with his own just yesterday.

'Er…yes,' he managed. 'Ask away and I shall endeavour to answer.'

'As well as you and your mother and your uncle, who else lives in Beechmount Hall?'

'My aunt.' He spoke shortly. 'My uncle's wife.'

Her eyes widened. 'I vaguely remember you mentioning her that night you had dinner in Ledbury House.' She flushed. 'I apologise for that deception—for not letting you know who I was until it had been decided that I would travel with you to Yorkshire.'

He waved this away. 'The situation was a difficult one. You did not know me from Adam. It was sensible of you and the other ladies to be cautious.' He grinned. 'I have never before been served dinner by a housekeeper and a lady's maid!'

She gave him a grateful smile. 'Can you tell me about your aunt?'

He hesitated, aware of the need for discretion. 'Aunt

Eugenia is, strictly speaking, my great-aunt—my mother's aunt.'

'So you are related to Mr Millthorpe through his marriage?'

He confirmed it. 'She is his second wife, and much younger than her husband. She has had…disappointments in life.'

'I see.'

Does she see? he wondered.

'They had no children.'

And his aunt would not appreciate this walking reminder of her own inability to give her husband a child.

'Ah.'

She lapsed into silence and he watched her attempt to put it all together in her head. This was a riddle as obscure as some of those they had exchanged in sport a few days ago, but one which had important consequences for her.

Robert could not help but wonder if his uncle's indiscretion had taken place during his marriage to Aunt Eugenia. If so, matters would be challenging indeed. He attempted to calculate Jane's mother's age, and then tried to remember what he had been told of his aunt and uncle's marriage. Without more information he was obliged to admit defeat—for now. However, he believed it unlikely. Mrs Bailey's mother seemed only a little younger than Aunt Eugenia. Therefore it was probable that his uncle had fathered a child before his second marriage…

His train of thought was interrupted by the realisation that Miss Bailey was agitated. She was staring out of the window, her face partly hidden by the poke of the straw bonnet he had come to know so well. In her lap, her hands twisted a fold of her dress—a clear sign of her inner turmoil.

'You are not alone, Miss Bailey.' His voice was thick with emotion, even to his own ears. 'I shall stand your friend.'

And in doing so I will not be alone either.

* * *

'I shall stand your friend.'

Mr Kendal's words echoed in Jane's ears and she held the sentiment close, knowing she would need every ounce of courage in the days ahead.

Suddenly her decision to travel to Yorkshire seemed more foolhardy than brave. Mr Kendal had tried to reassure her, but his innate honesty had meant he had felt compelled to hint at some unhappiness in Beechmount Hall.

Her grandfather sounded a little tyrannical, to say the least. Almost, she had been tempted to tell Mr Kendal of the estrangement between him and his son, but it had felt disloyal to her own papa to do so.

And Mr Millthorpe's second wife was clearly a troubled person. Still, perhaps she need not have to be in their company overmuch. She hoped to be quartered with the servants, and to make herself useful below-stairs even if her grandfather did not insist upon it. He might wish to have some conversation with Jane during her stay, but with luck she might avoid spending too much time in his company.

Mr Kendal's words were kind, and sincerely meant, but Jane knew the idyll she had shared with him was about to end.

Once they arrived at Beechmount Hall, she would live downstairs and he upstairs, and they both understood that this journey together had always been destined to finish.

The thought sent pain needling through her. *I must make the most of the last hour.*

She managed to reply with the appearance of equanimity. 'Thank you. Are we in country that is familiar to you yet? What can you tell me about the towns and villages we must pass through before we reach our destination?'

He obliged, and she watched his face as he spoke, as if committing to memory every feature, every word, every moment of their time alone together.

As the miles and the minutes ticked by she felt a strong sense of ending, of conclusion. Of farewell.

Dusk was falling as the post-chaise rattled up the drive towards Beechmount Hall. Leaden clouds hung heavily overhead, suffusing Jane's first glimpse of the house with a grey dullness that lowered her senses and heightened her sense of foreboding.

The house was massive—a solid, stubborn pile of blackened Yorkshire sandstone. It glowered over them, casting deep shadows over the greyed-out grounds, while a pall of smoke seeped sullenly from several chimneys.

Jane shivered, then felt the warmth of Mr Kendal's hand briefly squeezing hers.

'Courage!' he murmured.

The door opened, emitting a sliver of yellow light. Servants emerged as Mr Kendal alighted. Turning immediately, he assisted Jane from the carriage and they both thanked today's postilion. The man would be quartered with the grooms tonight, before returning to his inn on the morrow.

Two footmen were already unstrapping the trunks and bandboxes from the rear of the carriage. Neither looked at Jane or Mr Kendal.

Clutching her reticule, and reminding herself inwardly that it was a gift from Miss Marianne, *and* that it contained Mama's note, Jane shuffled forward and up two shallow stone steps into the hall.

She blinked at the sudden light. The hall was large and spacious, with a curving staircase, Ionic columns, and stucco friezes featuring Neptune and various sea nymphs. It was designed to impress—or, if you were a frightened serving maid, to intimidate.

'Mr Kendal! It is good to have you home again, sir.' A middle-aged butler with a kindly air was at once engaged in accepting Mr Kendal's cloak and cane.

'Thank you, Umpelby. It is good to be home—although

I still half expect you to address me as Master Robert and accuse me of raiding the orchard, or some such!'

Umpelby laughed. 'In truth, you were so angelic as a child that I was secretly rather pleased on those rare occasions when you *did* get up to some mischief.'

Jane, her anxiety temporarily subdued by this interesting piece of intelligence, was quite taken unawares when the butler turned towards her with a raised eyebrow.

'Er...' Mr Kendal looked a little uncomfortable. 'Miss Bailcy...er... Umpelby...'

He clearly did not know how best to introduce her, she was related to the family, yet still a servant.

She took matters into her own hands. 'I am Jane Bailey, sir.' She dipped a curtsey to the butler, offering him seniority.

He frowned fleetingly. 'I am pleased to make your acquaintance, Miss Bailey.' His tone and demeanour were warm and welcoming. 'We have prepared a room for you. It lacks an hour until dinnertime, so please take this opportunity to rest after your travels.' He beckoned to a young serving maid who had been hovering in the background. 'Nancy will take you to your chamber.'

'Thank you, sir.' She turned to Mr Kendal and put out her hand. 'And thank *you*, Mr Kendal, for accompanying me all the way from Bedfordshire.'

He looked at her hand, then took it slowly. His touch was warm—and, oh, she wanted to remember it.

'It was my pleasure, Miss Bailey.'

His deep voice reverberated through her, and for a moment she allowed herself to be lost in his silver-grey gaze.

Feeling herself flush, she broke away from that gaze even as she removed her hand. Umpelby seemed for an instant to be watching carefully, but when she focused on him properly his visage was a perfect mask of disinterested impassivity.

Following Nancy up the grand staircase, she was conscious that she was walking away from Mr Kendal. Their adventure together had truly ended, and now she was on her own.

Robert watched her go, her slight figure dwarfed by the majestic sweep of his uncle's elaborate staircase. He could still recall how large and cold and alarming Beechmount Hall had seemed to his eight-year-old self when he had first come to live here.

How brave she is!

He knew better than anyone how lost she must be feeling. And she had not even met the family yet.

Somehow, though, he believed Miss Bailey was equal to it.

She has more strength than she perhaps realises.

'Is my mother in her sitting room?'

Umpelby confirmed it, and Robert strode briskly to the small parlour at the back of the house that his mama had made her own. As a child, this had been the place he had felt most safe.

Opening the door, he was pleased to see her there, on her favourite couch, having a rest before dinner. She always preferred to lie down here during the day, rather than trail up to her bedchamber on the second floor.

'Well! And here I thought my own mama would be awake and anxiously waiting to greet her only child upon his return!'

She heaved herself upright. 'Oh! Robert! Robert, my dear!'

He embraced her, smiling at her confused sleepiness. 'Good day, Mama. I hope you are well.'

'I am—though everything is always better when you are here.'

He eyed her closely, seeking signs of strain. 'What have I missed? Have my uncle and aunt been tiring you out?'

'Oh, well…' She waved a hand airily. 'Nothing I could not manage.'

He frowned. 'Tell me.'

She swung her legs to the floor, her soft woollen blanket slipping to the carpet. He retrieved it and sat beside her.

'It seems my uncle omitted to tell Eugenia about—about this Miss Bailey.'

Robert's mind went back to the days before his departure, when he had been preparing for the trip. Surely the purpose of his journey had been discussed openly? But then he recalled that his conversations with his uncle had been mostly in his library. And Mama and he had talked of it here, not at dinner…

'Do you mean he did not tell her he had invited Miss Bailey?'

She shook her head. 'It is much, much worse. Eugenia did not even know of the girl's existence. She believed her husband to have no blood relatives at all, and is most put out.'

'I can imagine! Lord, what a muddle!'

'Tell me of her, Robert. Is she coarse and vulgar? Eugenia is sure of it. She says Miss Bailey is a young servant.'

'She is a servant, it is true—a lady's maid. But she is not at all coarse, and there is nothing vulgar about her. Nancy has taken her to her chamber, but you shall meet her before long.'

'I pity the girl, Robert. No one deserves Eugenia's anger—least of all a servant whose only sin is to be a reminder of Eugenia's childless state.' She patted Robert's hand. 'I always wondered if that explained Eugenia's antipathy towards us at times.'

'You are too kind, Mama. I always believed she was one of Macbeth's witches, and that she made evil potions with Henby in her chamber!'

They both laughed, but inside Robert there remained memories of that small boy who had felt his aunt's hostility without ever understanding it. She had lost her power over him, of course, now he was an adult, and yet on occasion both his uncle and his aunt reminded him of their coldness towards that eight-year-old boy.

Now his aunt's ire would be directed at Jane. And there was little he could do about it.

Chapter Twelve

'There must be some mistake. This cannot possibly be my chamber.'

Nancy the housemaid looked at Jane anxiously. 'I am sorry, miss. Is it too cold? I lit the fire an hour ago, as I did not know exactly when you and the young master would arrive. Perhaps the room is too small for your liking? I can ask the housekeeper for something larger. She just thought that this one would be easier to heat, it being February and all.'

Jane was bewildered. The chamber was enormous. 'Too *small*? No, not at all! And it is perfectly warm.'

'Then is it the bed? Not everyone can sleep well on a proper mattress if they are used to a feather bed. The only thing is, the master got rid of all the old beds with Harrateen hangings about three years ago, and replaced them with these modern ones.' She stroked the beautiful damask bed curtains, in a rich gold shade, then pressed on the mattress. 'See, miss? It is perfectly soft and comfortable!'

Jane's mind was in a whirl. She had cleaned many chambers that looked like this, but had never, ever slept in one. It was the height of luxury, with a sumptuous bed, a solid armoire, a washstand and a bow-front dressing table in mahogany, complete with an expensive oval mirror. There was even a painting on the wall above the fireplace—a still-life featuring vegetables and a pheasant ready for plucking. There were also three—yes, *three*—branches of candles in the room. Expensive wax candles, too—surely they could not be all for her?

Nancy moved to the window and closed the shutters, talking all the while. 'You only have an hour until dinner, and you will want to shake the dust from yourself before going downstairs. If you truly wish to change to a different chamber I can ask the housekeeper…'

'Oh, no,' said Jane in a small voice. 'I do not wish to be any trouble.'

There was a scratching at the door, which Nancy opened to admit two footmen, carrying Jane's trunk between them, along with her bandbox. On their heels was a young scullery maid with a jug of warm water, which she poured into the washing bowl on the washstand before leaving.

'Now then, miss,' said Nancy briskly. 'Let me help you with your buttons.'

And so, for the first time in her adult life, Jane allowed a maid to assist her with her toilette. She knew inside that it could not be right, but she was simply too overwhelmed to protest.

Nancy was around her own age, a pretty red-haired maid, with a sunny, talkative disposition. She unpacked Jane's trunk while Jane washed, selecting a plain evening dress in amber silk that Jane had washed many times when it had belonged to Lady Kingswood.

'Oh, but surely I shall be dining with the servants?' Jane protested weakly. 'That dress is much too fine for me. Indeed, I am not sure why my mama and my employer have packed me so many fine things!'

Nancy eyed her shrewdly. 'Perhaps because they anticipated what you did not, miss—that you will be dining with the family.'

Jane was aghast. 'What?' She gulped. 'Every night?'

As she spoke, she dimly recalled Mama and Miss Marianne suggesting this very possibility. Stupidly, she had discounted it, not wishing to hope for such preferment or luxury.

Nancy shrugged. 'I do not know. But my instructions for tonight were very clear. The master spoke to Mrs Thompson, our housekeeper, yesterday. He told her only that a young relative of the family would be arriving. Although raised as a servant, he said, she was to be given an upstairs room and brought to the large salon before dinner, suitably dressed.' She bit her lip.

'So all the servants know about me?'

Nancy's eyes danced. 'Of course! You know it is impossible to keep secrets in the servants' hall!'

'And—"suitably dressed"?'

'In truth, no one was sure if you would bring suitable clothing. The housekeeper will be relieved when I tell her about all this.' She indicated the pile of clothes on the bed. 'Although there is only the one evening dress. Now, can I help you with it?'

What else could she do?

Jane stood as Nancy buttoned her into what had been one of Miss Marianne's favourite gowns. The neckline was much lower than she was used to, and she had to resist the urge to try to pull it up.

'A perfect fit, miss!' Nancy beamed.

'Yes, Lady Kingswood and I are of a similar size,' Jane offered weakly.

'Please be seated, miss, and I shall dress your hair.'

Feeling as though she were in the middle of a strange but beautiful dream, Jane sat at the dressing table while Nancy brushed and pinned up her hair.

How many times have I performed this service for Miss Marianne?

Nancy then got to work with the curling irons that had been heating in the fireplace, and soon Jane was enjoying the sight of her own face framed by dainty, fashionable side curls.

'I love it!' she muttered thickly. 'Thank you, Nancy.'

Nancy beamed. 'It is easy to dress the likes of you, for you have so much natural beauty. Now, I did not notice any gloves in your trunk. Do you have any?'

Jane shook her head. 'Only cotton gloves for daytime wear. Nothing suitable for dining.'

'Never fear! Mrs Kendal will provide!'

Jane's heart skipped a beat. 'Mrs Kendal?'

Robert is married?

'Yes—Mr Kendal's mother.'

'Of course.' Her face flamed at her foolish error. How could she have forgotten that Mr Kendal's mother lived with him here? And why would she worry that he had a wife? Her mind was in complete disorder!

Jane pretended to study her side curls again in the mirror. Never had she looked so fashionable, nor so aristocratic!

Never forget who you are.

Was this what Mama meant? A wave of guilt laced with fear washed through her.

'Nancy…?' Her voice trembled.

'Yes, miss?'

'I cannot dine with the family. You know I am a simple servant—a lady's maid, like you?'

'Yes, miss.'

'Then, when I am here, am I to be a servant or not?'

'I have no notion. But tonight you are to be a guest.' She stood back. 'There! You are ready, miss. You look beautiful!'

Astoundingly, Jane could not disagree. Who *was* this vision she saw in the mirror? Her hair was expertly and fashionably styled, and her dress was both flattering and elegant.

'I never realised before that my eyes were so blue!' She flushed, conscious she was falling prey to vanity.

Nancy, smiling, would only repeat her compliments.

Ten minutes later, Nancy having returned with a pair of elegant white evening gloves, Jane was ready to descend for dinner. Nancy offered to lead her to the salon, where the family would gather—'For you'd easily get lost in this place, miss.'

Jane was grateful, but noticed that Nancy carefully stayed one step behind her as they descended the staircase.

Jane, her gloved hand sliding along the marble handrail, felt as though she was an actor in a play. After five days away from home—five happy days travelling with Mr Kendal—she had suddenly found herself walking on to a strange stage and playing a role for which she was entirely unprepared.

Nancy accompanied her down a long, elegant corridor. 'That's the dining room, miss.' She indicated a door to her left. 'The salon is the next one along here.'

They stopped outside the salon door. Jane squared her shoulders.

'Good luck, miss.'

Nancy's half-whisper sounded behind her. Jane nodded and went inside.

What seemed like a sea of faces turned towards her as she paused in the doorway and Jane found herself subject to the scrutiny of what felt like a dozen pairs of eyes. In reality, as well as an impassive footman, there were only four other people in the room. An old gentleman, seated by the fire. A tall lady next to him. Another lady, this one plump. And to her right Mr Kendal, magnificently attired in full evening dress.

He stepped forward. 'How do, Miss Bailey?'

His handsome smile was welcoming—it was clear he was attempting to reassure her. He bowed to her, then tucked her hand in his arm, drawing her forward into the room. The old gentleman turned his head sharply to stare at her.

My grandfather.

They looked at each other. He was slightly hunched as he sat in his chair, and his face was creased with the lines of advanced age. His eyes—as blue as her own—bored into her.

'Well?' he snapped. 'Come closer so I can see you properly, girl!'

Mr Kendal stayed with her, the warmth of his arm giving her fortitude. They stopped in front of Mr Millthorpe, whose narrowed gaze swept assessingly over her.

She let go of Mr Kendal's arm to make her curtsey. 'How do you do?'

He emitted a bark of laughter. 'The Runner had the right of it! Genteel, he said, and of good character.'

Jane's eyes widened. Runner? Oh, the Bow Street Runner who had found her. But he was speaking of her as if she were not present…

Remembering his treatment of Papa, she lifted her chin. 'And why should that surprise you, sir?'

'You have steel in you, then?'

His piercing stare increased her discomfort. She, not knowing how to respond, merely stood, keeping her gaze level.

I do—though I only discovered it recently.

The plump lady intervened, seemingly distressed by the tension in the air. 'Robert, I should like to make Miss Bailey's acquaintance.'

'Of course, Mama.'

He introduced them, and Jane was encouraged by the kindliness in Mrs Kendal's demeanour. Of course she would be kind. Mr Kendal must have got his good heart from her.

The other lady could only be Mrs Millthorpe. She had remained grim-faced throughout, and when Mr Kendal introduced Jane to her she gave only the slightest nod of acknowledgement.

Jane, who had seen many such interactions during her years as a servant, understood the subtle language of the cut. Mrs Millthorpe was making it clear she was not welcome. So be it.

The dinner gong sounded and Mrs Kendal immediately

moved forward to assist Mr Millthorpe to rise from his chair.

'I can do it!' he snapped, but he leaned his weight on Mrs Kendal's arm while she passed him a stout walking stick. He moved slowly towards the door, Mrs Kendal hovering solicitously by his side. Meanwhile his wife followed wordlessly, her face a mask of tight disapproval.

That left Mr Kendal and Jane to take up the rear.

He gave her a sympathetic grimace, then leaned forward to murmur, 'You look beautiful, Miss Bailey!'

His flattery soothed her spirits, and his company bolstered her courage as they entered the dining room. The table had been laid for five, with two places set on the long side facing the door. The others moved fluidly to what Jane assumed were their usual places—Mr and Mrs Millthorpe at the head and foot of the table, Mrs Kendal on the near side, and—

'You have been placed next to me, Miss Bailey,' said Mr Kendal, to Jane's great relief.

Mrs Millthorpe tutted. 'An uneven number of diners is so imbalanced. I declare it vexes me greatly!'

No one had any reply to this, though the comment made Jane's stomach lurch.

They all took their places and Mrs Millthorpe directed the footmen to begin serving. The food smelled delicious, but in truth Jane felt a little sick with nerves. Mr Kendal engaged her in conversation about her choices, and assisted her by serving some vegetables and sauce to accompany the soup. Jane slipped off her gloves, placing them in her lap like the other ladies, and tentatively began to eat.

Mrs Millthorpe, to Mr Kendal's right, claimed his attention.

'In what state are the roads, Robert? We are promised to Staveley House for their February soirée on Thursday next week, and the road to Staveley can be appalling in winter. Why, last year only two families managed to get through!'

As Robert replied Jane took the opportunity to study her grandfather's wife. Mrs Millthorpe was a tall, stately lady, with stiff posture and deep lines etched into her face. Jane glanced across the table. Mrs Kendal was probably of a similar age, but her face was creased with crow's feet and a few worry lines, rather than the deep unhappiness evident on Mrs Millthorpe's visage. The contrast was marked and, to her, significant.

Mr Kendal was in the middle of confirming to his aunt that the roads were generally in reasonable repair, and re-assuring her that, if the weather stayed dry, he had every confidence that they would get to Staveley House with little difficulty, when she suddenly cut across him—speaking in French, of all things.

'My husband tells me she is a servant.'

Jane understood every word.

Robert hesitated, a look of clear discomfort flitting across his features. He replied in English, 'Yes.'

'I cannot believe,' his aunt continued, still speaking French, 'that Mr Millthorpe can insult me this way. To sit at table with a *servant*—someone reared in service to her betters! Why, it demeans all of us!'

Jane glanced at her grandfather, whose eyes were alight with unholy glee.

He plays with all of us!

She dropped her eyes to her dinner, giving no indication that she could understand every word. Mr Kendal did not reply to his aunt's outburst, but turned to Jane with a mild query about whether she was enjoying the soup.

'Mmm, yes, it is delicious,' she managed.

In truth, her hand shook, and she was desperately try-ing not to cry. To feel such hostility from someone she had never even met before was disturbing.

Thankfully Mr Kendal covered her distress with a stream of bland conversation, to which she only had to contribute the occasional monosyllable. But as the second course was served Mrs Millthorpe reverted to French again.

'Just look at her hands, Robert! A *servant's* hands— disgustingly red and chapped!'

It was all Jane could do not to flinch and hide her hands. Yes, they remained chapped—although they had healed enormously during the journey—but to hear part of her referred to as 'disgusting' was truly upsetting. It also fired her anger. Mrs Millthorpe had never had to work. How dared she sit in judgment over those who did?

Mrs Kendal, who had been eating in silence opposite, lifted her head and gave Mrs Millthorpe a long look. This was met by a bold glare from Mrs Millthorpe. Mrs Kendal dropped her gaze.

Somehow Jane managed to endure the ordeal. She ate very little but stayed in her seat, and she managed not to cry or to answer with a defiant outburst. It was strange to feel angry and upset at the same time, and to force both to bow to her own self-control. But she survived it.

Finally the servants moved in to clear away the last course and Mrs Millthorpe rose to lead the ladies out. 'Let us leave the gentlemen to their port,' she declared.

Oh, no! I must leave Mr Kendal and go with her! At least his mother will be with me.

Heart thumping, Jane rose and followed Mrs Kendal out of the room. As she walked, she could feel Mr Kendal's gaze on her back.

If only I could stay here with him!

Chapter Thirteen

Once in the salon, Jane waited until the other two ladies had seated themselves, then chose a hard chair near a side table, closer to Mrs Kendal than to Mrs Millthorpe.

'I suppose,' Mrs Millthorpe declared generally, 'this is the first time you have sat at a formal dinner.'

Jane started. *Is she speaking to me?*

She eyed Mrs Millthorpe cautiously. That lady was staring fixedly at a Chinese vase at the far side of the salon.

'Have the manners to answer my question!' Mrs Millthorpe was now glaring at her.

'I…um…no, I have not dined formally before.' Jane's voice shook a little.

'What sort of accent is that?'

Jane looked at her in bewilderment.

'Where are you from, girl? Where were you raised?'

'In—in Cambridgeshire, ma'am.'

Mrs Millthorpe seemed to be expecting more.

'Although I now live in Bedfordshire. I confess I was unclear as to your meaning as I am not conscious that I have an accent. But of course I can hear that you are from Yorkshire, so it is logical that there is something about the way I speak that is different to you.'

'Are you daring to suggest I have a *Yorkshire* accent?' Mrs Millthorpe's eyes were bulging with outrage.

'I believe we all have different accents,' offered Mrs Kendal tentatively. 'Although yours could never be described as Yorkshire, Eugenia. I am sure that was not Miss Bailey's meaning.'

'No, indeed,' lied Jane.

What is wrong with having a Yorkshire accent, anyway?

'Hrrmph! Where have you worked? How many positions have you held?'

For the next hour—though it seemed longer—Mrs Millthorpe questioned Jane on her work as scullery maid, housemaid, then lady's maid. Jane carefully omitted the year after Papa had died, unwilling to expose herself or Mama to Mrs Millthorpe's contempt. Being a servant was perfectly respectable. Being a near pauper—though it had not been their fault—would have left Jane and Mama open to her scorn.

Mrs Millthorpe was also interested to know about Jane's mother and the course of her work. Jane remained composed, answering her questions calmly and politely. In this, her servant's training stood her well. She simply pretended inside that Mrs Millthorpe was her employer, and therefore entitled to question her.

Never forget who you are.

At least it allowed her to contain her temper.

The illusion created by the side curls and the silk dress that she was anything other than a servant had been shattered by Mrs Millthorpe's pitiless examination of her past and her background. And as the time went on Jane became more and more distraught.

Through it all Mrs Kendal looked distressed, but each time she tried to intervene she was silenced by Mrs Millthorpe.

By the end Jane felt as though she had been forced through a mill—tumbled and crushed and broken into pieces. Mrs Millthorpe had been relentless, ruthless and heartless. Jane was barely managing to retain control of her emotions. She felt like running from the room, from the house, from the entire county of Yorkshire.

At last the door opened, admitting the gentlemen. Mr Kendal was slightly behind his uncle, and his eyes immediately searched hers. She could give him nothing—no sign of welcome or even of animation. She was exhausted. Empty. Crushed.

A slight frown marred his brow briefly, but he instantly smoothed it away as he greeted the ladies. Mr Millthorpe took his seat in the same armchair he had used earlier, and they all conversed generally about the weather and the Staveley House soirée.

Jane sat silently, empty of thought, word and emotion.

'We shall use the small carriage,' declared Mrs Millthorpe.

'Oh, but, my dear Eugenia…' Mrs Kendal's hands were fluttering in distress. 'You forget there are five of us now. We should never fit comfortably in the small carriage.'

'Five? *Five?*' Mrs Millthorpe's voice was shrill. 'There are but *four* who will be seen in public at the Staveley soirée.'

All eyes turned to Mr Millthorpe for adjudication, but he was staring into the fire, seemingly lost in thought.

Jane's anxiety reawakened. She wished to be anywhere but Beechmount Hall. If only she were at home with Mama. Or downstairs with the servants. Or—

'Miss Bailey!' Mr Millthorpe's voice creaked with age, but his authority was unmistakable.

'Yes, sir?' Fear pooled coldly in the pit of her stomach.

'I shall retire shortly, but I wish to speak with you on the morrow. Be in my library at ten o'clock!'

'Yes, Mr Millthorpe.'

Soon afterwards Mr Millthorpe's valet came to attend his master. He cursed the man, who demonstrated remarkable patience as he assisted his master from the room. Jane watched in trepidation, for fear he would address her again, but he ignored everyone.

A little later his wife poured tea—refusing to place a cup into Jane's hand but instead resting it on the table. The intended insult was noted, but Jane was now past the point where she was able to feel anything.

Once she had drunk her tea, Mrs Millthorpe too, retired. Pointedly, she bade Robert and his mother a loud goodnight. When the door closed behind her, Jane's inward sigh of relief could not have been more heartfelt.

'Now, then, Miss Bailey...' Mrs Kendal was all smiles, 'You shall sit with me and Robert and we can be easy for a while.'

Warily, Jane joined her on the settee, and Mrs Kendal proceeded to regale them both with tales of all the domestic dramas her son had missed during his time away. In the absence of the Millthorpes she positively sparkled with warmth and charm, and Jane's spirits revived a little in her company.

Mr Kendal did his share too, with questions and explanations for Jane as to who the characters were. She felt her shoulders start to drop, and the tightness in her chest loosen a little. They both offered to take her on a tour of the house tomorrow, to which she agreed with gratitude—so long as Mr Millthorpe permitted it, of course.

'He is not the man he was,' said Mrs Kendal, with a hint of sadness. 'Now he spends most of his days in silence—a far cry from the vital, robust man he used to be.'

Mr Kendal grimaced. 'In truth, Mama, I see a change in him after just a couple of weeks away. When did he become so frail?'

Mr Kendal spoke softly, but Jane could sense the distress behind his words. Despite her fear of her grandfather, she could see that both Mrs Kendal and her son held him in some affection.

There must be more to him, then, than the tyrant I encountered this evening.

Her throat closed in sympathy. Not for her grandfather, but for Mr Kendal.

Mrs Kendal patted his hand. 'It has come upon us all so

gradually that none of us noticed—save the man himself, I suspect.' She eyed Jane shrewdly. 'It is why he so particularly wished to meet you. Oh, do not fear! I have no intention of questioning you as Eugenia did.' She paused. 'My aunt can be…difficult…but you should understand she has had much unhappiness in her life.'

Jane raised a sceptical eyebrow. Could that really excuse her harshness?

But Mrs Kendal was still speaking. 'My dear, you have been through enough for one day.'

'Indeed, I am rather fatigued.' *To say the least!* 'I should like to retire.'

'You need no permission to do so!' Mrs Kendal smiled.

They wished her goodnight, informing her of the usual arrangements for family breakfast.

'Oh, but…shall I continue to eat with the family?'

Mrs Kendal nodded. 'I should think so. At least until my uncle decides otherwise.'

'None of us truly knows what his intentions or his wishes are regarding you, Miss Bailey,' Mr Kendal offered.

'Actually,' his mother reflected, 'I am not sure my uncle does either.'

As she climbed the stairs Jane reflected on this. Although she had enjoyed dressing like a lady earlier, her pretence had soon been spoiled by the reality of Mrs Millthorpe's displeasure. Somehow, in the morning, she must convince her grandfather to allow her to live and eat with the servants for the remainder of her stay. For one night, though, she would enjoy the luxury of her grand chamber.

She went inside, surprised to discover Nancy waiting for her.

'Oh, miss, I have built up the fire for you again, and placed a warming pan in your bed. It shall hopefully keep you warm through the night. Now, may I help you undo your buttons?'

'Nancy! There was no need to wait up for me! I am perfectly able to look after myself.'

Nancy looked shocked. 'Indeed not, miss. I would be remiss in my duties if I had not waited—as you well know!'

'You are using my status as a servant against me?' Jane asked, but could not help smiling.

As Nancy began unbuttoning her dress, a sudden thought struck Jane.

'How have the other servants responded to my arrival?'

'Oh, you know… Different ones have different things to say.'

'Oh, yes?'

I can imagine!

'Well, Eliza was first asked to attend you, but she whined so much about it that Mrs Thompson was quite put out. That's when I offered.'

Jane swallowed. 'Who is Eliza?'

'She's one of the other housemaids, but she thinks too much of herself. She has been wheedling Henby—Henby is the mistress's personal maid. I think Eliza wants to be recommended to see to the young master's wife when the time comes.'

'Mr Kendal is to be married?' Jane's heart plummeted to the approximate level of her evening slippers.

'Oh, no! Least, not that anyone knows—though a fine-looking young gentleman like him will have no difficulty finding a wife when he so chooses.' She leaned forward to add conspiratorially, 'Given he is in line to be the master's heir, he can have his pick of any maiden for a wife.'

Jane could only nod. The thought of Mr Kendal's wife had, it seemed, robbed her of speech.

'So, Eliza was whining, saying she would not serve a servant, and I just piped up and said I'd do it.' Nancy picked up Jane's dress as she stepped out of it. 'I shall take this away and look after it for you.'

Jane knew exactly what that meant. Nancy would wash

it, dry it, iron it, and mend the slight tear in the side. She glanced at Nancy's hands. They were red and chapped.

'I am used to looking after my own mistress's clothes,' she offered. 'I can certainly take care of my own.'

'Ah, but *can* is not *should*—not when the master has decreed you are to have an upstairs bedchamber and eat with the family.'

'He said that—that my bedchamber should be upstairs?'

'He did. And so—Eliza or no Eliza—you shall be treated like a guest if I have owt to do with it!'

Jane could have hugged her. 'Thank you, Nancy.'

Ten minutes later Jane was alone, snuggling into her warm bed, with the fire slowly dying and a bright beeswax candle burning on the table beside her. Even if this were just for one night, at least it was happening.

But Mrs Millthorpe did not want her here—that was clear—and nor did some of the servants.

The thought caused her stomach to tighten. Jane was unused to being disliked or unwanted—even noticed. It did not sit well with her.

But for one evening I dressed like a lady. I had curls and a silk dress and I ate with the family.

She smiled to herself, blowing out the candle.

And Mr Kendal shielded me.

The thought sent a comforting warmth through her. She turned over in the sumptuous bed, closed her eyes, and drifted off to sleep.

Robert rolled the brandy around in his glass, enjoying the play of candlelight in the amber liquid. Alone in the salon— for his mama had retired soon after Miss Bailey—he was taking the time to allow his thoughts to swirl and settle.

Jane.

As a serving maid she had been beautiful. He still remembered his first encounter with her…his appreciation of her rosy cheeks, attractive figure and deep blue eyes. Then he had likened her in his head to the goddess Diana, and had saluted her beauty in an act of unaccustomed lyricism.

Tonight she had been Venus. That yellow-bronze silk dress had clung to her feminine form in all the right ways, and the low neckline had afforded him a glimpse of heaven. Her hair had been different as well, emphasising her delicate cheekbones and the colour of her eyes, and accentuating the beauty he had seen from the first.

His heart had been pounding as he'd walked forward to draw her into the room, and he had been conscious of a strong urge to protect her from his aunt and uncle's characteristic plain speaking.

She had held her own, though, meeting his uncle's gaze with confidence—exactly the right way to handle the old curmudgeon. Aunt Eugenia had been bursting with indignation, of course, and Jane must have felt it. When his aunt had addressed him in French at the table—deliberately aiming to exclude Miss Bailey, while also criticising her—he had been conscious of a sense of shock and embarrassment.

Miss Bailey, who was no fool, had not needed to understand French to sense the hostility emanating from her hostess.

He shook his head. He was now very familiar with Miss Bailey, and the quiet, timid creature by his side this evening, who had barely eaten or drunk, was not the girl he had come to know. And as she had left the dining room with the other ladies he had watched her go knowing she was feeling bereft.

Once the door had closed behind them he had turned his head to see his uncle watching him keenly.

'A good-looking chit, is she not?'

'She is fairly handsome,' he had replied coldly. He had not wished to discuss Miss Bailey.

'The Bow Street Runner who found her told me in his report. Pretty, he said, with a good figure. I had hoped it would be so.'

Robert had frowned. 'Why should it matter to you how she looks?'

'Oh, it ain't me it matters to. But it suits me very well that she is a well-formed lass.' His uncle had chuckled to himself. 'Not got much to say for herself, has she?'

'Miss Bailey is a level-headed young woman, with sensible notions on many matters.'

'Ha! Don't you get on your high horse with me, Robert! I ain't criticising her.'

'She knows she is not welcome.'

'Not welcome? I sent you all the way to Bedfordshire to fetch her, did I not?'

Robert had nodded.

'So how can she feel unwelcome?'

'My aunt—'

'Pfft! Never worry about Eugenia. I long since stopped doing so!'

His uncle had gone off into a guffaw, which had changed into an alarming cough. By the time Robert had patted his back and soothed him with brandy the conversation had been lost.

An hour or so later his uncle had suggested joining the ladies.

Miss Bailey's desperation had been clear when he and his uncle had joined them in the salon. He had caught just a glimpse of it as their eyes had briefly locked. What had surprised him was the force of his reaction to it. In taking responsibility for her during the long journey north, he had, it seemed, formed something of an attachment to her.

But given how attracted he was to her, and the fact that her status was unclear, such an attachment was dangerous. Unless their stations were equal he could not consider marriage. If their stations remained unequal, making her his mistress was the only option—yet, knowing her, that could never be.

He groaned. The thought of her in his bed had been

haunting his mind since their first meeting. Being thrown into her company had served only to make it more intense. Allowing this attachment to develop further could only lead to heartache.

I must be resolute. I must remind myself that she is simply someone I came to know in unusual circumstances. What I am feeling is a tendre, a temporary infatuation, nothing more. It will pass.

He emptied his glass and rose to seek his bed.

It must.

Chapter Fourteen

Jane entered the library on Mr Millthorpe's command. The room was well-lit, via two long multi-paned windows, and what seemed like thousands of fascinating-looking books were huddled together on the dark wood shelves. A small fire burned in the marble fireplace.

Jane's palms felt a little moist and her heart was fluttering.

What will he say to me?

'Ah, there you are! Come here, child.' His tone was curt and stern.

'Good day, sir.' She curtseyed, then approached him.

Seen in daylight, her grandfather looked positively ancient. His body was thin and bent, and his skin resembled aged pale parchment. He was impeccably dressed, in morning wear in the style of twenty years ago, and he wore a ruby ring on his right hand. His hair was fine, thin and white, and his face was a mass of lines. His eyes, a startling blue, pinned hers with keen intelligence.

'Be seated.' He indicated an ornate chair covered in yellow satin. 'Pull it closer.'

She obeyed, moving the chair closer to his. At his side was a small table with a glass and a brandy carafe. He poured himself a large measure, glancing sideways at her as he did so.

'Do you disapprove of my brandy habit so early in the day, eh?'

'Not at all. It is none of my concern.' She folded her hands in her lap, every inch the dutiful servant.

'Hmph! Eugenia and that fool doctor try to tell me to drink less, and to eat only meat and gruel, but—' he snapped his fingers '—I have never been complaisant, and I do not intend to change the habits of a lifetime. I have little time remaining on this earth, and no one shall deprive me of the few pleasures I have left.'

'Indeed, sir.'

His eyes narrowed. 'Last night I believe I caught a glimpse of the girl behind the servant's mask. Who are you, Jane Bailey?'

She frowned. 'I am not sure of your meaning, sir. I am simply Jane Bailey.'

'Bailey—that very name is meant to injure me. And nothing in this situation is simple. You know I am your grandfather?'

She inclined her head. 'My mother told me.'

'Your mother…' He shook his head. 'My Edward was always headstrong, but when he announced that he wished to marry a servant girl I could not countenance it.'

Thoughts of herself and Mr Kendal sharing a kiss suddenly assailed her. A gentleman should not, *could* not marry a servant.

'I understand that.'

'You do? There is, then, no rancour, no bitterness about the life you might have lived if you had been raised as my granddaughter?'

She considered this. 'It is a subject that has never occurred to me. I am content with my life.'

Was that completely true? What of her wish for security, for a home? If she had been raised as a lady perhaps she might even have married a gentleman. A gentleman like—

'You are most unusual, Jane Bailey.'

She remained impassive. 'Am I? It does not seem so to me.'

Inside, she was all turmoil. His question had raised hopes and wishes she should never consider. What if Mama had reached out to him after Papa's death? What if he and Papa had reconciled years ago? What if—?

He grunted. 'Edward and I discussed the matter of his planned marriage in the most direct terms.' His eyes became unfocused, as if he gazed at something unseen, something remembered. 'I told him that if he married this woman then he was no longer my son.'

His Adam's apple bobbed in his throat as he swallowed with strong emotion. He looked at her.

'I never expected him to actually do it.'

Jane's stomach lurched. He was a fool! They had both been fools!

'I am sorry, sir.'

He waved this away. 'Once I came to my senses I tried to find him. I did not realise he had changed his name. Your grandmother was Eleanor Bailey when I met her. By taking her name and rejecting mine he was repudiating me as I had repudiated him.'

She stared at him in shock. 'Then—you wished to reconcile with him?'

'I did.' His blunt statement hung in the air between them.

'I wish he had known. I wish Mama and I had known.'

It felt as though the ground was shifting under Jane's feet. The boundaries of her life, the beliefs upon which she and Mama had lived, were false. So much wasted time!

She shook her head sadly. 'If only you had found each other again. Papa was a good man.'

'He was also wilful and headstrong.'

Jane raised an eyebrow.

'Ha! Yes, I know he got that from me.' He tapped a long white finger on the arm of his chair. 'After he left I married again—my Eleanor had died years before. In my head I believed I should sire another son—that the best thing would be to forget about Ned and Eleanor and everything that had gone before. I forbade everyone even to speak of him. I believed myself to be master of my fate.' He nodded pensively. 'I was, I believe, entirely bacon-brained.'

'I do not believe any of us can claim to control fate.'

'It took a very long time for me to understand that lesson.' He had turned reflective again. 'I know my days are numbered. These old bones cannot last much longer. I cannot remake the past, but perhaps I can make an ending to some of it, at least…'

Shaking himself, he took a sip of brandy.

'This past year my mind has turned away from the present and towards memories from years ago. Not six months ago it suddenly occurred to me that Ned might have used his mother's name, so I commissioned a Bow Street Runner to find him.' His hand gripped the arm of his chair like a claw. 'He returned with the news that Ned was long dead, but that he had sired a daughter. You.'

'We have the same eyes.' Her voice was thick with emotion. 'You, me and Papa. I see him in you.'

And as she spoke she realised her words indicated an acceptance of their familial bond.

'As I do in you, child.'

He reached a hand towards her and she took it, marvelling at the strength—and the frailty—of his grip. Jane's chest tightened. How could this be happening? A lifetime of anger, of regret—all based on a misunderstanding fuelled by stubbornness. Part of her was furious at the loss of a life she could have had—*should* have had.

Might Papa have lived?

Despite her rage, she could not help but respond to the man in front of her. An angry old man, finally understanding the impact of his errors, his implacable obstinacy. Yet Papa had been just as inflexible. Two fools! Two hardheaded men, facing off like rutting stags. And they had suffered for it, as she and Mama had.

It took him a long moment to regain control of his emotions. Jane, surrendering to hers, felt her throat tighten and her eyes moisten.

Such waste!

'Now, now, child.' He patted her hand.

She sniffed and reached for her handkerchief. 'You and Papa were both fools!' Her tone was fierce.

His eyes widened. 'You wound me!' He sat back. 'Yet I must acknowledge the truth of what you say.'

'Mama is a good woman.' Her tone was defiant. 'She could make no one ashamed.'

He shrugged. 'I do not recall ever meeting her. All I could focus on was her status as a servant. I believed she could never be part of my social circle. I did not wish such a life for my son.'

'It was *his* life. He had the right to make his own decisions.'

He sighed, a hint of bitterness in his expression. 'I wish I had had your wisdom then.'

She grimaced. 'What is done is past. It cannot be changed.'

'Not all of it, no. But some things may be put right.' His eyes narrowed. 'Now, tell me… Are you comfortable here?'

'Yes, sir.' Confusion washed through her at this abrupt change in topic. But perhaps he could not bear to dwell for too long on what occurred.

'The truth, now.'

'My chamber is beyond comfortable—although I fear it is too much luxury for me.'

'Too much luxury? For my own granddaughter? I think not!'

Her heart skipped. 'But, sir, you know I am a servant.' She held up her hands for his inspection. 'See? And after I leave here I shall return to serve my mistress.'

She raised her head proudly. She refused to apologise for who she was. And she refused to play his games. She would not allow herself to be tempted into impossible dreams.

He opened his mouth to say something, then closed it again. After a moment, he enquired about her journey.

So he had chosen not to claim her fully as his granddaughter? Then she was right to be guarded.

'It was very long, sir, but the carriage was comfortable and we suffered no accidents.'

Trying to think of something to say that would help put behind them memories of Papa, she decided to tell him of Farmer Lingard and his unfortunate mishap. Her tale engaged his interest, and he guffawed aloud at the part where she had arranged for Mr Kendal to drive the cart.

'I see you leading him a merry dance! Good that you can shake him out of his cautious ways now and then.'

'Is Mr Kendal cautious?' She reflected for a moment. 'Yes, I can see that in him. But he is also determined, and can himself be terribly strong-willed on occasion. Why, he even—' She stopped, conscious that she was being indiscreet.

'He even what? Do continue, for you have piqued my interest.'

She was helpless against the devilish glint in his eye, and so she responded with a twinkle. 'He berated one of the landlords we encountered to the extent that the poor man thought his reputation would be quite ruined!'

He chuckled. 'Robert the Unruffled? Now, *this* is a tale I must hear in full!'

She obliged, telling it in such a way as to emphasise the humorous aspects, and was rewarded by his laughing loudly and merrily. From there, they discussed matters such as the state of the roads and the variation in posting inns.

When she had run out of travel tales he responded with stories of his boyish adventures, when he had slipped away from his tutors to fish in the dene or wander over the hills, and it was only when his valet arrived, to take him to his chamber for what was apparently his customary nap, that they realised almost three hours had passed.

Was that an approving look in the valet's eye? Certainly Mr Millthorpe seemed in fine fettle and brimful of vivacity—a decided contrast to the morose, flat air he had carried last night and earlier.

I enjoyed his company today, she realised with a pang. *Even though I am angry with him—with them both. And my pleasure is partly because I know he is Papa's papa. His stories matter because through him Papa is alive to me again.*

She followed them out of the library. But then, abruptly realising Mr Millthorpe did not wish her to observe his slow progress up the stairs, made off along the main corridor with an air of confidence, despite having no clue where she was going.

She walked all the way to the end, where a door gave way to what was clearly a servants' staircase. With a pang of recognition, she moved to the first step, then paused.

Oh, I so wish to descend, but really I should not do so.

She retreated, closing the door, then proceeded back along the corridor with a great deal of uncertainty. What should she do? She had to give Mr Millthorpe a little more time to ascend before seeking sanctuary in her own chamber. She could not be with the servants until he gave her leave to mix with them, and she had no idea where to find the family.

In the end she returned to the library, curling into the window seat and gazing out at the windswept February landscape. Her mind was whirling with new knowledge—although she could not, for now, make sense of it. She craved distraction, but could not find it. She would have loved to read a book, but did not dare touch Mr Millthorpe's property.

Her eye fell upon a lone robin, huddling miserably on a bare branch outside.

Poor robin! I know just how you feel!

Yet her isolation was not just physical. She simply had no idea where she belonged. Or even if she belonged anywhere.

After a time, the view became soothingly familiar—the same trees bending with each gust of wind, the occasional bird circling or resting on a bare branch. Her eyes grew heavy, so she closed them…just for a moment.

'So here you are!'

A delicious voice penetrated her pleasant dreams. Instinctively her attention turned towards it, merging it with her dream.

'I might have known not to worry,' the voice continued.

Worry? Why should anyone worry? Fighting through layers of sleep, she opened her eyes—to find Mr Kendal's amused cool grey eyes smiling into hers.

'Good day, Miss Bailey.'

Through a fog of sleep-induced stupidity she could only smile. What a wonderful way to wake up.

He seemed to groan, then stepped back towards the fireplace, where the two chairs she and Mr Millthorpe had used were still angled closely together.

Somehow she had ended up curled on her side on the long window seat, her feet tucked up and her hand under her cheek. Oh, Lord! Had she been drooling? Did she have a hand mark on her face? Were her curls crushed?

She swung her legs to the floor and sat up. Patting her head, she discovered her side curls had not been destroyed during her unplanned nap, and that her face was devoid of spittle.

Now she was properly awake, she felt the full force of uncertainty about her position.

Who am I? How must I behave with Mr Kendal? Does he know that my gr—? That Mr Millthorpe regrets the estrangement from Papa?

'Sir, I apologise. I did not intend to fall asleep. I was simply—'

'You were simply…?'

'I had planned to go to my chamber, but my—Mr Millthorpe and his valet were going upstairs, so I decided to wait until they had gone.' She stood, smoothing the folds of her simple day dress.

'Ah. You have realised, then, that my uncle is frustrated by his own infirmity? He hates to be reminded of it, or for others to see how feeble he has become.'

'His mind does not seem subject to the same decline.'

He considered this. 'Yes and no. When he turns his attention to something—or someone—his mind is as sharp as ever. Recently, though, he has tended to spend long periods of time unfocused—or perhaps he is simply lost in his own thoughts.'

He sat in his uncle's chair, inviting Jane to join him with a gesture.

She walked towards him, feeling decidedly uncertain. 'He told me his memories of forty years ago seem closer to him than events which happened last week,' she said.

Mr Kendal nodded. 'It is often so with older people.' He looked closely at her. 'Now you are awake—at least I *believe* you are awake—should you like to tour the house, as we discussed last night? My mother and I would enjoy showing it to you.'

'Yes, of course!' She could feel herself flushing. 'I do not know what came over me! I never sleep during the daytime.'

'It is not entirely unexpected, when you consider you have been travelling for five days and have now found yourself in an entirely novel situation.'

'House servants have been dismissed for less.'

'That may well be true, but you would do well to remember something.' He leaned forward. 'Today, you are not a servant.'

'Not a servant…' She echoed his words half-dreamily, conscious of little else save his nearness.

If only that were properly true. If only she had been raised as part of Papa's family. She could then maybe expect another kiss from Mr Kendal some day…

Mr Millthorpe's words came back to haunt her. Had she told the truth when she had said she did not yearn for that other life? A life in which she was Mr Millthorpe's acknowledged granddaughter, in which she had grown up in this house, and in which would be entitled to kiss Mr Kendal on as many occasions as they both wished…

She stopped her thoughts from pursuing that particular quarry. 'But I shall always be a servant, so I must not allow this visit to give me notions.'

'Notions?' He raised an eyebrow. 'Notions are often the most delightful things, and even a servant may enjoy unexpected luxury. Now…' He rose, holding out a hand to her. 'Let us go and find my mama, for she likes nothing better than showing the house to visitors.'

And so it proved. Mrs Kendal led them both from the attics to the kitchens, even showing Jane all the bedrooms save Mr Millthorpe's. When it came to showing Jane Mr Kendal's room, his mother regaled them both with a history of how she had persuaded Eugenia to allocate such a grand chamber to her son once he had left the nursery.

'I told her I thought it would be good for him to have a bright, south-facing room, rather than the small chamber at the other side of the house which was what she had initially suggested.' She leaned forward to add conspiratorially, 'I also told her that if his room was here, near the main family's bedchambers, he could run errands for her more easily!'

'I declare I never knew this, Mama! My poor aunt!'

'Well, why should I not speak up for my son? This bedchamber is much more comfortable than any of those in the other wing!'

'What I should like to know,' Jane interjected, 'is whether he did, in fact, make himself useful!'

'Of course I did! Why, I was the most obedient child!'

His mama sighed. 'He was—that was unless he decided to be obstinate. In general he has the sweetest, kindest nature, but now and again he will stamp his foot about something and then there is no reasoning with him.'

She patted her son's arm, to take any sting from her words, but Jane could not resist sending him a saucy look.

'Slander!' was his only comment, but Jane saw both the humour in his eyes and the affection between mother and son.

As she followed them out of the room she could not resist glancing at his bed. She had studiously avoided looking at it before, but just for one moment she allowed herself to envisage him lying there, and wondered what it might be like to feel his strong arms around her in the dark.

It was the first time she had tested herself thus since the heady kiss they had shared.

Heat raced through her, closely followed by shock at her own wanton thoughts. There was some anxiety underneath, but no overt fear.

'I apologise—what did you say?' They were both looking at her.

'Just that my uncle is sleeping, so we shan't disturb him.' Mr Kendal indicated the door opposite.

'Oh, yes, of course.'

He frowned slightly, but the moment passed as they moved towards the staircase.

My room is in the other wing, not this one. I wonder if that means something?

She actually felt a little better about the unaccustomed grandeur of her own chamber now that she knew she had not been housed in the family wing.

Visiting the servants' quarters was equally disturbing—although for very different reasons.

On a number of occasions in Ledbury House, Jane and the other servants had had unexpected visits from Miss Marianne, showing someone around. Such breaches of the unwritten border between the two worlds had always been uncomfortable for the servants, who had tended to stand impassively, briefly ceasing their work while the visitors passed through. This time Jane trailed behind Mrs Kendal and her son, desperately trying to look composed, as if she were used to being in such an exalted role.

Umpelby, genial and unconcerned, introduced her to Mrs Thompson, the housekeeper, and to the cook, and then to Henby, Mrs Millthorpe's personal maid. This lady, who was as tall, as thin and as self-important as her mistress, gave Jane the shallowest of curtseys, and Jane flushed in deep discomfort.

Thankfully Mr Kendal and his mama seemed to have missed these hints of tension. Or perhaps they had never learned to see them. Mr Kendal was clever, and perceptive, but he had not been raised among servants. Again, this served as a reminder of the differences in their station.

It is as if I am two people here.

Part of her was being forced into the role of guest, uttering suitable words of admiration regarding the beautiful chambers, elegant furniture and impressive public spaces—including the grand ballroom at the back of the house. The other part of her noticed everything from a servant's perspective.

Resisting the urge to give voice to any of these thoughts, she focused instead on aping the behaviour of *tonnish* guests she had seen all her life. She knew how to exclaim, and compliment, and ask suitable questions about settees and fireplaces.

Mrs Kendal seemed pleased with her, which was good.

Mr Kendal just seemed amused.

'So that is everything—well, everything in the interior. Robert, you shall show Miss Bailey the gardens and the lake tomorrow, if this rain ever stops! I declare Eugenia is right about the soirée at Staveley next week. All the roads shall be mud after this!'

Mr Kendal reassured her that so long as it was dry next Tuesday and Wednesday the roads would be fine for their trip to Staveley House on Thursday next.

'It is always fixed around the date of the February full moon, for we do not stay the night and so everyone travels there and back by moonlight.'

Jane was only half listening. She would not be accompanying them on any outings to visit the local gentry. Impossible. Last night Mr Millthorpe had had the opportunity to include her in their plans, yet he had not done so.

She was struck by the realisation that she would still be here then. Two full weeks at Beechmount Hall had not seemed so very much when she had agreed it with Mama and Miss Marianne. Now it seemed an eternity. How was she to work out how to behave? Was she a servant or not? Was she permitted to be Mr Millthorpe's granddaughter within this house, or must that not be spoken aloud?

She focused then on the other challenge. Given that her grandfather seemed to have decided not to claim her in public, and yet she was living here as if she were part of the family, how was she to keep reminding herself that there must be nothing between a lady's maid and a gentleman? Especially when she was expected to spend time in Mr Kendal's company every day of the week?

She sighed inwardly. There were no easy answers.

Chapter Fifteen

'How I have missed seeing you in that bonnet, Miss Bailey! Now, do not blush. It becomes you!'

They had just stepped outside the front door and Robert was determined to ensure she had a favourable impression of Beechmount Hall. For some reason it mattered very much to him that Miss Bailey should like his home.

She patted her plain straw bonnet, making a self-deprecating comment.

Yes, he thought, *it is plain. It has no fancy ribbons or feathers or fake fruit on top—just a simple blue ribbon which she ties under her ear to keep the bonnet from flying off in the wind. And yet...*

'You look beautiful.' The words were out before he had time to consider them, or how inappropriate they were.

She blushed, and almost tripped as they stepped down the shallow stone steps to the gravel filled drive.

'Oops! How silly of me!'

Her rosy cheeks were adorable. He, of course, had to reassure her that she was not at all silly. As he did so he was conscious of a strange feeling of elation, which he understood was caused just by being alone with her. He berated himself inwardly. This *tendre*, he reminded himself for the hundredth time, was transient in nature. He should just enjoy the sensation while it existed. When she left, inevitably all would be peaceful again.

He led her towards the parterre, laid out by some Millthorpe ancestor a hundred or so years ago. The fashion then had been to control nature, to contort gardens into rigid geometric shapes and patterns. He mentioned his distaste for it, but she disagreed.

'But it is so elegant! Just look at these little hedges, and how neat everything is!'

'I much prefer the wilderness of the park beyond. There we have oaks and elms dotted about as if at random—I believe it is much more pleasing on the eye.'

She laughed. 'I believe it is the servant in me who seeks tidiness everywhere! But of course you are right. The wildness is beautiful in a different way.'

They conversed amiably on a range of matters as they ambled through the gardens towards the lake. He could not resist telling her something of his childhood adventures there.

'Why, you sound just like Mr Millthorpe!' she exclaimed. 'Yesterday and this morning he was telling me tales of his own childhood adventures and mishaps. His stories are uncannily similar to yours. Boys are eternally boys, I suppose.'

'So you sat with my uncle again this morning? It is becoming quite the habit.'

She stiffened. 'Oh, but there is nothing in it!' Her brow was creased. 'I am not trying to come between you, or to take your place in his affections.'

He chuckled. 'I know that, Miss Bailey.'

Her innocence was clear to see—there was no guile in her.

'I shall be gone very soon and I shall never return,' she repeated earnestly.

'Indeed.'

Although her assertion had been an attempt to reassure him, and it echoed his own thoughts from earlier, it also created in him a sense of foreboding.

Never to see her again?

They walked in silence for some minutes before he belatedly realised that hers was the silence of anxiety. 'What is it, Miss Bailey?'

She looked at him, clearly considered pretending that nothing was the matter, and then thought better of it. How well he could read her now!

'I am pleased to have had the opportunity to meet my— to meet Mr Millthorpe, but I am perfectly content with my life. I told him so yesterday.'

'I am glad to hear it.'

My grandfather. That was what she'd almost said. Was she ready to acknowledge her background, then?

He decided to proceed with caution. 'Was your mother reluctant for you to travel here?'

She grimaced ruefully. 'She has no reason to like Mr Millthorpe, so I am glad she agreed that I should come. I wonder how they are all going on at Ledbury House? It is strange to think of it now. My existence here is so different—so peculiar and unnatural.'

He raised an eyebrow.

'Oh, please do not think I am not respectful of your family, and your life here. It is just—it is entirely foreign to me.'

As she spoke, a robin on a nearby branch tilted its head, as if listening to her.

I agree, he told it silently. *Even when she discusses commonplace subjects she is fascinating.*

'Tell me of the differences. What would your typical day involve as Lady Kingswood's maid?'

She did so, and he drew her out on the details.

In the end, he had to exclaim, 'I declare my eyes have been opened! I did not realise maids worked so hard.'

'Oh, but my work is easy compared to some,' she offered earnestly. 'When I was a scullery maid—now, *that* was hard work indeed!'

He was interested to hear more, and they passed the time doing so as they walked to the two-mile point at the far side of the lake before turning back.

By this stage he had had a fair education in the hard

physical work involved in keeping fires lit, chambers clean and vegetables cut. Such services he had always taken for granted. His own valet magically ensured he had a selection of crisp white cravats and spotless shirts when he needed them, and the man spent hours each day polishing his boots.

He glanced down. His boots—glossy and clean when they had stepped outside—were now daubed with mud. 'Oh, dear!' He pointed out the mess. 'I now feel guilty for the mess I have made of my boots!'

She moaned. 'And just look at my dress—oh, Lord, poor Nancy!' Her tied-up skirt had a few spatters, while the hem of her petticoat was brown with mud. 'I shall clean it myself.' She nodded decisively.

'Really? And how would you feel if Lady Kingswood suddenly decided to wash her own clothing to save you from having to do it?'

She clapped a hand to her mouth. 'Lord! I should feel unwanted, and useless, and I would worry about being turned off.'

He decided on judicious silence.

After a few moments she asked, in a small voice, 'So you think I should allow Nancy to see to my clothes?'

'Only you can decide what you wish to do. But sometimes a situation that seems straightforward is in fact complex and entangled.'

'Entangled…yes.' She glanced at him. 'Thank you.'

He nodded, and they proceeded in perfect amity.

Entangled. Complex. Like you, us…this.

He wanted nothing more than to take her into his arms and thoroughly kiss her, yet he could not. Too much was uncertain. Her future. Her status. How much she had been harmed by what she had suffered at seventeen. His mind delineated all these reasons, yet nothing dimmed the impulse, the yearning for her.

Summoning every ounce of self-control, he walked on by her side.

* * *

During the next few days Jane felt the comfort of an emerging rhythm to her time in Beechmount Hall. In the mornings she ate a meagre breakfast—years of early-morning work meant that her stomach was not ready for food on first waking. She would then sit with Mr Millthorpe until noon, and after nuncheon she would walk with Mr Kendal in the gardens and grounds.

Sometimes, if the day was dry, they would climb to the small tree-crested hill that gave the house its name. She could sense Mr Kendal's love for the place in the way he talked of it, and in the certain look in his eye when he gazed at the house and grounds from that vantage point.

At times she thought she imagined another look in his eye—something that called to her, leaving her breathless and hoping for a kiss. Yet it never happened.

In the evenings, after dinner, she would sit with the ladies in the salon until the men joined them. She and Mrs Kendal were forging a firm acquaintance. She was, of course, predisposed to like Mr Kendal's mother, and in truth found her engaging and warm, if a little yielding.

She frowned. She could not say the same of Mr Kendal, for all that he chose not to engage in some of his battles.

Mr Kendal was habitually reserved, she had found, and she thought it surprising that the relaxed, candid gentleman who was her friend could become so taciturn and even aloof at times in the company of his uncle and aunt.

Perhaps he worries for his mama.

Mrs Kendal often seemed anxious in Mr and Mrs Millthorpe's company, despite the fact she had lived there for nigh on twenty years.

In truth, my grandfather is something of an autocrat, Jane acknowledged ruefully.

Mr Millthorpe generally made his wishes and opinions known in no uncertain manner, causing much unneeded tension and conflict in the family. At times, the glint in the old man's eye made it seem to Jane that he was deliberately trying to get a rise out of Mr Kendal, who steadfastly and coolly refused to give him the satisfaction of engaging with him. Mr Kendal was as stubborn in his own way as her grandfather.

And Mrs Millthorpe was full of opinion—much of it ill-informed or simply untrue. As a servant, Jane was used to buttoning her lip and not speaking of family controversies, but on occasion she was severely tempted to respond to the outrageous statements of her grandfather's second wife. This was especially difficult when that lady was critical of Mr Kendal, who did not escape her jibes. But Jane's instinctive wish to defend him had to be suppressed. He did not require her aid.

To be fair, Mr Kendal often looked amused by these barbs, and they were tempered by the occasions when his aunt spoke fawningly of him. These tended to be the moments when her husband had displeased her, so Mr Kendal was temporarily elevated from irritant to paragon in comparison.

He took her praise with the same indifference as he did her criticism. It seemed it simply did not matter to him.

Of all of the family, Mrs Millthorpe was the only one Jane struggled to like. She was habitually sour-faced, irritable and judgemental, and she seemed to take delight in the misfortunes of others. Her contribution to the household seemed only to be to trouble others.

On Sunday they all travelled by coach to the small chapel in Arkendale. It took Mr Millthorpe almost ten minutes to get from the carriage to what was apparently his usual pew, but he managed it. Jane, who could see the pride in his eyes as he sank gratefully into his seat, felt a sudden lump in her throat at watching him.

During the service she was conscious of the relentless scrutiny of the congregation. A stranger in their midst—especially one staying at Beechmount Hall—was clearly of great interest to them. Immediately afterwards Mrs Millthorpe whisked her straight into the closed carriage, before she might be questioned, and they waited inside with the curtains closed for the others to join them.

'Thank goodness,' her hostess muttered. 'For a moment I thought I should be forced to introduce you to Mr and Mrs Dodsworth.' She shuddered. 'A servant…sitting with the family in church!'

All of this was clearly aimed at Jane, although Mrs Millthorpe had maintained her peculiar habit of talking indirectly *at* Jane, rather than *to* her. As such, Jane did not feel able to reply, for fear of being accused of impertinence. So they sat in silence, Jane trying not to move or even breathe loudly.

Eventually they were joined by Mr Millthorpe, Mrs Kendal, and finally Mr Kendal. He gave her a keen look as he entered the carriage, but said nothing.

The other three were in the sought-after front-facing seats, and Jane and Mr Kendal were seated together in the rear-facing position. Jane looked down, enjoying the sight of his leg so close to hers. If she closed her eyes she would better feel the sensation of warmth coming from his body, where it was near hers.

I do not care that I am rear-facing, for he is beside me.

No more than three hours after the service, and just when Jane and Mr Kendal had returned from their usual walk, the sound of a carriage was heard outside the window of the salon.

'Visitors!' exclaimed Mrs Kendal. 'Well, now, I wonder who it could be?'

She addressed Mr Millthorpe, who was half dozing in his chair by the fire.

'We have visitors, Uncle.'

'Eh? Visitors?' He lifted his head. 'Blast it! What do they mean by disturbing our peace in this way? Who is it?'

Mrs Kendal had gone to the window and was peeping

out from behind the curtain. 'It is Mrs Dodsworth. And her husband, too. Oh, and *Miss* Dodsworth is with them.' She looked directly at Mr Kendal.

Jane's senses were suddenly fully awake. Why had she addressed that last part to her son?

Inside, she was still struggling with the undoubted pull she felt towards him. Like a flower turning towards the sun, she was drawn to him in company, and she blossomed and shone when they were alone together. He had become the friend she had never had, although she was even now unsure as to his opinion of her at times.

Mama was Mama, and Miss Marianne was Miss Marianne, but neither were as interesting as Mr Kendal. Nor were they as interested in her—in her opinions, her thoughts, her history… Certain topics were off-limits for both of them, but in general there was an affinity between them that she had never experienced with anyone else.

That does not mean it is special, she told herself. *It may just relate to my sheltered life so far. Perhaps he has felt this partiality for many women before me.*

Her body's reaction in his presence continued to be intense, confusing and exhilarating all at once. Occasionally as they walked his arm would brush hers, or he would assist her with a brief hand on her elbow. Invariably her insides would melt, her heart would pound a now familiar tattoo, and her breath would catch. These exhilarating moments would not awaken the fear inside her, and she was becoming increasingly confident that her strong connection to Mr Kendal was healing some of the brokenness inside her.

As she was pondering all of this, she suddenly noticed Mrs Millthorpe staring at her. A level, fixed, implacable stare.

She started, finally understanding what was expected of her. 'Oh! I should—I must go to my chamber. I have—I have things to do.' She stood.

'What things?' barked Mr Millthorpe.

'Well, I should write to my mama.'

'Again? I paid for a letter to go just yesterday.'

She flushed. 'I do not think I should be here if you have visitors.'

'Nonsense!'

'My dear—' began his wife.

Mr Millthorpe's gaze swivelled around to her. 'Do you have something to say about the matter?'

Eugenia subsided, her lips a thin line of disapproval.

Helplessly, Jane sank back into her seat.

The footman admitted their guests, and Jane rose with the others, shrinking inside. She recognised them from the chapel—a middle-aged couple with a pretty daughter about Jane's own age. They were greeted warmly by the others, Mr Millthorpe even going so far as to warmly welcome the lady and her daughter, while shaking the gentleman's hand.

Miss Dodsworth had fair hair, deep blue eyes, and a warm smile. She was dressed elegantly, Jane noted, in a celestial blue crape frock, worn over a white satin slip. There was a deep border of net lace around the bottom, and pretty blue embroidery. Jane sighed. Her own printed muslin seemed drab in comparison.

Jane was introduced simply as, 'Miss Jane Bailey, visiting from Bedfordshire.' She made a curtsey, feeling an air of dreadful strangeness as she did so.

Miss Dodsworth's eyes sought Jane's and they were filled with curiosity. Jane gave a shy smile, and was rewarded with a smile in return.

'Miss Bailey, eh?' Mr Dodsworth lifted a quizzing glass to peer at her through it. 'You'll be related to the Farnham Baileys, I'll wager.'

Before Jane could even think how to answer this, Mrs Millthorpe cut across her visitor to address his wife.

'My dear Mrs Dodsworth, I apologise for not being able to speak to you directly after church this morning. A twinge of colic sent me scurrying to the carriage.'

'Colic? Oh, my dear, how dreadful! I declare there is nothing worse than colic!'

Mrs Kendal added her support to this position, and the three ladies then engaged in a prolonged discussion about the gastric sufferings they had endured. Mr Dodsworth, lifting his eyes to heaven, moved to sit with Mr Kendal, and they were soon engrossed in a wide-ranging discussion about politics and farming.

Mr Millthorpe had lapsed into his customary silence, and was currently contentedly engaged in looking into the fire.

'Miss Bailey!' Miss Dodsworth had come to join her on the yellow satin-covered settee. 'I am delighted to find another young lady in the district.'

'Oh, but I am here for only a fortnight. I shall return home to Bedfordshire after that.'

'What a shame! I confess to be missing the company of people of my own age.'

'What of Mr Kendal? Surely he—?'

Miss Dodsworth made a dismissive sound. 'Oh, Robert is like an older brother to me! No, there is something particularly delightful in meeting a lady near my own age.' She smiled sunnily. 'I myself am three-and-twenty.'

'I shall also be four-and-twenty on my next birthday, in August.' Jane tilted her head on one side as a sudden thought struck her. 'How old is Mr Kendal?' She grimaced. 'I apologise if that is an impertinent question.'

'Not at all!' A dimple peeped in Miss Dodsworth's cheek. 'I shall make a bargain with you. You shall guess, and then I shall give you the answer.'

Jane tried to work it out. 'He came here when he was around eight, I think… And he mentioned being here more than fifteen years…perhaps twenty. Is he five-and-twenty or thereabouts?' She frowned. 'But that cannot be right.'

'Why not?' Miss Dodsworth gave her a puzzled look, and then she giggled. 'Let me divine it: you think he cannot be five-and-twenty because…' she leaned forward to whisper '…because he acts so much older!' She straightened. 'There! Now it is I who am being impertinent!'

Jane could not help chuckling a little. It was indeed Mr Kendal's dignity and sense of reserve that had left her feeling as though he must be older.

And yet I have seen another side to him.

She recalled certain moments when they had laughed together over some trifling matter. He had always seemed young and carefree then

Mr Kendal had caught the sound of their laughter, and was eyeing them both quizzically from the other side of the room.

'Oh, dear! He has divined us! Now he will plague us to know what is so amusing!' Miss Dodsworth was refreshingly irreverent.

Jane threw him a saucy look. Their conversation, though indeed a little impertinent, was harmless. She would tease him about it later.

He replied with narrowed eyes and a mock glare, which sent Miss Dodsworth into a peal of laughter. Jane was conscious of an unexpected thrill of enjoyment. She *liked* Miss Dodsworth. And she liked Mr Kendal. And she relished this raillery and jesting. It was entirely new to her.

She smiled broadly and made her decision. 'I declare Mr Kendal to be nine-and-twenty. No more and no less.'

'Close! He turned eight-and-twenty in November.'

Jane nodded sagely. 'I am content with my supposition.' She considered for a moment. 'He should slacken more… devote some time to his own interests.'

'He has taken on the burden of responsibility from Mr Millthorpe as he has aged.'

Jane glanced at her grandfather. He was apparently engaged in observing the different conversations, his blue eyes sharp and alert. Jane felt an unexpected wave of affection for the elderly patriarch. Despite everything, she found herself more and more in charity with him as time went on.

Tea was served, and they all clustered around Mrs Millthorpe as she passed them each a dish of tea, coffee, or in some cases a glass of wine. She even put the teacup directly into Jane's hand.

The maid then returned with sweetmeats. No one looked at her except Jane, who was again feeling disconcerted by her exalted status.

Soon afterwards the Dodsworths rose to depart, with Miss Dodsworth pressing Jane to return the visit. 'Robert!' she declared, 'you shall bring her tomorrow!'

Robert bowed his head in assent.

Mrs Millthorpe looked decidedly grim, but had to paste a false smile on her face as Mrs Dodsworth reminded her of the Staveley House soirée, planned for Thursday evening. They all held the now familiar conversation about the state of the roads, then the Dodsworths took their leave.

No sooner had the salon door closed behind them than Mrs Millthorpe sank into her chair with an air of exhaustion. 'Well! I thought they should *never* go!'

Mrs Kendal looked perplexed. 'But they stayed only the usual length of time. And you have always welcomed them visiting before?'

'Oh, for goodness' sake! I declare you are positively bird-witted at times, Niece!'

Mrs Kendal seemed quite startled by this, and a little hurt.

Mr Kendal frowned.

But Mrs Millthorpe was not done, and this time her venom was directed towards Jane. 'I have never before,' she declared, 'had to endure a visit where I must hide the fact that a *servant* is in the salon, dressed like a lady and aping her betters!'

Chapter Sixteen

Mrs Kendal gasped, and a wave of mortification washed over Jane. Although she *was* a servant, there was no need for Mrs Millthorpe to be so cruel. She bit back an impertinent retort, and felt a sudden lump in her throat. Her eyes stung.

Do not cry!

'Eh? What's that?' Mr Millthorpe fixed a beady eye on his wife.

At the same time Mr Kendal rose from his seat and walked across the room to sit with Jane. He did not speak. He did not need to. The unlooked-for support tightened Jane's chest with gratitude. His cool grey eyes found hers and he nodded slightly.

She gave him a misty half-smile. It was all she could manage.

'Well!' Mrs Millthorpe was addressing her spouse, an air of defiance in the toss of her head. 'You cannot expect me to be easy about it.'

Her husband spoke slowly. 'About *what*, exactly?'

Mrs Millthorpe was angry, but there was a deep hurt there too. One her grandfather could not see.

'About having *her*—' she jabbed a finger in Jane's general direction '—in my home.'

Here it was—finally. All the anger she had been suppressing since Jane's arrival had finally slipped its leash.

'She has every right to be here.' Mr Millthorpe's tone was disturbingly soft. 'As she is my only living blood relative.'

Two spots of colour appeared on Mrs Millthorpe's cheekbones. 'The daughter of a by-blow, I assume? What would your first wife, the sainted Eleanor, have had to say about *that*?'

Jane gasped. *She does not know I am Edward's daughter! He has never told her!*

Her hands clenched into fists. She had not realised her grandfather had been so disrespectful to Mrs Millthorpe! Why on earth had he not told her the truth?

Husband and wife glared at each other from opposite sides of the fireplace. Between them the fire blazed, crackled and spat.

This should not be happening—and it is all because of my presence.

She stood. 'I do not wish to distress anyone. I—'

'Sit down, child.' Mr Millthorpe's tone was harsh.

She sat, trembling. Mr Kendal put his hand on hers briefly, his touch warm. She sent him a worried glance.

Mr Millthorpe sat up straighter in his chair. 'I have never had a by-blow.'

There was a stunned silence as the impact of his words was felt.

Jane felt Mr Kendal stiffen beside her.

Mrs Kendal was the first to find her voice. 'Then…then who is Miss Bailey?'

'Her father was my son—Edward.' Mr Millthorpe's voice cracked a little. He coughed to disguise the emotion, then carried on, addressing Mrs Kendal. 'We were estranged before you and Robert came to live here. Before my second marriage.'

Mrs Millthorpe's mouth was hanging open. She turned to Jane. 'You are *Edward's* daughter?'

'I am.'

'I did not know… I thought…' She addressed her husband. 'You should have told me.'

They eyed each other, the only sound in the room the crackling of the fire.

Then he nodded. 'You are right. I should have told you. I

myself only discovered her existence recently, through the offices of a Bow Street Runner. She is Edward's only child and his legitimate daughter. He took his mother's surname when he left here.' He looked at Jane. 'Dodsworth was right, you know. You *are* related to the Farnham Baileys. Your grandmother's people still live there. You have countless cousins in Yorkshire on your grandmother's side.'

'I do?' Jane was astonished.

Just a fortnight ago I had only Mama. Now I have a grandfather and 'countless' cousins.

She could barely take it in.

There were, however, more pressing concerns.

Mrs Kendal had moved to her aunt and was gently patting her hand. 'Oh, Eugenia, I had no idea! I had heard about Edward, of course, but we all thought him long dead.'

'He *is* long dead!' Mr Millthorpe banged a fist on the arm of his chair. 'And through my own headstrong obstinacy I never had the chance to put things right.' He looked at Jane. 'Until now.'

All eyes turned to Jane.

He meant to put things right? But how? He could not bring Papa back. Could not undo her life growing up as a servant.

Jane frowned, her mind whirring with racing thoughts. She could almost *see* the shifting perceptions in the room. She dared not look at Mr Kendal, but was conscious of his continued rigidity beside her.

Finally Robert spoke up, his tone harsh. 'You should have talked of this before. You should have told us.'

Mr Millthorpe glared at him. The two of them locked gazes as the air in the room hummed with uneasiness. After a long moment, Mr Millthorpe dropped his gaze.

'Yes.'

The single word resonated in the room like a booming gong.

'In truth,' he continued, 'I could scarcely believe she existed and had been found. I put myself through agonies of apprehension—that the Runner had erred, that she was not truly Ned's daughter, that she would not come.' He looked at Jane. 'It is not just your Millthorpe eyes that convinced me, but your Millthorpe fire.'

'Fire? But I am not fiery!'

He laughed at this. 'You were fiery enough to put me in my place when I told you of my estrangement from Ned. As I recall, you described me as a fool.'

'I described both of you as fools! And I stand by it!'

Frustration rose within her again. Her grandfather had made a muddle of all. He had held grudges when he should have let go, and he had kept secrets when he should have been open. What a catastrophe he had created!

Mrs Millthorpe put a hand to her head. 'Then you mean to take her to the Staveley House soirée on Thursday…?' She addressed her husband.

He nodded, his expression briefly rueful. 'I do. I have waited to establish if she will be a suitable person in looks and in manner. I believe we can all see that she is.'

Jane bristled with indignation.

How dare he sit in judgement on me?

'And,' he added, 'she will be presented as my grand-daughter.'

Jane gaped.

He means to claim me after all?

Mrs Millthorpe's shoulders slumped in resignation. 'But what is she to *wear*?'

Mr Millthorpe looked a little taken aback by his wife's question. Jane, too, was a little bewildered by it.

'Wear?' He looked Jane up and down. 'She has always looked perfectly presentable to me.'

Mrs Kendal and Mrs Millthorpe looked at each other, their cynical expressions a mirror of each other.

'And that shows how little you know of fashion!' declared his wife.

'I am proud of it!' he retorted.

They were back on familiar ground, and the disquiet in the salon had eased considerably. Still, an undercurrent of shock persisted. Again Jane, rendered almost speechless, could sense the shifting perceptions eddying and swirling all around her.

They had not known—they had thought her illegitimate!

Suddenly much became clear. Mrs Millthorpe's hostility. Mr Kendal's lack of concern about the possibility of his being ousted. Now that she thought about it she realised she had never spoken to him about the estrangement between her papa and his father.

I must speak to him. He must not think I intend to displace him from his inheritance.

She glanced at her grandfather. He would not do that to Mr Kendal, would he?

Mrs Kendal turned to Jane. 'Miss Bailey—'

'Call her Jane. We are all family here.' Mr Millthorpe's tone made clear that this was unmistakably an order.

Mrs Kendal gave a half-smile. 'Jane... I have seen you wear the same dress each night since you came here—the amber silk. Is that your only evening gown?'

Jane nodded. 'It is. I did not know I would need even one evening gown.'

Was this really happening? Must she go out in public as if she were a proper member of the family? Her caution about her grandfather's intentions was, it seemed, now unnecessary.

He means to recognise me in public.

What this meant for her future was unclear. Suddenly there was quicksand beneath her feet again. Although such a change represented unlooked-for good fortune, it took away many of the certainties in her current life—including her role as lady's maid. She felt lost, engulfed, as if Jane Bailey no longer existed. She was drowning in a wave of change and fear and insecurity.

Mrs Kendal was frowning. 'Aunt Eugenia, how quickly can Henby and Eliza make up a gown?'

Her aunt had not been idle during the past moments. She had clearly been working herself up into a state of righteous indignation.

'So now I am to be further inconvenienced, am I? My own personal servant taken away to make a gown for your guest? It is insupportable!'

She fished a lace-edged handkerchief from her reticule and dabbed at the corner of her eye.

'She is *our* guest,' her husband retorted. 'And you will treat her with respect.'

'Please,' said Jane, desperate to avoid further disagreement. 'I do not wish to cause trouble. I do not even wish to go to the soirée!'

Her cry came from the heart. The very thought of attending filled her with dread.

'It pleases me that you should go,' said Mr Millthorpe curtly.

Mrs Kendal, catching her eye, shook her head slightly. And as Mrs Kendal soothed her aunt with words of reassurance Jane finally plucked up the courage to glance at Mr Kendal. He looked grey-faced and grim, and did not turn his head to meet her gaze.

Jane swallowed. Mr Millthorpe's announcement had changed everything. Now she must begin again with people who had thought they knew who and what she was.

But I am the same as before. I am Jane, raised as a servant. Being Edward's daughter changes nothing.

Even as she tried to reassure herself she knew it was not true.

Finally Mr Millthorpe's valet arrived, and took him away to rest. Mr Kendal took the opportunity to leave with him, muttering some vague excuse. Jane, eyeing his closed face and stiff posture, wished she had never come to Yorkshire.

'Oh, dear, Robert…' was his mama's response. 'Yes, of

course. We shall discuss—' she glanced at Jane '—everything later.'

'I shall call for Henby,' said Mrs Millthorpe, walking to the bells.

Jane's mind was awhirl. The events of the last half-hour were almost too much for her to understand. But she had sensed the shift in the air. The feeling that she was culpable of an unnamed crime. The feeling that Mr Kendal was displeased with her.

And as she sat there, dressed in finery and with inappropriate curls in her hair, she was conscious of feeling deserted, solitary and friendless.

In truth, she had never felt so alone.

Robert marched directly to the stables, stopping only to don his boots and his wine-coloured riding jacket. Blacklock, his stallion, gave a whinny and a nuzzle of greeting, and Robert as ever slipped him a piece of carrot. He saddled the horse himself, needing the familiarity of buckle and bridle, girth and stirrup to divert his racing mind.

His uncle's revelation had been entirely unexpected and he cursed his own stupidity.

Mounting in the stable yard, he took the horse across the cobbles at a trot, enjoying the familiar sound of steel on stone. Stone setts gave way to gravel, then grass. Once free of the parterre, he urged the stallion to a canter, then a full gallop, and as his speed increased the battles in Robert's head were momentarily forgotten. A crow briefly aligned its flight with theirs, but it could not keep up, and soon wheeled around towards a venerable oak tree nearby.

We are flying faster than the birds, he thought, and the thought was closely followed by the recognition that the knot in his stomach was beginning to loosen. *This never fails.*

All his life Robert had loved riding—some of his earliest memories were of sitting on the back of a pony. It had been his solace and his comfort on many occasions when he had needed it—when his uncle's cantankerousness and his aunt's criticism had been too much to bear, or when his dear mama had been talking to him for too long, or when he was possessed by the simple requirement for his own company and the need to escape the house.

His horse knew the route well. Having descended the gentle slope at the front of the house, they wheeled around to half circle the lake, then began the climb to the rise behind Beechmount Hall. Robert slowed the pace to a walk, unwilling to exhaust the poor creature.

'Good boy. Well done.'

He patted Blacklock's neck before dismounting. Tying up the reins so they would not trip the stallion, he walked to the edge of the hill to look down on his home.

There it squatted—a solid, ugly and yet beautiful stone pile. The day was dull and overcast, and the heavy grey clouds on the horizon blended effortlessly with the grey-black Yorkshire stone. As obstinate as its master.

He gave a short laugh. He had always known his uncle to be headstrong, immovable, and taciturn on matters of importance. But he had had no idea he was holding a secret such as this!

The afternoon was almost gone, and the gathering dusk was beginning to settle around him like a weighty damp cloak. He mounted the horse again, and together they picked their way carefully down the hill.

The last thing I need is for Blacklock to break a leg on an unseen rabbit hole.

They passed the lake—home to many of his fondest childhood memories—and began ascending the park.

The glow of yellow candlelight from multiple windows was both comforting and unfamiliar all at once.

Is this still my home? My future? All is changed now and I know not what to make of it.

Chapter Seventeen

Branches of candles had been lit, and the brightness inside the salon meant that Jane could no longer see the gardens outside. Dusk was falling and Mr Kendal had still not returned. They had all seen him two hours ago, passing the salon windows on a glorious black stallion, his face set with dark determination.

'Oh, dear…' Mrs Kendal had murmured.

'Well,' her aunt had replied cryptically, 'he has only himself to blame. He should not have run that particular errand.'

Had they been speaking of her? Was the errand she'd spoken of his trip to Ledbury House to bring her here? She had caused such trouble…

Jane bit her lip. Talk of Edward—and Jane's very existence—had hurt Mrs Millthorpe and caused discord between her and her husband. It would have been better for them if she had not come.

And yet even now, feeling as small and as upset as she could remember, she could not be completely sorry. Meeting her grandfather and penetrating his sour temper to find the interesting, lively mind beneath had been enlightening.

He is part of me, she thought. *And I am part of him.*

Seeing her father in those eyes every time she was in Mr Millthorpe's company had brought back long-buried memories of Papa.

And meeting Mr Kendal, too, would have been impossible without the errand that had sent him all the way to Bedfordshire.

I cannot regret that!

And yet there remained an undoubted uneasiness in the air. It had been somewhat dissipated by Mr Millthorpe's departure from the salon, but afterwards his wife had embarked on a long list of the ills, slights and knocks she had been subjected to during the long years of her marriage.

Mrs Kendal had made soothing comments from time to time, but in truth Mrs Millthorpe had seemed largely unaware of her audience. Jane had been content to remain silent, allowing the angry words to wash over her, hearing clearly the pain beneath them.

Mrs Millthorpe's personal maid, Henby, had arrived in answer to her mistress's call, and Mrs Millthorpe had drawn her into the litany of complaints, asking for affirmation that her claims were true.

Henby had replied soothingly that Mrs Millthorpe was right, and her every word just. This might have been merely the empty words of a servant, meeting her mistress's needs, but the glare she had thrown towards Jane at one point had made it clear who Henby thought was to blame for her mistress's distress.

'And now I am to find a dress suitable for her to wear at the Staveley House soirée. On Thursday! *Thursday*, Henby! And today is *Sunday*!'

Henby had tried to soothe her mistress, telling her she would contrive something, and this seemed to have had the desired effect, for soon afterwards Mrs Millthorpe's tirade had finally slowed, then halted. Henby had brought her a tisane, and Mrs Millthorpe had lain down on the settee for a nap.

Jane had remained seated, hardly daring to move.

After a time Mrs Kendal, too, had dozed in her chair.

Gradually the silence in the room had allowed Jane's nerves to settle. She hoped Mrs Millthorpe would feel better after her rest. Jane was not sure how much more of her anger she could take.

She reflected on the row between her grandfather and his wife. Something about today's exchange had been deeply unsettling. Despite the fact they had been married for twenty-five years and more, Mr and Mrs Millthorpe did not seem to share the sort of amity Jane would have expected.

They are both unhappy people, Jane reflected. *Is that the reason for the discord, or simply its result?*

After a long hour Mrs Millthorpe stirred, stretched, yawned, and sat up. Mrs Kendal, seemingly attuned to her aunt's needs, also woke at this point, and helped Mrs Millthorpe settle herself upright with a comfortable cushion behind her back and an offer of tea.

'Not tea, no.' She glanced at the clock on the mantle. 'We shall have to prepare for dinner in an hour. No doubt,' she said spitefully, 'we shall be treated to that same amber silk we have seen every evening.'

Jane flushed, aware that the knots in her stomach, which had eased a little during the silence, had now renewed their twisting.

Be brave.

She swallowed. 'My mistress, Lady Kingswood, gave me a number of day dresses, but only one evening gown. In truth, I would prefer not to eat with the family, since it is clear my presence causes some distress. I should also prefer not go to the soirée. Perhaps—'

Mrs Millthorpe's steely gaze swung around towards Jane. *'You!'* Her face was suffused with purplish rage. 'You would have done better not to have come at all!'

Mrs Kendal gasped, then tried as ever to be peacemaker. 'Now, then, my dear Aunt Eugenia, we must simply contrive, as Henby says, to make do.'

She sent Jane a sympathetic glance.

Thank goodness for Mrs Kendal! Jane knew she was not completely friendless. But how angry Mrs Millthorpe was! And surely Mrs Kendal must be concerned about her son's inheritance?

Jane's stomach twisted.

'Henby! Ring the bell for her so we may discover what

must be done.' Mrs Millthorpe's eyes narrowed. 'Has Robert returned?'

Mrs Kendal looked a little bewildered. 'I have no idea, for I also slept.' She glanced at Jane, who gave a tiny shake of the head. 'I think he has not yet returned.'

'Hmm… I intend to speak to my husband on the morrow. I shall have a great deal to say to him—including plenty about protecting my own and my nephew's future!'

Mrs Kendal, with a quick glance towards Jane, gave a non-committal answer, but Jane noticed the slight frown she wore eased a little afterwards.

Did they genuinely believe she was there to steal Beechmount Hall away from them? The notion was absurd. Had they forgotten she had been raised to be a servant? It was impossible even to consider someone like her being gifted such a place, such responsibility—especially since Mr Kendal was the master in all but name.

She shook her head ruefully. Mr Millthorpe remained master, for all his frailty. But Mr Kendal was clearly meant to be his heir.

Jane realised she must now expect that her grandfather would ensure she no longer needed to earn her living as a servant. But she had not been raised to be heiress to such a place as this! Surely everyone could see it would be most unsuitable?

Her ears caught the sound of hooves on the gravel outside and her pulse instantly quickened.

It must be him!

Her reaction to Mr Kendal's return was much too strong. *I should hate to lose his good opinion.*

Strangely, at this moment, amid thoughts of inheritances and her being claimed as a legitimate granddaughter, Mr Kendal's good opinion was her primary concern.

Henby arrived with news for her mistress. 'We have found some trunks in the attic, ma'am. They contain old dresses from years ago that can be unpicked and remade, for the fabric is good. There is plenty of satin, silk and lace, that may be used.'

Jane felt a flicker of interest. Of all her duties, dressmaking was a joy, not a burden. If she was forced to go to this soirée perhaps she could wear a new dress.

'Well, have them brought down here, for I have no intention of climbing up to a draughty attic!'

Henby assented, adding that she would ask Eliza to join them, as she would be assisting with the stitching.

Jane was now only half-listening, as she had caught the sound of Mr Kendal's voice in the hallway. As he passed the salon she distinctly heard him ask for a bath to be drawn in his room. The sound of his voice always did strange things to her insides, and now she had an image of him in his bath to contend with.

As scullery maid, she had often had to heave jugs of water upstairs, when a member of the family had bathed, and of course she had occasionally seen servant men washing half naked in lakes and streams. She knew what a male torso looked like unclothed, and had no difficulty in imagining Mr Kendal's firm chest, arms and back.

Her mind strayed to the thought of Mr Kendal in his bath. Why, even now he would be disrobing upstairs. He would likely await the hot water in his dressing gown, and would be naked as a newborn underneath it…

Heat spread through her and she had to resist the strong urge to fan herself. Thankfully no one was paying her any attention, and soon afterwards Henby returned—this time accompanied by Eliza, and by two footmen carrying an enormous trunk.

This was deposited in the middle of the floor, and the footmen left as Henby opened it.

'Just look!' she announced, lifting the first garment—a painted silk dress festooned with flowers and leaves.

'Ooh!'

Jane, Mrs Millthorpe and Mrs Kendal all made a similar sound—the eternal sigh of a woman of fashion.

'And this!' Henby held up a striped pink satin gown, festooned with a line of bows down the bodice. The waist was low and the hips and rear extremely wide.

'Obviously made to be worn with a rump and panniers,' said Mrs Kendal. 'I remember my own mother wearing a grand dress like this for a ball one time.'

'It's beautiful,' sighed Jane, running her fingers over the smooth satin. 'And so well preserved!'

Henby flipped it over. 'There are yards of fabric in the skirt and train. The sleeves need work, and we would need to fashion a new bodice and underdress, but it will do.' She did not request Jane's opinion. 'Eliza and I shall unpick it this evening and start remaking it in the morning. I have some plain pink that will do for the underdress, and we shall size it on one of Miss Bailey's other dresses.'

'Can you do it in time?' Mrs Millthorpe sounded rather anxious. 'Whatever my personal feelings on the subject, it is a matter of pride that no one in my party shall be ill turned-out for the Staveley House soirée.'

Henby clicked her tongue. 'There is a prodigious amount of work to be done. The gown will have to be simple, with very little embellishment.'

'But it must not be *dowdy*!'

'Eliza and I shall do our best.'

Henby exchanged a look with Eliza—a look which seemed to Jane to have an element of slyness in it.

Why, they have no intention of ensuring it is fashionable!

Jane was quite shocked. Were they intending to disobey their mistress because they resented *her*?

She thought quickly.

I am my mother's daughter. I have my own strength.

'Perhaps I can assist,' she offered diffidently.

'You can sew? Good!' Mrs Millthorpe seemed pleased. 'You might as well make yourself useful.'

'I shall concentrate on the bodice and sleeves, if you like, and leave you two to create the main form of the dress.'

Jane was addressing the two servants, but again it was Mrs Millthorpe who answered.

'Capital! Go you and start unpicking the pink. We shall amuse ourselves by exploring the trunk further.'

The servants curtseyed and left, taking the pink striped satin with them.

Jane watched them. Would they 'accidentally' destroy it, or carry out some other means of ensuring she had no suitable dress for Thursday?

She considered this, but soon realised that, much as they might wish to make Jane as unattractive and shabby as possible, they would not dare to face their mistress's displeasure if there was no dress at all.

'May I come in?'

Robert sighed inwardly.

I am in no mood to discuss this yet.

'Of course, Mama!' Freshly dressed after his bath, he ran a hand through his wet hair and pulled two bedroom chairs forward to accommodate the conversation that his mother had clearly planned.

'Did you enjoy your ride?' Her eyes were scanning his face.

'I did.'

She took a breath. 'What do you make of today's news?'

He shrugged. 'My uncle has always enjoyed playing with us as puppets. This is more of the same.'

'But—your inheritance…'

'What inheritance? I am related to him only by marriage. He may dispose of his property in whatever way he wishes.'

'Robert, please. We both know there has been an expectation—'

He spoke curtly. 'Expectations are not reality. We must

deal with circumstances as they are, not as we once believed them to be.'

'Do you think…? Miss Bailey seems innocent and honest. Is it possible that she knew?'

Inwardly, the answer came instantly. Of course she knew.
Her mother would have told her. So why had she kept the
information from him? Was she truly as guileless as he had
believed her to be?

He tried to deny it, but there was a sense of hurt—of
betrayal, almost. He had thought they had built a level of
trust between them. Why, then, had she not told him of
her true status?

'She must have known. Edward was her father. She is
a legitimate grandchild—his only blood relative, as Uncle
said himself.'

Mama bit her lip. 'So where does that leave us?'

He sensed her anxiety. 'We shall manage, Mama. I make
a good living from my importing business. We shall live
perfectly comfortably.'

He could not believe he was being forced to say this to
her. Beechmount Hall was her home. He had thought they
would live there for the rest of their lives.

She nodded and lifted her chin. 'You are right, of course.
I can be brave and start again if needs be.'

His heart went out to her. She should not have this uncertainty at her age. What a disaster his uncle had contrived!

He could not even think of Miss Bailey right now.

Dinner that evening was a strange affair. Jane's amber
silk dress made its customary appearance, but evinced no
comment. Mr Kendal, who took his usual seat on Jane's
right, was quiet and withdrawn. Mrs Kendal looked anxious. Mrs Millthorpe politely furious.

She had clearly decided to ignore her own husband pointedly—something to which he responded with garrulous
glee, making wide-ranging comments on a range of top-

ics and drawing unwanted attention to Jane by asking for her opinions.

When the footmen finally cleared the table Jane was conscious of a sense of relief as the ladies left the gentlemen and made for the salon.

There, Henby was waiting, with the huge sleeves from the pink dress as well as some offcuts from which she indicated that Jane was to attempt to fashion a bodice.

'Oh, but—'

Jane bit her lip. There was no point in asking for a single piece now. Henby and Eliza had clearly cut the dress up in such a way that had left only these smaller pieces for Jane.

'When we looked at the skirt more closely we found parts were infested with mildew and had to be discarded.'

'Mildew? But—'

Again, she choked back her words. Jane had not noticed any mildew earlier. Besides Henby, as a lady's maid, would know full well that mildew could be easily removed by washing in diluted white vinegar.

Although to be fair, if it had been on the dress for a long time, the mildew might have caused staining, or even a weakening of the fabric. If indeed there *was* any mildew. In addition, Jane was not at all convinced that there were genuinely only these small pieces left to be used to create the bodice.

'I have left you the spare sewing box that our housekeeper uses.' Henby indicated a wicker box on the side table.

'Thank you.'

Once Henby had gone, she considered the pieces in front of her. The bodice would have to be made in four parts, with central seams down both the front and the back in order to line up the pattern. The sleeves were more straightforward. She picked one up. The shoulder would not require much adjustment, but the bottom needed to be changed completely. The sleeves were elbow-length, with large gathered gauze cuffs and self-fabric hems.

Already her mind was working out possibilities, testing and discarding options. First she would need a trim…

She was surprised to discover a certain fierceness inside her. Despite the best efforts of Henby and Eliza, she refused to be unfashionable. She could not control her grandfather, nor mend the breach among his family. But if he meant to take her to this soirée Jane would make her mama and papa proud. She refused to be the pauper among them, or to be sneered at.

She went to the corner and fished in the trunk again. Finding what she needed, she set to work.

All too soon tea was served, and the gentlemen came to join them. Mr Millthorpe was still in a buoyant mood—Jane had the sneaking suspicion that he had actually *enjoyed* the earlier tension.

Setting down her sewing with considerable reluctance, Jane moved to the main part of the room, near the fireplace. Near Mr Kendal. Near the dangerous eddies and maelstroms of the Beechmount Hall family.

'Emma Dodsworth is such a *dear* girl!' Mrs Millthorpe announced, to no one in particular. 'So elegant! So refined! So well-educated! One can always tell the quality of a young lady after a very short time in her company.' She gave Mr Kendal a sideways look. 'Did you not think she was particularly delightful today, Robert?'

'It is always a pleasure to see Miss Dodsworth,' he replied slowly, 'apart from on those frequent occasions when she delights in baiting me!'

Mrs Millthorpe tittered, causing Mrs Kendal to look at her in wonder. 'Oh, Robert! Why, you and Miss Dodsworth have such an easy relationship. I declare I have always sensed an affinity between you.'

Mr Kendal frowned. 'We have been friends since childhood, it is true.'

'And who would have thought she would grow into

such a beautiful young lady? It is down to her breeding, of course.'

Mr Millthorpe rubbed his hands together. 'Breeding, aye. I have often noted that adding common blood to stock seems to make them hardier. Healthier too.'

His wife sniffed. 'We are not speaking of *stock*, but of people. And Miss Dodsworth's ancestry is beyond reproach!'

'That's what *you* think! Why, in these parts we all know Dodsworth's grandmother played her man false. Her only son had a remarkable resemblance to one of the grooms!'

Mrs Millthorpe's eyes widened. 'Indeed? I never knew that. How interesting—er…how shocking, I mean!' She pondered on this a moment, then recalled herself to the present. 'Anyway, my point is that when one has been raised to be a *lady* it is instantly apparent. Miss Dodsworth's grace, her manners, her skill upon the pianoforte—why, her music has enlivened many an evening.'

'She is a charming girl, and she plays the piano beautifully,' agreed Mrs Kendal, in the silence that followed this. 'I shall look forward to hearing her play at the soirée.'

'All the ladies will be invited to play or sing, and we shall have a delightful evening!'

Mrs Millthorpe's tone was one of triumph. She threw a quick glance towards Jane, who had managed to remain impassive. *So far.*

'I have no doubt Miss Dodsworth will be dressed in the first stare of fashion.'

'She will, eh?' Mr Millthorpe's keen gaze was fixed on his wife. 'And you will ensure that Jane is well turned out, I am certain.'

Her face hardened. 'It is in hand.'

'Good.'

This, finally, seemed to silence her, and as the servants returned to take away the tea cups Jane, with a great deal of relief, retired to bed.

Chapter Eighteen

Jane walked along the hall to the library, but before she could knock on the door she paused, hearing raised voices inside. Mr and Mrs Millthorpe were, it seemed, engaging in strong debate.

She made out Mrs Millthorpe saying something about 'living with my sister' before she realised the impropriety of listening at the door and fled before she could be discovered.

'Oof!'

She crashed into sudden warm hardness. Mr Kendal put his hands out to steady her, and for the briefest of moments it felt as if she was in his arms. He smelled of soap, maleness, and something that was uniquely him. She stored the memory for later.

'Oh, Mr Kendal, I do apologise. I was—er—that is to say—'

'Yes?'

He was not helping. His expression was closed, his mouth a thin line of reserve.

'I came to speak with Mr Millthorpe, as I usually do at this time, but his wife is with him, so I came away.'

He raised an eyebrow. 'Arguing, are they?'

'I cannot say.'

'I learned a long time ago that it is best to stay away during their—er—debates.' He grimaced, adding slowly, 'Can I invite you to the small parlour, where you will be safe from all of it?'

A wave of relief washed over her, tempered by a sense of trepidation.

Everything is wrong here!

'Thank you.'

He led her inside and closed the door. The sounds of debate could clearly be heard, even through the thick walls. Thankfully, they could not make out any words.

'You may be at ease,' he said neutrally. 'They never come in here.'

A flash of insight came to her. 'You would come in here as a child?'

'I still do, even now. Mama, too. She uses this parlour as her own sitting room in the afternoons.'

He invited her to sit, then seated himself opposite.

'My uncle and aunt are all that is good, of course, but their engagements can be wearisome for others. Mama would often take me in here and read to me during those times.'

'Did anyone ever try to—to settle their disputes?'

'Lord, no! We discovered years ago that they both glory in opposition. Strange as it may sound, they quite relish their quarrels.'

She nodded thoughtfully. 'How peculiar!' She paused. 'I was very surprised to discover that no one here knew that I am Edward's daughter.'

He eyed her evenly. 'Indeed?'

This was not in the least encouraging.

'I assumed everyone knew. But I think that people may have thought I was…not legitimate.'

'It seemed the most likely explanation.'

'My papa died far from home and with little money. The estrangement from his father and his home must have hurt him deeply.'

Nothing. He just sat there, listening.

Where has my friend gone? Lord, have I ruined everything?

'My mama and Lady Kingswood both advised me to be circumspect. Mama in particular has no reason to love Mr Millthorpe.'

'I see.' He sounded uninterested. 'Now, enough about family matters. How vexed are you about this dashed soi-rée?'

His tone and manner were all politeness, yet there was no warmth in his eyes. Her heart sank.

'Oh, well, I should much rather not go, but—' She squared her shoulders. 'If I am to go, I shall make the best of it.'

He eyed her thoughtfully, and looked as though he was about to say something. After a long moment, he gave a slight shake of the head. 'As a lady's maid, did you assist with such evenings at Ledbury House?'

That is not what he was going to say.

'Only if it was a very large celebration. I usually stayed in my mistress's chamber, in case she needed me. There have been times when I was needed to sew a hem or a torn flounce. And of course I waited up until she was ready to retire…helped her be comfortable.'

That is, on the nights she retired alone. When my lord was there…

She blushed, remembering some of those nights when she had fled in confusion as Lord and Lady Kingswood had clearly planned amorous activity.

Why must I think of such things right now?

She knew the answer. It was there in her quickened heartbeat and in the warm feeling in her chest. It was as though there was a lit candle inside her when she and Mr Kendal were in the same room. In truth, she would love to do the things with him that she had understood Lord and Lady Kingswood must do…

'Tell me,' she said, to cover her confusion. 'Does Mrs Millthorpe have a sister?'

He nodded. 'She does. She is widowed and lives in Knaresborough. She and my aunt see each other regularly. Why?'

'I overheard Mrs Millthorpe mention her.'

'Is that the way of it?' He jerked his head towards the library. 'My aunt frequently threatens to leave and live with her sister, but then, when she is calmer, she says her duty to her husband keeps her here.'

'I see.'

The entire household would be more tranquil if Mrs Millthorpe did live elsewhere. She bit her lip at such an uncharitable thought. But of course Mrs Millthorpe could not leave—not without causing a local scandal.

She is trapped here. And everyone feels her unhappiness.

'I have no complaints about my life, Miss Bailey,' he said.

His insight was impressive.

'Are my thoughts so transparent to you?'

He looked startled at this impertinent question.

Confused, she rushed on. 'Of course you do not. But do you not sometimes wish circumstances were different?'

His eyes widened, and then a strange rigidity developed in his bearing. 'I cannot. I must deal only with reality.' His tone was flat.

He looked at her for a long moment, then rose abruptly, walking to the window.

'I think it will stay dry. We shall go to visit the Dodsworths around three, if that pleases you?'

'Yes, of course.'

'Good.'

He bowed, and left, leaving her discomposed and more than a little confused. She sat there, feeling deflated at the breach between them. Since yesterday things had changed.

How I wish we could go back to that easy friendship!

It was only now, when it was gone, that she could truly understand how important it had been to her.

Mr Kendal, it seemed, was something of a whip. When Jane stepped outside with him, to travel to the Dodsworths' home, she could not hold back an exclamation.

'A curricle! How exciting!'

She was determined to be cheerful and friendly, and at all costs to hide her unhappiness. The knowledge that he was displeased with her was draining her confidence and occupying her mind to the detriment of all else.

She moved forward to inspect the carriage. The body was a bright yellow, trimmed with black, and the black hood was folded down. The two wheels were enormous, and far, far above her head was the seat where she would sit in close proximity to Mr Kendal.

It would have been perfect if they had only been in harmony, like before.

'Let me assist you.'

His tone was polite, neutral, pleasant. It was killing her, slowly and agonisingly.

She held on tightly as he climbed up and slid in beside her. His left thigh was pressing against her right one in a most exciting way and his upper arm was in full contact with hers. Her body immediately awoke, demanding impossible things.

No, I must not lean into him, nor move my leg so I can feel the friction with his, nor—

'This is a little like our journey north,' she said, all in a rush.

As soon as she heard her own too honest words she closed her eyes briefly in horror.

He seemed unperturbed.

'I was just thinking that.'

He was?

He lifted the reins. 'Hiya!'

His proximity was briefly forgotten as the two matched greys stepped out and the curricle lurched forward. Fear of imminent death immediately replaced the desire that had been flooding through her a moment ago.

'Is it safe?' she asked fearfully, stealing a glimpse at the ground, which looked very far away.

'Are you questioning my driving abilities?'

'Oh, no, of course not! I would never presume to— Oh! You are teasing me!'

His familiar grin flashed briefly. 'Yes, it is safe. I know how to handle the reins, and I know my horses.'

'I have only ever been in a cart or a gig, and now and again in Lord and Lady Kingswood's coach. Never have I been up so high!'

'I surmised that.'

'Is—is that why you have brought the curricle today?' she asked shyly.

'You think I have done it simply to please you?'

'Oh, I—no, of course not!'

'I have missed driving the curricle these past weeks,' he continued smoothly, seeming to ignore her consternation.

'Of course.'

Jane turned her head away, hoping her bonnet was hiding the feelings she was sure were transparent on her face. Why was she suddenly so tongue-tied around him? Where was their previous easy amity?

The feeling persisted throughout the journey, and during their visit with the Dodsworths.

They stayed for an hour, during which Jane became conscious of two things. First, that she dearly wished she could have Miss Dodsworth for a friend. Second, that Mrs Millthorpe had been right to hint at the suitability of Miss Dodsworth as a possible wife for Mr Kendal.

Having known each other from childhood, they used first-name terms as easily as they did the more formal adult titles, and Miss Dodsworth teased Mr Kendal continually. Her parents, too, were on great terms with him, and they all fondly regaled Jane with memories of Mr Kendal as a child and a youth.

It was fascinating and strangely heartbreaking all at once.

Once back in the curricle, Jane decided to maintain the air of forced cheerfulness she had adopted earlier. 'Miss Dodsworth is such a lovely young lady!' she offered. 'So kind and accomplished—but I do not know what I shall do if I am asked to play the piano on Thursday, for I have never played so much as a note!'

He frowned. 'I had not considered that before. But there are many ladies who do not play the piano.'

'But if they do not play the piano then they play the harp! I shall be exposed as an intruder in their midst. In truth I felt deeply uncomfortable even just now.'

'You did? It seemed to me that you were at ease with the Dodsworths?'

'Oh, I was! Such a warm, welcoming family! But even as I was feeling welcomed and included, I also knew I should not be there.'

He shook his head. 'Your situation is complicated, indeed.'

He looked ahead, lapsing into silence.

He still will not speak to me of it, then. Perhaps it is too late, and his good opinion of me is lost.

Seated up there, high above the realities of daily life, and driving along quiet roads, they might be the only two people in all of England. If only he would smile at her again. Just once more. She would keep the memory of it for ever.

'Hiya!'

They had reached a wide, empty stretch of road and he drove the horses faster. Amidst the thrill of speed, Jane was conscious of a stabbing pain in her heart. She suspected he had deliberately broken the uneasiness of the moment with the gallop.

A lump formed in her throat. It all contrasted starkly with his efforts to know her better during their journey northwards.

He does not wish to deepen our acquaintance now. All is changed. I would do well to accept that.

The words in her mind made perfect sense. Her heart, however, was not listening.

Robert kept his eyes fixed on the road ahead, knowing that to look at her would not be helpful to his peace of mind. The shock of his uncle's revelation was beginning to dissipate, and along with it came a welcome return to an improved clear-headedness.

He had listened carefully to her explanation and it had rung true. He believed his first instincts were correct and she had not intentionally misled him. But the hurt remained, and with it a certain wariness, yet at a deeper level his desire for her was resurging.

These shifting sands continued to trouble him. He was yet to figure out how the situation might unfold, but one thing was certain.

I need to tread carefully.

Chapter Nineteen

Jane caught her breath. Over the years she had had many moments of triumph in her dressmaking efforts—moments when she had seen Lady Kingswood in one of her creations and known—just *known*—that her mistress would outshine all the other ladies at the ball or rout she was attending.

But this time it was not Lady Kingswood wearing the dress. It was her.

'My word, miss!' Nancy's voice was an awed whisper. 'You look—you look like an angel!'

Jane could not speak.

Is that really me?

From the dark curls clustering around her forehead to the pink satin slippers at her feet, she looked every inch the elegant lady. The dress was a triumph. Henby and Eliza had created a plain pink satin slip under the pink stripe, and Jane had added her bodice to it with ease. Her natural talent for dressmaking, her keen eye for detail, and her years of painstaking learning and skill had combined to ensure this dress would be the best she could possibly manage.

After stitching together the bodice, and connecting it to the main part of the dress with tiny, neat stitches, she had finished it with small details that lifted the dress from ordinary to stunning—a gold trim and a line of fabric roses under the bust, gorgeous Brussels lace around the low neckline and the short, puffed sleeves.

Working deep into the night last night, she had even added a fall of lace around the hem, and pink fabric roses to her plain pink slippers.

Her exhaustion had been an excellent distraction from the agony her heart was experiencing. From the breach with Mr Kendal that occupied her every thought, her every waking moment.

They had gone from being strangers to friends, and then to something more than friends. Now it seemed they were back to being strangers again. In company, she managed to maintain her equilibrium—years of servant discipline combining with a desire not to shame her papa and mama. In private, it was an entirely different matter.

Her spirits were low…lower than she could ever remember.

After Master Henry's attack she had been in a perpetual state of fear for a time, and had afterwards felt shamed and disgraced by what he had done to her. He had destroyed the belief that she had been building in her seventeen-year-old self.

Since then she had worked hard not to listen to that lowering voice within her. The one that told her she was unimportant. She was worthless. She was nothing.

For years she had battled to make herself new, and she had, she believed, been succeeding. Apart from the memory attacks—which were becoming less frequent—she had become ever more successful in believing that she was strong and competent and capable.

All that work was now hanging by a thread.

Master Henry was reasserting himself within her soul, threatening to rise up and overpower her at any moment.

I am trouble, her broken self whispered. *I am useless. I am incapable even of sustaining a friendship that was important to me.*

No! she replied to that self with passion. *I am a good lady's maid. I am a competent seamstress. I am a good daughter.*

But thoughts of her mama, so far away, threatened to undo her. Thoughts of Mr Kendal frequently did.

Nancy must know how she cried at night, for the housemaid had, without any request on her part, placed clean handkerchiefs under her pillow and on her nightstand.

Now Nancy helped her don Mrs Kendal's old evening gloves, and then she was ready.

At least I look like a lady, she told herself fiercely.

She might not be able to play an instrument, and her arrival might have caused untold trouble in this household, but at least her appearance was nothing to be ashamed of.

Still, she could not prevent the wave of uneasiness flowing through her as she made her way to the salon.

Shall I disgrace myself tonight? Shall I embarrass my grandfather? What will Mr Kendal think of me?

Her stomach lurched as she imagined herself being disdained or laughed at by dozens of unknown people.

She was last to arrive, and as she entered the salon all conversation stopped. Both Mrs Kendal and Mrs Millthorpe surveyed her quickly, from head to toe, while Mr Millthorpe lifted the quizzing glass tied to his breeches in order to scrutinise her more exactly.

Mr Kendal—oh, Mr Kendal's eyes were suddenly ablaze with admiration, sending a warm glow through her.

Could he still have some regard for me?

Her heart leapt.

All of this she took in in an instant, before Mrs Kendal broke the stunned silence to bustle forward and envelop her in a warm embrace. 'My dear, you look charming!' She turned to stand beside Jane, one arm still curled around her waist. 'Does she not look *splendid*, everyone?'

Jane could feel her colour rising. 'Oh, no…' she protested weakly. She had forgotten Mrs Millthorpe's propensity for plain speaking.

But… 'You will not discredit me,' she pronounced, with a regal nod. 'So long as no one knows the truth about your background. Are those fabric roses?' she added, her curiosity getting the better of her.

Jane confirmed it.

'Well, Henby and Eliza have done an excellent job! Who would have thought an old dress could be reworked so well?'

'Eh? What's that?' Mr Millthorpe's gaze sharpened. 'Is this an *old* dress? Where did you get it from?'

'There was an old trunk in the attic, stuffed full of them,' his spouse explained.

'I thought that pink stripe looked familiar,' he responded cryptically. 'Help me up!'

Mrs Kendal dashed forward to do so. Meanwhile her son strode directly towards Jane.

From the day she had first caught sight of him at Ledbury House, Jane had known him to be handsome. Tonight, in full evening wear, he looked simply magnificent. Magnificent, handsome, and, oh, so dear to her.

Lifting her gloved hand, he looked directly into her eyes. 'Beautiful.'

The single word reverberated through Jane, sending a glow of happiness radiating out from her chest to every part of her.

'Come with me, child!' Mr Millthorpe hobbled past them, moving more quickly than was his usual habit. He was clearly animated about something.

Jane cast a brief questioning glance at Mr Kendal, who replied with a slight shrug.

Silently she accompanied Mr Millthorpe down the corridor, her heart still racing at Mr Kendal's reaction just now.

Mr Millthorpe paused outside the door of one of the smaller sitting rooms, seemed to ready himself for a moment, then opened the door.

It was a pretty room, with the typical large, low windows looking out towards the back of the house, a marble fireplace, and a collection of elegant furniture. The shutters were closed against the winter darkness, and a single branch of candles on the mantel suffused the room with soft warm light.

Although the fireplace was empty, the room did not feel cold. The chairs and sofas were finished in blue satin. Jane now remembered that Mrs Kendal had told her it was known as the Blue Parlour.

Mr Millthorpe made his way directly to the fireplace and stopped, gazing at the portrait above it. Jane's gaze followed his—and she gasped.

It showed a woman in a pink striped satin dress, her hair powdered and her lips curved in a merry smile. Around her neck was a simple string of pearls, and by her side stood a small boy, his blue eyes smiling at the artist.

'My father? And—my grandmother?'

He nodded.

Jane had seen this portrait just days ago, when she was being shown around the house, but had not understood its significance. She had, of course, been looking for family resemblances in the various family portraits hung around the house, but the same blue eyes were everywhere—clearly a strong feature of the Millthorpe line. Never before had she seen an image of her father as a child.

He cleared his throat. 'Eleanor. Edward. Both gone.' His voice was thick with emotion.

Without thinking, she slipped her hand into his and they just stood there for a long moment, unspeaking.

He squeezed her hand briefly, then released it. 'Bring the candles.' He made his way towards a writing desk near the windows.

She did so, and watched as he opened the desk and re-moved a small box.

'This was Eleanor's favourite room. Here she would write and read, entertain her friends and play with young Edward.' He indicated the room with a gesture, his hand trembling a little. 'No one uses this room now, but I insist it is kept spotless and lit by candles in the evening. She is still here, you see. In this room.'

It ought to have sounded sinister, yet strangely Jane felt only a sense of comfort.

'Yes, she is.'

Her heart, already pounding from the hope Mr Kendal had set alight within her, now lurched with fresh emotion.

From the box her grandfather drew out a string of pearls, each one a perfect miracle. In the candlelight they glowed with lustrous iridescence. Jane had never seen anything so exquisite. She set the candles down on the desk and reached out to touch the jewels.

'They are beautiful. Are these the ones she wears in the portrait?'

'Yes. They belonged to her own mother before they came to her.' He eyed her keenly. 'Eleanor's mother was a Bailey of course. Her name was Jane.'

'Jane Bailey?' Jane's voice trembled. 'So Papa named me…?'

'After his grandmother. Yes.'

This was entirely unexpected. Jane's mind could barely take it in.

'Turn around.'

She obeyed, and stood in shock as he draped the pearls around her neck. Her hand reached up to touch them as he fumbled with the clasp.

'There.'

She turned back to face him, wiping away a small tear. 'I am honoured to be permitted to borrow these for the evening. I shall try to make her proud of me.'

'Borrow? No, these are yours, child.'

Jane gaped. 'Mine? No, I cannot accept them! It would not be fitting.'

'Not fitting?' He raised an imperious eyebrow. 'Well, who else should have Jane Bailey's pearls other than Jane Bailey, her own great-granddaughter? My granddaughter!'

'Yes, but I am not *really* your granddaughter. In the eyes

of society it will never be right for a former servant girl to accept such a gift.'

He brushed this aside with the irreverence of old age. 'Society? Pah! This is not a *gift*, child. It is your rightful inheritance. Now, why have you not said thank you? Am I to accuse you of being rude or ungrateful?'

He has me with that.

'I am sorry, sir. Thank you from the bottom of my heart.'

And by forcing her to thank him he had tricked her into accepting the pearls, the wily old curmudgeon!

'And do not call me "sir". Grandfather will do very well.'

'Yes. Grandfather.'

The word hung in the air between them and his eyes were glistening in the candlelight.

'And now we are late—we shall be in trouble with the ladies for delaying them,' he said gruffly. He offered her his arm. 'Let us go, Jane.'

Staveley House was a large manor—probably almost as large as Beechmount Hall. As it was full dark when the Millthorpe party arrived, the moon being obscured by cloud, Jane had only the slightest impression of its exterior—a substantial silhouette, with flaming torches to aid the guests on arrival, and a veritable army of grooms and footmen to assist each coach.

They had, of course, travelled from Beechmount Hall in the large travelling coach, as the smaller carriage could not have accommodated them all. Jane had, as ever, been seated backwards-facing, with Mr Kendal by her side. How comforting it had been to feel the warmth of his body next to hers, especially now she had some hope of restoring their friendship.

Comforting—and yet discomfiting at the same time. For his closeness had caused the usual flutterings inside her. Now, believing he still liked her, Jane wondered if might he kiss her again some time…

She smiled inside. A headiness was threatening to over-come her.

Perhaps I shall not disgrace myself tonight after all. I have the dress, and my grandfather, and actual pearls! And I have Mr Kendal's regard.

The glow had returned, suffusing her body with a heady mix of confidence, warmth and desire. Just for now she would allow herself to enjoy this giddiness.

But deep within her the turbulence of the last few days remained. Master Henry was not far away, and with him were the doubting voices.

Right now, though, in the glow of pearls and the dress and Mr Kendal's regard, she felt stronger than she had done in days. The events of the past half-hour had pro-vided a much-needed veneer of confidence, of elation, that skimmed over her deeper troubles like thin ice over a dan-gerous lake.

It will get me through the evening, she told herself firmly, ignoring the brittleness of her own façade.

Mrs Millthorpe had maintained a litany of empty anxiety about the muddy roads the whole way to Staveley House, but they had managed to get through without mishap. It was hard to know whether her desire to be proved right was stronger than her desire to reach their destination.

Lost in her glow of happiness, Jane smiled inwardly at Mrs Millthorpe's dilemma. Recent events had given her a fresh sympathy for Mrs Millthorpe, and a better under-standing of her unhappiness.

The carriage drew to a halt, and instantly Jane's nerves returned in full measure. As she followed the others in-side she was acutely conscious of the footmen and house-maids deployed to assist with the removal of cloaks, hats and boots, and the donning of evening slippers for men and women alike.

As Jane slipped her feet into her pink satin slippers she remembered an old fairy tale Papa had used to read to her—about a serving girl who normally lay by the cinders but who, through magic, attended three balls with a prince.

There will be no royal wedding for me, she thought ruefully.

Yet, here she was, as delighted as the girl in the story to be wearing fine clothes in the company of a handsome man.

Their hosts, Mr and Mrs Foster, were there to receive them, along with three of their five children.

'The two younger ones,' Mr Kendal murmured in Jane's ear as they awaited their turn, 'are not yet out of the nursery.'

His breath tickled her ear, sending a delicious shiver through her.

When it came to Jane's turn, her grandfather stated simply, 'Miss Bailey—my granddaughter.'

'Ah! Is that the way of it?' asked Mr Foster obscurely. 'You are welcome, Miss Bailey. Why, the whole district has been agog and wishing to find out more about you!'

Jane was unsure what to say to this. But Mr Foster, thankfully not expecting a response, had moved to shake Mr Kendal's hand and Jane found herself greeting Mrs Foster, Mr John Foster, and the two Misses Foster.

They all seemed friendly and welcoming, and Mr John Foster's gaze held something of admiration in it. He was around her own age, tall and handsome, with deep brown eyes and dark wavy hair. If her entire being had not already been taken up by Mr Kendal, the look in those brown eyes might have had some impact on her vanity.

'It is a pleasure to meet you, Miss Bailey.'

He bowed and smiled and Jane's anxiety decreased a little. It seemed they did not know the whole truth about her. Perhaps tonight would not be so bad after all.

Chapter Twenty

John Foster moved on to greet Mr Kendal. 'Good to see you, my friend.'

Mr Kendal, Jane noted, was fairly glowering as he shook John's hand.

John looked a little startled, but then his eyes narrowed. He smiled, and there was a hint of defiance in it 'And thank you for bringing such a delightful guest!'

'The delight, I assure you, is all mine!'

There was definitely a challenge in Mr Kendal's answering grin.

Strange.

The two Misses Foster were younger, and clearly excited.

'How do, Miss Bailey?' said Miss Mary. 'We are to have ices later!'

'Hush now, Mary,' admonished her big sister. 'Miss Bailey has ices every day of the week where she lives!'

'Really?' Miss Mary's eyes grew round.

'Oh, no, I honestly don't!' Oh, the irony, that they thought she was from a wealthy background! 'In truth I have only ever had ices once, when I visited London.'

'You have been to London? *Actual* London?' Miss Mary was clearly awestruck.

'Um…yes.'

She had gone when she and Mama had run away, after Master Henry had attacked her, and they'd had to seek positions in a new household.

'Did you go to Astley's? And the Tower? Did you see Princess Charlotte and the Prince Regent?'

'Mary, please do not tease Miss Bailey so!' Mary's older sister spoke sternly.

'I am sorry, Miss Bailey.'

'Think nothing of it!' Jane assured her, but she was conscious of a slight feeling of relief as Mrs Millthorpe finally completed her greetings with Mrs Foster and they all walked further in to the house.

'Well done!' It was Mr Kendal, his eyes smiling. 'I had not anticipated such inquisitiveness.'

'Nor I!' replied Jane, with fervour.

That initial encounter set the tone for Jane's evening. While the other guests were less direct than Miss Mary Foster in their questioning, nevertheless Jane found herself continually fending off politely worded questions about her life and her background.

She took her lead from her grandfather. Mr Millthorpe was open about his estrangement from his son, and the fact that Edward had taken the name Bailey when he had left home and married Jane's mother. Her grandfather did not, however, mention that Jane and her mother worked as servants.

Jane found the scrutiny troublesome. Ever conscious of the footmen and the maids, carrying out their duties in the large salon where the guests had congregated, she watched them serving drinks and directing people to the comfort rooms when needed.

If she had been among them she would have known exactly what to do, what to say, how to behave. She wished she were here as a housemaid, not a guest. And yet…and yet…

Miss Dodsworth was there, with her parents, and her delight at seeing Jane was so genuine that Jane could not help but respond warmly to her. Mr Kendal, too, seemed to wish to stay by Jane's side as much as he could—that was, until two new guests arrived.

By that point there were, Jane calculated, somewhere between thirty-five and forty people present. So when the new arrivals appeared in the doorway Jane was initially only mildly curious. Until, that was, Mr Kendal groaned and rolled his eyes at Miss Dodsworth.

'Oh, Lord!' she muttered. 'I had heard the Haws were away, visiting with relatives. They are clearly returned.'

All curiosity, Jane eyed the pair in the doorway. The woman was sixtyish, stout and sallow, with an eager eye and a fluttering fan. She wore a satin puce dress and three enormous feathers in her headdress. The gentleman with her looked to be nearing forty. He was tall and thin, with a sharp nose and a wet mouth.

Jane shuddered. 'Who are they?'

'Mrs Haw and her son, Marmaduke. They are received everywhere, but…' Miss Dodsworth's voice tailed away.

'I shall tell you what my kind-hearted friend refuses to say.' Mr Kendal grimaced. 'Which is that they are vulgar.'

'I see…' Vulgarity, Jane knew, was unforgivable among the gentry and aristocracy. 'So why are they received?'

'Their lineage is impeccable, sadly,' replied Miss Dodsworth.

The Haws began working their way around the room, and Jane noticed the moment one of the ladies told them about her, for both Mrs Haw and her son immediately turned to stare at her. Instantly Mrs Haw bent to whisper something in that lady's ear. The lady gasped, then looked at Jane. Cold fear flooded her stomach.

She watched the Haws intently after that. Each time they conversed with someone new the same thing would happen. Mrs Haw would adopt a confidential manner, and the person she was confiding in would react in some way. Surprise. Shock. Puzzlement.

Jane was desperately trying to interpret the looks.

It cannot be me she is speaking of! I do not even know her! How could she possibly…?

An instant later, comprehension came to her. 'Mr Kendal,' she managed, her voice croaking slightly, 'is there any connection between Beechmount Hall and Mrs Haw's residence?'

'Connection? No.' He looked surprised. 'As far as I know the Haws have no relations in the district.'

Jane shook her head. 'I mean in terms of the servants.'

He frowned. 'Let me think…' His brow cleared. 'Yes! One of their grooms has a sister who is a servant in Beechmount Hall—a housemaid. Eliza, I believe is her name.'

Eliza. Suddenly it all made sense.

Miss Dodsworth had gone to speak to the young Misses Foster, so Jane was standing alone with Mr Kendal. The Haws had reached the group next to them and were even now taking their leave.

Will they speak to us next?

'I think,' she said slowly, 'the Haws know about me.'

'Dash it all!' he murmured. 'Brace yourself, Miss Bailey.'

'Good evening, Mr Kendal! What a delight to see you!' Mrs Haw was all effusiveness. 'And in such fine looks! I declare, apart from my own dear Marmaduke—and Master John, of course—there is no man so handsome as you!'

A hint of ruddy colour appeared on Mr Kendal's cheek. 'Good evening, Mrs Haw,' he managed. 'And Mr Haw.'

The gentlemen bowed to each other—a formal gesture, Jane noted, with nothing of amity in it.

Mrs Haw's protuberant blue eyes swivelled to Jane, then passed on as if they did not see her.

Mr Kendal's jaw hardened. 'Miss Bailey—may I make known to you Mrs Haw and Mr Haw, her son? Miss Bailey is Mr Millthorpe's granddaughter.'

Automatically Jane replied with a polite remark, even as it dawned on her what Mr Kendal had done. Nearby, eyebrows were raised and mutterings paused as other guests watched and waited.

Mr Kendal had, in the manner of his introduction, given Jane the honour of being a higher rank. Mrs Haw's eyes narrowed, and a slash of colour appeared on her cheeks. She looked as though she were biting back bitter words.

Mr Kendal waited, seemingly unperturbed, while Jane shrank inside. Her heart was pounding with anxiety.

'I see.' Mrs Haw gave a slight inclination of her head. It was enough. She did not cut Jane.

Jane exhaled in some relief. Mr Kendal's risk had worked out. He had accurately calculated that, if forced to do so, Mrs Haw would defer to the Millthorpe name and connections.

Mr Marmaduke Haw took a different approach.

'A delightful young lady! Such a divine dress!'

He lifted Jane's hand to his wet lips. Jane was glad she was wearing gloves.

'Such a pretty young thing!' he exclaimed again, lifting his quizzing glass to inspect her bosom more closely. 'I must say I welcome these new fashions in evening gowns. What say you, Kendal, eh?'

'I have nothing to say on the matter,' returned Mr Kendal coldly.

His tall solidity beside her gave Jane immense comfort. How much more difficult this would have been without him!

Inside her soul, the ghost of Master Henry stirred and flexed…

Mrs Haw slapped her fan against Robert's arm. 'Mr Kendal! There is something I have been meaning to discuss with you.' She lowered her tone dramatically. 'It is something of a delicate matter, so would you be willing to sit with me on that settee over there while I tell you the whole?'

Mr Kendal had little choice.

He assented, his expression unreadable, bowed and walked away. Jane, already struggling to maintain her equilibrium, felt entirely bereft.

Mr Marmaduke Haw was determined to make the most of his opportunity. Instantly he laid a hand on her gloved arm, sliding his fingers upwards until he encountered bare flesh. As he did so her stomach tightened with sickness.

'Miss Bailey!' he continued smoothly. 'I am so delighted to find a new young lady in our midst. Especially one who… Why, to think I was not sure whether to come here tonight!'

His eyes were roving all over her, concentrating particularly on her chest. She wanted to pull her dress up as far as it could go. Fear was rising within her, mixing with unwanted memories. She felt sick.

'But,' he continued, 'in the end I said to myself, "Marmaduke, it is the Staveley House February soirée. Everyone will be there and your mama wishes to go. You must do your duty."' He lowered his voice and bent his head towards her ear. 'And never has duty been so desirable.'

The last word was almost a whisper, as his foul breath reached her nostrils.

She stiffened as deep within her the nightmare began again. A memory attack was building. She had to go!

Mr Haw, in essence, was similar to Master Henry. She sensed it. She knew it. In the way in which he had just spoken to her, touched her, looked at her body…

I need to leave ! Now!

She turned and walked away from him, giving no reason, no polite excuse. And as she did so she saw his jaw drop.

She focused on keeping her breathing steady, on delaying as best she could the overwhelming terror building within her.

As she hurried towards the door she was conscious of the interested looks on the faces of those around her—all of whom had been observing the little drama.

*Oh, I know! s*he thought bitterly.

She should not have left him so rudely. A true lady would have found a way to extricate herself gently.

But I am not a lady. I am me. Jane Bailey. Serving maid.

Chapter Twenty-One

She half ran down the corridor, and was relieved when a maid indicated that a door on her left was the designated retiring room. Thankfully, the room was fairly quiet, with two ladies just leaving to return to the salon and two languid housemaids there to assist.

Ignoring them, she sank into a soft armchair and closed her eyes, allowing the memory attack to take over her body. Her heart raced and her breathing quickened, sending panic through her.

I have not enough air!

Pins and needles pricked her hands and feet and her stomach churned.

I cannot be ill here!

Then came the dizziness. She tried opening her eyes, but that only made it worse.

Henry was on her, his face twisted with Marmaduke Haw's leering smirk, and she could not escape. It was as though Henry was there now, attacking her now, and Mama was yet to rescue her.

The reaction in her body was always just as intense as if the memories were real.

Go to the ending, her mind screamed.

This worked occasionally. Desperately she tried moving the memory to the point at which Mama had rescued her, but to no avail. She was stuck in an endless moment of Henry/Marmaduke's weight on top of her, his hand on her breast, his foul breath in her nose.

Come back to now.

This helped a little.

She focused on the feeling of the chair beneath her. Not

the table where it had happened. A soft chair. Cautiously, she touched it with both hands. Smooth satin. Carved wood. Her feet were planted on the floor. She wriggled her toes. Dancing slippers.

She opened her eyes. The housemaids were looking at her anxiously. Vaguely she remembered them asking her if she would like something—hartshorn? A tisane?

'A tisane would be wonderful,' she croaked. 'Thank you.'

Her racing heart was beginning to slow a little. Deliberately she closed her eyes and played out the rescue part of the story. Strange how it never seemed as real as the terror.

He reminded me of Master Henry...even before he touched me and looked at me in that way.

Tonight she did not have to wonder why she was trembling from head to toe.

Gradually the pace of her pounding heart slowed and the feeling of terror subsided. She sipped the tisane provided by the maid, and after a time felt reasonably calm again.

She should return to the salon, she thought, as three matrons entered the retiring room. She had been gone from there a very long time. They glanced at her curiously, but did not speak to her, reminding her of the fact that her secret was now known, and of the rude way in which she had cut Mr Haw.

If she had truly been raised to be a lady then she would have found a polite way to end the conversation, as well as an excuse for leaving the room. In truth, she was no lady. Inside, she would always be a servant.

She had hurried out in clear distress.

She had embarrassed her grandfather and the rest of the family.

She had let Mr Kendal down—and after he had made the effort to support her so publicly.

She chastised herself. She should be better now! It had been years since it had happened. And she had thought Mr Kendal's kiss had cured her.

She closed her eyes again, deliberately invoking the memory of his wonderful kiss. It took a moment, but there it was. Desire. Need. Hunger. And underneath a sense of safety—the knowledge that Mr Kendal was not the same as Master Henry.

There was hope for her recovery, then, even after this.

Her thoughts returned again to the salon, and to her own rude behaviour. She should have been stronger. Her mother had taught her not to put up with any nonsense from lecherous men.

'End the conversation and get away,' had been Mama's advice.

It had served Jane well on the dozens of occasions when she had been importuned, by everyone from farmers to footmen. It was a normal part of life for women. On most occasions a memory attack had not followed, and she had been suffering fewer and fewer of them as the years went on.

So why was tonight different?

Dimly, she understood. She had been vulnerable tonight, given the turmoil of the past days. In addition, she had not expected something like this here, while she was dressed as a princess.

Such men were everywhere, it seemed. Even her fine gown and her aristocratic hairstyle had not saved her. Marmaduke Haw had judged her a servant, and believed he could behave towards her according to his whim.

She shook her head, reasserting her will. But she had not allowed it. She had been master of the situation, not he. He had expected her to allow him to behave so towards her, to be cowed by politeness, by society's rules for the behaviour of young ladies. But she had her mama's steel within her. She was a proud servant.

She nodded, filled with sudden vehemence.

I shall go back. Face them all.

Summoning her courage, she rose, gave a slight smile to the two housemaids, and made for the door.

As she opened it, she collided with the lady who was just entering.

'Sorry!'

'Oh, I am sorry!'

It was Miss Dodsworth.

'Oh, there you are! Thank goodness! Robert is distracted with worry and has sent me to find you!'

They stepped out into the corridor together.

'He is?' Jane was bewildered by this news. 'Why?'

Isn't he angry?

'I am not entirely certain,' Miss Dodsworth confessed. 'Something about Mr Haw upsetting you? I did not see you leave the salon.' She grimaced. 'Mr Haw does not always behave as he should…'

'Indeed he does not!' Jane replied hotly.

'Oh, dear!' Miss Dodsworth was sympathetic. 'Most of us know to keep away from him. Normally, he does not actually *do* anything—he is just vaguely lecherous. But Robert fears he overstepped the mark with you.'

'He did.' She did not elaborate.

'How did he get the opportunity? Was Robert not with you?'

'Unfortunately Mr Haw's mother drew Mr Kendal away.'

'Ah, that explains it.'

'Explains what?'

'Why Robert is so animated. He clearly feels a sense of responsibility for you. Although…'

'What?'

'Oh, nothing.' She laughed. 'Just a fanciful notion. Now, you and I shall stay together, and Mr Haw will have no opportunity to behave badly towards us.'

Jane looked directly at her. 'Do you really believe he would have behaved so towards *any* woman? Or is it—?'

She gathered her courage. 'Is it because he knows I was raised as a servant?'

Miss Dodsworth's kind expression did not waver. 'His mama has been telling anyone who will listen about your humble upbringing. But I and my parents judge people as we find them, and I think others will as well.'

'But I saw the shock and disbelief on people's faces.'

'I am sure they wish your father had raised you in more comfortable circumstances,' Miss Dodsworth replied slowly. 'But many people here—particularly the older generation—remember him with fondness. I confess until tonight I did not even know of his existence!'

'So—what would you advise? Should I stay in the retiring room or return to the salon? And what of Mr Haw?'

Miss Dodsworth sent her a keen glance. 'I believe you were already resolved on returning to the salon when I came to find you. And as for Mr Haw—why, everyone knows how shockingly vulgar he and his mother are. Until now they have managed to walk on the edge of acceptability. Mr Haw may have overstepped the mark tonight by upsetting you. Let us see how it will unfold.' She grinned. 'Besides, if the Haws disdain you it is likely to make everyone else even more determined to like you!'

'I see…' Jane wasn't convinced, but it was kind of her to offer such reassuring words.

They turned the corner into the main hall leading to the salon. Mr Kendal was there, pacing up and down. His hair was tousled, as though he had run his hand through it in some agitation. He looked beautiful.

Why was it that when Mr Kendal looked at her with admiration it filled her with heat and confusion, and yet other men just reminded her of Master Henry?

Indeed, she acknowledged with a gulp, *I still believe I should delight in having Mr Kendal touch me intimately.*

She felt her heart skip at the thought, even as Mr Kendal strode towards them.

'Miss Bailey! How do you?' He took both her hands in his.

'I am well.'

It was true. She felt drained, exhausted, but the terror had settled. And seeing his concern, feeling his warmth, was immeasurably healing.

He raised a sceptical eyebrow. 'You are pale and your hands are trembling.'

'They are?'

He nodded.

'I am much better now.'

He knows. He understands what happened, and why.

'Also, they all know I am a servant.' She said it bluntly.

He shook his head. 'The fact you were raised a servant is only troublesome to the most rigid and the most inflexible among our local society.'

'Th-there are at least some here who judge me as being lesser?'

Strangely, given her encounter with Mr Haw and its aftermath, her worries about status now seemed less acute, less significant.

His gaze bored into hers. 'You are here tonight as your father's daughter—as your grandfather's granddaughter. Frankly, if some do not like it I do not give a tinker's damn. Pardon me!'

He tagged on an apology for his warm phrasing. She shrugged it away, her heart swelling at his words of support.

'I apologise for leaving you with *that man*.' His loathing was obvious. 'Tell me, if you can, what did he say to you?' His brow was creased with concern.

'It wasn't the words. It was *how* he said it.' She shuddered.

Mr Kendal's jaw hardened. 'He plays games with society's rules…always acting on the edge of acceptable behaviour. How I should love to call him out on it!' He eyed her keenly. 'How do you now?'

His voice was deep, his concern clear. It made Jane's heart sing.

'Better.' She nodded. 'Much better.'

'There is a little colour in your cheeks now. I am glad of it,' he said simply. 'Are you ready to go back inside?'

'Yes.' She squared her shoulders. 'But I know my departure was rude, and—'

'Think nothing of it! Everyone here knows what Mr Haw is. Your actions were perfectly reasonable in the circumstances.'

He was being kind. Nevertheless she was grateful.

'Let us all stay together when we go back in,' added Miss Dodsworth, who had been eyeing them with keen interest during this exchange.

They looked at her.

'Yes, I thought you had both forgotten my presence,' she murmured. 'Let us go!'

Mr Kendal let go of her hands, offering an arm to each of them. 'I am fortunate indeed!' he murmured. 'A beautiful lady on each side!'

Miss Dodsworth gave a suitably tart response to that, while Jane simply *glowed*.

On entering the salon, they realised that in their absence supper had been served. This provided the perfect distraction, since nobody paid them any notice as they merged with the crowd, choosing their preferred foods and then finding a settee.

Mr Kendal stood beside them, and they shared the same side table for their plates.

Jane was grateful that no one seemed to be paying her any mind. It allowed her to look about her and feel reassured that nobody was noticing her.

They are all much too well-bred to do so.

She perused the guests, trying to remember the names of the various people she had been introduced to.

Mr Haw and his mother had retired to the far corner. Jane

eventually dared look in their direction—to find Mrs Haw eyeing her with open hostility. Her heart sank.

Mr Kendal, still alert to Jane's distress, followed her gaze. 'Do not be alarmed,' he said softly. 'Earning Mrs Haw's enmity is an accomplishment in these parts. Is it not, Emma?' he enquired of Miss Dodsworth.

'Oh, beyond doubt! Robert and I used to compete for the honour of who would be the first to irritate her. To be fair to her, she does not hold grudges, and the next time you meet she is likely to be all charm again.'

'Then, as I am unlikely ever to meet her again, I shall endeavour not to worry.'

'Not meet her again? But—forgive me—the distance between you and your grandfather has been healed, has it not? I am hoping you will be a regular visitor to the county after this.'

Jane did not know what to say to this. She could perhaps see herself living with Mama, in an out-of-the-way cottage somewhere. If her grandfather intended to settle something on her then she and Mama would have an end to their money worries, but they certainly would not go out in society.

Miss Dodsworth looked to Mr Kendal, whose expression remained impassive. 'The situation is delicate...' he muttered.

Miss Dodsworth frowned slightly, but was too well-mannered to question further.

Jane glanced across to her grandfather. He was seated in his favourite spot in any room—by the fireplace—and laughing at something his host had said. He was clearly in high spirits, enjoying the company and the occasion. Jane could not help smiling. Thankfully her dramatic behaviour did not seem to have been widely noticed.

'He is wide awake tonight,' commented Mr Kendal.

Jane could hear the affection in his tone.

'Yes—normally by this time he has had his brandy and retired.'

Miss Dodsworth interrupted. 'Ooh, it is time to begin the performances. I do so love music!'

Mrs Foster had opened the lid of the grand pianoforte that stood in the centre of the room. A footman brought a box full of sheets of music and placed it on top, while another two moved a large harp from the corner into the centre of the room. The two Misses Foster, looking decidedly nervous, came forward—the elder to sit at the piano, while the younger took up her position behind the enormous harp.

Once the noise levels in the room had quietened to a suitable level, Mrs Foster nodded at her elder daughter, who began to play. After a moment the sweet sounds of the harp joined the piano, and the final few conversations ceased.

Jane had been lucky enough to have had music in her life from the start. Papa had been an excellent singer, and Jane remembered singing with him—at first simple folk songs, but then pieces of increasing complexity. Naturally, however, she had never had the opportunity to learn to play an instrument. But Lady Kingswood could play both the piano and the harp, and had encouraged Jane to keep singing.

Right now Jane was captivated by the beautiful sounds the two girls were making, and the sure way in which their fingers played the keys and plucked the strings in perfect time.

I could never be so talented.

Of all of the luxuries ladies commanded, surely the ability to play an instrument was the most delightful?

When the piece finally ended, Jane sighed in appreciation before joining the others in heartfelt applause. The girls then each performed a solo piece, before stepping away from their instruments and curtseying.

'Oh, I think I am to be next,' murmured Miss Dodsworth, seeing Mrs Foster's gaze wander around the assembled guests.

And so it proved. Mrs Foster called her forward to the piano, and Miss Dodsworth played a country reel, followed by a more intricate piece by Beethoven. They all clapped, and Miss Dodsworth returned to her place beside Jane and Mr Kendal.

'Well done, Emma!' Mr Kendal smiled.

'That was wonderful!' gushed Jane. 'That second piece was really difficult, but you managed it with ease!'

'I had to concentrate!' Miss Dodsworth grinned. 'I do enjoy playing, but I am always relieved when my piece is successfully completed.' She raised an eyebrow. 'Do you play the piano or the harp, Miss Bailey?'

Jane gaped at her, aghast. 'Neither! Mrs Foster will not ask *me* to play, will she?'

'Er…normally all the young ladies sing or play during these soirées. But perhaps given the circumstances…'

Mrs Foster had called upon a lady in a green dress, who came forward to play a single piece on the piano. Jane barely heard it, so great was her anxiety. The lady in the green dress was followed by two sisters singing a duet, and then came the moment Jane had feared.

Mrs Foster called her name.

Chapter Twenty-Two

Instinctively Jane looked to Mr Kendal. He had no answer. But just feeling the connection of his eyes locking with hers gave her the courage to carry out the wild plan that had come to her just moments before.

She lifted her chin, and turned to Miss Dodsworth. 'I could perhaps sing, if you will accompany me on the piano?'

'Of course!'

They walked together to the centre of the room. Mr Kendal's uneasiness was palpable.

Jane knew she was about to look foolish—and, what was worse, she would make her entire party look foolish. While she was used to singing, she had never performed. She glanced towards the Millthorpes. Mrs Millthorpe was twisting her hands round and round. Mrs Kendal was frowning with worry. Mr Millthorpe remained impassive.

'What do you wish to sing?' Miss Dodsworth took a sheaf of papers from the box and began flicking through them.

Jane's heart sank.

I do not know any of these!

With a trembling hand, she removed some more.

Nothing.

Miss Dodsworth removed the last remaining papers and began sifting through them while Jane watched.

'Wait!' She held out a hand. 'What was that previous one?'

'"Ruhe Sanft."'

'Can I see it?'

Jane perused it. While she could not read music properly, the words were all there, and now the tune came to her.

'I think I know this one.'

Miss Dodsworth's eyes widened. 'But it is one of the most difficult pieces to sing! All those high notes! And Herr Mozart writes such beautifully complex music— Are you certain you wish to sing this one?'

I have no choice. It is the only piece I know.

She nodded, and moved to stand close to the piano, where she could see the words on the sheet if she needed them. Her grandfather was directly ahead. She dropped her gaze.

I cannot look at him now.

Thankfully Mr Kendal was to her left, outside her direct view.

Miss Dodsworth moved the sheets to the music rack in front of her. Mrs Foster raised an arm to indicate to her guests that the performers were ready, and silence fell.

Why was it totally silent? Why couldn't some of them keep conversing, as they had with the other performers? It was clearly the novelty of having a stranger in their midst. A servant, at that.

Knowing that was no help at all.

Miss Dodsworth played the opening bars and there was a murmur of surprise in the room—clearly some of them recognised the music. Jane began to sing at the right time— and thankfully in the right key—but she knew she was singing much too quietly. Her voice, quivering with trepidation, was being drowned out by Miss Dodsworth's piano-playing.

Instantly Miss Dodsworth played more softly, perhaps erroneously believing that Jane was singing quietly for dramatic impact.

Jane sang in the original German, its meaning playing in her mind.

What was, what will be, should not chase you any longer...

Keeping her eyes fixed on Miss Dodsworth's hands, she let the message of the aria flow through her. Everything she had been up to now did not matter. Maid or lady. Servant or mistress. What would happen in the future was also unknown.

Sorrow and grief, fear and doubt should not plague you...

As she sang, gradually her worries vanished. She stood straighter, and allowed her voice to strengthen and soar. *'"Ruhe Sanft, lass los..."'*

Rest gently, let go...

The words were perfect. She reached the final bars, allowing the song to resonate around the room. And as the last notes rang out and faded away she stopped, slightly breathless.

There was utter silence.

Fearing the worst, she raised her eyes to meet her grandfather's. His were wet with tears.

An instant later resounding applause rang out.

Miss Dodsworth rose and enveloped Jane in a fierce hug. 'That was *beautiful!* I have never heard anyone sing so well!'

Mrs Foster came forward to gush, and to compliment, and moments later Jane found herself surrounded by well-wishers, all eager to tell her how wonderful a singer she was and how her piece had affected them. Mrs Kendal hugged her, and Mr Foster thanked her profusely for 'deigning to sing' at his 'humble soirée'.

Jane, dumbfounded, could only murmur vague thanks. Her mind was awhirl. Mostly what she felt was relief. Through a gap in the crowd she saw her grandfather lift an imperious finger.

'My grandfather is calling me,' she explained, glad to get away from the unexpected attention.

The man sitting beside Mr Millthorpe jumped up to give her his seat as she approached. 'Delightful!' he muttered. 'Truly delightful!'

'Thank you,' she replied politely, sliding into the seat.

'Well, Jane?'

Her grandfather had dried his eyes, she noted, but he still looked shaken.

'Well, Grandfather?' she returned softly.

'Edward was a fine singer.'

'Yes, he was. We would often sing together.'

He reached for her hand and squeezed it firmly, overcome.

'And my Eleanor…'

She waited.

'It was as though her voice was singing through you. I have missed it these forty years and more.' His voice cracked. 'Thank you, child.' He leaned forward and rested his forehead briefly against hers. 'Thank you.'

It was so soft she barely heard it.

She swallowed back tears and tried to give him a misty smile. 'I want to know more about her.'

'And so you shall.'

The next performer—a young matron who was extremely proficient on the harp—began to play, and Jane sat silently, still holding her grandfather's hand.

But what of Mr Kendal? He had not come forward like the others.

But then, she reminded herself, *he is naturally reserved.*

She sent a sideways glance in his direction. He was staring fixedly at the harpist, his handsome features devoid of emotion. He might have been carved from granite.

Suppressing a pang of disappointment, she chided herself for her vanity. Was it not enough that so many in this room had enjoyed her singing? Must she have his approval as well?

The answer came immediately.

Yes. Yes, I must.

Her heart sank as distress spread through her. Of all the people in this room, his was the opinion she valued most.

Not even her grandfather's approval could satisfy her. She must crave Mr Kendal's regard. But why?

Because he is important. He is my—my friend.

She frowned. 'Friend' was too little a word. Miss Dodsworth could be her friend. Mrs Kendal, even. No, what she felt for Robert Kendal was altogether more complicated than mere friendship. But she had no name for it beyond 'friendship' 'amity' or 'esteem'.

None of these even came close to reflecting her burning need for his company, his approval, his regard.

Strangely reluctant to pursue the thought, she distracted herself by focusing, once again, on the music.

Chapter Twenty-Three

Having arrived home hours after midnight, they all slept late the next morning.

Jane woke from a nightmare-free sleep with a delicious feeling of contentment. Despite her worries, and the unpleasant incident with Marmaduke Haw and his mother, the soirée had gone rather well in the end. Miss Dodsworth was a darling, the Foster family warm and gregarious, and most of the neighbours had seemed welcoming and kind.

But, Miss Dodsworth apart, she could not imagine local society tolerating her for very long.

'The situation is delicate,' Mr Kendal had said, depressing Miss Dodsworth's innocent assumption about the depth of the family's welcome for Jane.

Although there had been her singing, and the gratifying response to it.

She turned over in her comfortable bed, hugging the memory close. She had accepted compliments about her voice all of her life, yet last night was the first time she had ever truly performed.

I should like to do it again. But next time I will watch Mr Kendal for his response.

She pictured him smiling, clapping. But then the doubtful voice in her mind tripped her up with an image of him from last night. He might be frowning or, worse, looking uninterested. And, of course, she would never have the opportunity to be in such society again.

At least she had had last night.

There was a gentle scratching on the door.

'Come in! Oh, good morning, Nancy.'

'Properly speaking, miss, it is afternoon,' Nancy replied cheerfully.

'What?' Jane sat bolt upright. 'Never in my life have I slept so late! I am quite ashamed of myself!'

'But why, miss? You did not retire until after three, so you had every right to sleep on.' She opened the heavy curtains, allowing pale winter light into the room. 'Only Mr Millthorpe is downstairs. The others have not yet emerged from their bedchambers.'

'My grandfather is downstairs already?' Jane's sense of guilt increased. 'I must go to him.'

Fifteen minutes later, dressed in a simple printed muslin with a yellow ribbon around the waist, Jane tapped lightly on the library door.

'Enter!' he called imperiously.

She went in. 'Oh! I do apologise, Grandfather. I had not realised you were with your steward.'

'Stay, stay, child. It is of no matter. I had finished anyway.' He addressed the steward. 'Make sure he comes tomorrow, if you can. And tell him to bring that clerk of his!'

'Yes, sir.' The steward gathered his papers, bowed to them both, and departed.

'Good day, child.' He embraced her warmly. 'Now tell me, for it has been perplexing me, how did you learn to sing like that? I know the source of your talent of course, for as I told you Eleanor had as fine a voice as I have ever heard, but your singing has more than raw talent. You have honed it, learned technique. How, and when?'

'I cannot remember a time when I did not sing. As I said last night, Papa sang with me even when I was a baby, so Mama says, and when I was older I used to sing with Miss Marianne all the time. When she became Lady Kingswood she encouraged me to keep singing.'

He nodded thoughtfully. 'But how did you know that Mozart piece? Why not simple country airs?'

'When Miss Marianne was growing up she had to learn

to play the harp and to sing. She had to practise the harp every day. I was so envious that she was being allowed to learn an instrument, which always puzzled her. She said when I sang with her it made the practice more interesting. Eventually she insisted I be present and a part of her lessons with music tutors.' She smiled softly, remembering those far-off days. 'I was always happiest when I had music.'

'Just like Eleanor. That's where Edward got his talent—a talent he passed to you.'

She beamed at her grandfather, loving the feeling of connection to her past.

The sound of hooves on gravel drew their eyes to the windows. Robert, looking magnificent on his black stallion, was just leaving.

'He always rides when he is troubled about something,' said Grandfather quietly. He sat back in his chair. 'Tell me, child, how did you and Robert deal together on your journey to Yorkshire?'

This was unexpected. 'Um…very well.'

His eyes narrowed, and she felt her colour rise.

'He was—he was most gentlemanlike.'

He snorted. 'By the sounds of it he was far *too* gentlemanlike, if you ask me!'

She had no answer to this.

'Do you still walk with him in the afternoons?'

She had not known he knew about their walks. 'Yes, unless the weather is bad.'

'Good.' He patted her hand. 'Now, let me tell you more about Eleanor's singing…'

Robert was livid. With himself.

'I am the greatest fool in Christendom!' he announced, making Blacklock's ears twitch backwards. 'No, not you,' he said reassuringly, patting the stallion's neck.

They continued slowly to the top of the mount, where the beech grove crackled with copper leaves and beechnuts underfoot, the canopy above bare to the leaden sky. Robert dismounted and the horse began foraging for winter grass among the carpet of last autumn's windfall.

Stomping across to the edge of the hill, he cursed his situation and his own foolishness in the strongest possible terms.

Eventually he calmed a little, and talked himself through the mess he had created.

It had all begun the moment he had laid eyes on Jane. He was a full blooded man, and as such he always noticed attractive females, but from the start there had been something particular about the way her pretty face and fine form had continually drawn his eye.

'My fair Diana!' he said now, remembering his foolishness on the night he had first met her.

Could he even then have read the signs? He shook his head. It was not unreasonable to assume his interest in a random serving maid had been no more than a momentary diversion.

Even when I spent most of that dinner at Ledbury House being distracted by her presence?

During the journey he had convinced himself that what he was feeling was simply the effect of propinquity—that he would have become fascinated with *any* attractive young lady if he had been thrust into her company for a prolonged period of time.

And there may well be an element of truth in that, he acknowledged wryly.

But without the long journey, would he have ever come to truly *know* Jane?

Their arrival at Beechmount Hall had changed things. No longer had it been simply Robert and Jane, spending all day and all evening in each other's company. Most of the time now he was limited to enjoying her society in the presence of his aunt, his uncle and his mother.

Not exactly the ideal situation for courtship, he noted wryly.

For courtship was what he now wanted.

Although he had not consciously been pursuing her at the time, he now realised his afternoon walks with her, his delight at being seated next to her at dinner every evening, his impatience to join the ladies after the evening port—all were indications that his heart, not just his fancy, was engaged.

Her burgeoning relationship with her grandfather was a joy to observe. Despite the implications for his own future, Robert could not help but be glad to see how the old man lit up in her company.

And why should I not enjoy seeing it? For I respond to her in just the same fashion.

He knew his aunt and his mother were worried about him being cut out by Jane, but Robert was at peace with it. His uncle's estate was not entailed; he could dispose of it as he pleased. And what better way to honour his beloved first wife and his lost son than by transforming the life of his only granddaughter, his own flesh and blood, by lifting her from servant girl to mistress of Beechmount Hall, with all the wealth and status that entailed?

He frowned. She had not been raised to such responsibilities. He must ensure the staff supported her. The lawyers, too. The steward would need to be patient with her.

Idly, Robert wondered if she would accept him as an adviser.

He shook his head. Possibly not. It might seem unlikely to all her other advisers that he could support her with a genuine lack of bitterness, so they might advise her to stay away from him.

The thought sent a pang of pain through him. He could cope with losing the inheritance he had always assumed to be his, yet the thought of being estranged from Jane filled him with agony.

He strode across to his horse, mounting via a fallen tree trunk that lay nearby. As they picked their way downhill he reflected on last night's events. First, the journey—the delicious proximity to her, the heat of her thigh against his... He had been glad of the darkness covering evidence of his overwhelming desire for her. Seeing her in that pink gown, the satin clinging perfectly to her form and the low neckline exposing her white skin to his covert gaze, had threatened to drive him to madness. Never had he felt desire such as this!

To see Marmaduke Haw ogling that same décolletage had filled him with disgust and rage. Yes, most men were interested in the female form. But most men behaved respectfully towards ladies even while appreciating their beauty.

Haw has no class, no breeding. Jane, raised a servant, is worth a hundred of him!

Finally he allowed himself to remember her singing. Not knowing the prodigious talent she had hidden from them all, and assuming she would have to give some excuse as to why she could not play an instrument, he had awaited with dread the moment when Mrs Foster's eyes would alight upon Jane. Although the rumour of her upbringing as a servant had spread around the salon, his neighbours could not have known if Jane had any of the accomplishments expected of a young lady. They would all have been agog, many expecting her to fail.

Once he had seen her step forward with Emma and realised she was going to sing he had been rather relieved. Even a simple country air would have been enough. The fact she had sung a complex Mozart aria had been entirely unexpected. The realisation that her singing was not only good, but astonishing, had slowly dawned on him.

He was not a man much given to flights of fancy, but as her voice had dipped and soared he had felt as though she pulled at his very soul. Afterwards, when her angelic song had ended, he had been unable to respond, or move, or even think. He had belatedly come round, as if waking from a deep sleep, to find that the applause had ended and people had clustered around her to congratulate and exclaim. Then she had walked towards her grandfather, and Robert had seen in his uncle's expression something of his own reaction to Jane's divine melody.

Mozart, he reminded himself. Mozart wrote it.

Ah, but it was my Jane who rendered it real in that room last night.

Jane. The woman he loved.

Of course he loved her. It was blindingly obvious.

Now what?

I love her, yes. But should I speak to her of my feelings?

As Blacklock made his way up towards the house Robert imagined himself making a declaration to Jane. What might her response be? There had been times when he had believed her to hold warm feelings towards him, but he honestly could not say how strong those feelings were. She had responded delightfully to their kiss in the carriage, despite her past, and she looked to him for comfort and for friendship. He knew she enjoyed his companionship…

Yet none of this could be seen as certain indication that she was on the way to being in love with him. Why should she not turn to him for friendship? She was a stranger among relatives she had never met before. Of course she would rely on him as a friend whom she trusted. It did not mean for certain that she felt anything stronger for him.

A warm glow developed in his chest as he considered the remarkable trust that had grown between them. That trust had been shaken these past days. Yet last night's events had gone some way to healing the breach between them.

What if I break that amity with an ill-judged declaration?

His heart sank as another problem occurred to him. It was a declaration she would be bound to accept. A former serving maid receiving a proposal of marriage from a wealthy young gentleman? She would have to be deranged to turn him down.

The thought gave him no comfort.

Was it prideful of him to wish she would accept him for who he was, and not because their stations were unequal and she would be 'marrying well'?

On the other hand, he mused, if his uncle planned to make her his heiress it would seem to everyone—including Jane—that Robert was nothing more than a fortune-hunter! How could she trust his proposal when it would appear to everyone—including his own mother—that inheriting Beechmount Hall was a prime consideration in his declaration? They had only met eighteen days ago.

He shook his head. It seemed longer.

It feels as though I have known her a lifetime, and yet there is so much more to learn about her.

At least he now knew his own heart. Fool that he was, it had taken a blinding flash of realisation during her song to bring him to wakefulness on that score. That had been less than a day ago. There was time yet to consider his best course of action.

I must not misstep on this—it is too important.

Chapter Twenty-Four

Her grandfather was busy with matters of business all day on Saturday, so Jane missed her usual cose with him. On Sunday, however, she ended up spending many hours in his company, for while they were out at church he had caused the footmen to bring downstairs the trunks containing his first wife's possessions, and small items relating to both Eleanor and her child.

He and Jane sat in Eleanor's sitting room, surrounded by the debris from the things they had gradually unpacked—things consisting of memories, dreams, and important moments in their lives.

After a late nuncheon, Mr Kendal joined them. He had come looking for Jane, for it was time for their usual afternoon walk, but Jane did not want to stop exploring the trunks with her grandfather. At the same time, she did not wish to forego the pleasure of her time with Mr Kendal—one of her favourite times of day.

She hesitated, torn.

'You may stay, Robert, if you wish,' her grandfather said diffidently.

Mr Kendal eyed him questioningly, then agreed. And so it was that Jane spent almost the entire afternoon in their company.

Mr Kendal seemed genuinely interested in discovering more about Eleanor and Edward, and handled Eleanor's letters and Edward's christening gown with great care.

'She seems so close to me now,' her grandfather murmured as they examined the last of the treasures. 'I am glad you came here, Jane.'

'As am I.' She reached out a hand to him and he took it.

'I should add that I, too, am glad you are here, Miss Bailey,' Mr Kendal added in a low voice.

He was looking at her intently, in a way that made her heart flutter madly.

I have never seen such a look in his eyes before. What does it mean?

'Miss Bailey? Why do you insist on such formality?'

Jane regarded her grandfather blankly, for she had been momentarily lost in Mr Kendal's gaze.

'It must be Jane and Robert,' her grandfather continued, 'and I will not be disobeyed on this!'

'Yes, Uncle.'

'Yes, Grandfather.'

They spoke in unison, then looked at each other and laughed.

The clock on the mantel struck the hour. 'That is it now. All is accomplished,' declared her grandfather obscurely. 'Jane, ring for my valet. I shall rest these old bones before dinner.' He eyed them both. 'Can I trust you two to look after all this?' He made a vague gesture.

'Of course, Grandfather.'

'Good.'

'We shall pack it away carefully,' added Robert.

Robert! I can address him by his true name now. Robert...

She tried it out in her mind, enjoying the delicious thrill of the imagined syllables on her lips and tongue.

'You shall look after it now and always. Both of you.' With this obscure comment, Grandfather shuffled forward in his chair. 'Well, help me up, then,' he muttered testily, and they both rushed to comply.

After the valet had accompanied him out of the room Jane and Robert set to work, sitting on the carpet to carefully rewrap the precious papers, personal possessions and other treasured items her grandfather had hoarded.

'For all his crusty exterior,' Robert commented, stowing

away a carved wooden horse that had belonged to Jane's father, 'my uncle is remarkably sentimental.'

'He feels things profoundly, I believe,' Jane said soberly. 'I think he loved Eleanor deeply. And he loved my father.' Tears sprang to her eyes. 'That they remained estranged for so many years is a tragedy.'

'It is.' Robert paused for a moment, then looked directly at Jane. 'I wonder if his undoubted love for Eleanor accounts for my aunt's unhappiness? Everyone talks of the fact that she bore no children. But perhaps it is not only that.'

'I believe you may be right.'

They looked at one another for a long moment, and then once more they both spoke at the same time.

'I'm sorry!'

'No, you first.'

'Thank you.' She took a breath. 'I was just going to say it makes me miss my mama and my home. I thought I should be bereft, away from my mother and Lady Kingswood, but I have been surprisingly content these past weeks. Yet just now, seeing my grandfather's sorrow...'

He swallowed. 'I see. Yes, of course you must be missing them.'

He dropped his gaze, seemingly busy in carefully wrapping a small wooden box.

Suddenly, he lifted his head to look at her directly. 'You would not think of living in a different part of the country, then?'

Shock rumbled through Jane. 'Of course not! My place is with Mama. And Lady Kingswood is important to me.'

She had been picturing a cottage near Ledbury House, where her and her mother would live in comfort and ease. Yet even as she spoke she was conscious that she was not completely comfortable with her own assertion.

What is happening? she wondered.

Was she actually daring to imagine a life here, near

Beechmount Hall. Or even *in* Beechmount Hall? Away from her real life?

She shook her head. Her grandfather had invited her for a short visit. That had been clear to her from the beginning. She now had an understanding that he probably meant to bestow a legacy upon her, in honour of Papa. But Beechmount Hall must be given to Robert. Only Robert had the skill and the knowledge to manage it.

'I have only two nights left here,' she said aloud. 'I will set out for home on Tuesday, as planned.'

The words sounded strange to her own ears.

'Of course!' Robert replied briskly. 'Now, pass me that pile of letters, for there is space for them in the corner of this trunk.'

Afterwards, while dressing for dinner, it occurred to her to wonder what he had been about to say.

It must not have been important, she told herself, *for he did not pursue it.*

At dinner, there was a peculiar feeling in the air. Jane sensed it as soon as she entered the salon. Mr Kendal—Robert—seemed distracted, and she did not get the usual welcoming smile from him. What was worrying him? She hoped he had not reverted to his coldness of a few days ago.

Mrs Millthorpe was complaining vaguely, and Mrs Kendal was offering sympathy. Her grandfather was late, which was most unlike him.

The dinner gong sounded and they all looked at one another.

'But where is my uncle?' asked Mrs Kendal.

Thankfully, a footman appeared, to explain that the master had gone directly to the dining room as he had only just descended. When they entered he was taking his seat at the head of the table. He looked resplendent in full evening dress.

'Well?' he snapped. 'Why are you all gaping at me?'

Mrs Millthorpe looked taken aback. 'My dear! I have not seen you wear that evening coat in an age. It becomes you.' She walked towards him and saluted him with a kiss on the cheek.

He patted her hand. 'Ah, you are a good woman, Eugenia.'

They took their seats, Jane and Robert exchanging glances that indicated a shared confusion about this break from the usual pattern.

The first course was served, and after filling his plate Jane's grandfather addressed her directly.

'Jane, when you were singing the other night…'

'Yes?'

'Your German pronunciation was impeccable. Do you have an ear for such things?'

Jane sent him a mischievous smile. *It is time to reveal my learning.*

'Actually, I can speak German,' she said. In perfect German.

There were gasps all around the table before a clamour of questions erupted.

'But how…?'

'Truly…?'

'You speak German?' Robert was all amazement. 'I am impressed. Each time I think I know you, you surprise me with something more.'

She dimpled at him. 'I also speak Italian.' She revealed this in its own language, enjoying the amazed reactions of everyone around the table.

Once they had got over their initial astonishment she explained how it had come about—a combination of Miss Marianne's love of teaching and her own love of learning.

'I have easily learned spoken languages while I was busy dressing her hair or helping her dress. We have been doing it for many years. And, yes—' she glanced at her grandfather '—I do have an ear for languages. I believe it is connected to my musicality.'

He tapped a thoughtful finger on his chin. 'Your Lady Kingswood will also, I presume, understand and speak French. Did she not teach you that language?'

Here it is. Shall I admit it?

'Yes. Yes, she did,' Jane replied in French.

All eyes turned to Mrs Millthorpe.

'Well! I was never so astonished!' she declared, without a hint of embarrassment. 'And yet you never said a word when I was speaking French on your first evening.'

Belatedly, she seemed to realise everyone was staring at her.

'Well, how was I to know that Jane had been raised with such an education? It is most unusual.'

'It is highly unusual, I know,' Jane replied in a conciliatory tone, keen to show Mrs Millthorpe that she did not bear a grudge. 'And my mama will be astounded when I return to her, for my hands are now fully healed—as you see.' Jane held them up for everyone's inspection.

'I am glad of it, Jane.' Grandfather's tone was positively affectionate.

Jane beamed at him.

Will my hands ever be chapped and sore like that again?

The notion filled her with confusion. The change in her circumstances—the *possible* change—was too enormous to take in quickly. If it did happen, she hoped she could become accustomed to luxury instead of hard work.

There was silence.

Beside her, Robert's shoulders seemed suddenly tense.

Then a clatter of metal on china sounded to Jane's left. Her grandfather had dropped his knife.

He is unwell!

Instantly Jane divined the problem. He was choking on a morsel of food and struggling to breathe. He was eerily silent and trying to stand. As one, they all rose and went to him. Robert slapped a hand on his back, and after a few attempts a piece of food flew out. Grandfather sank into his chair, desperately breathing in air. His wife patted his shoulder as he gasped and strained.

'Uncle!' Mrs Kendal's face was creased with concern. 'You are not well!'

Jane saw it too. One side of his face had dropped—the contrast between each half of his visage was striking. His eye and the corner of his mouth both sagged. One arm also seemed to have gone limp. As they watched, his eyes closed.

Jane realised what was happening.

Apoplexy.

'Umpelby!' Robert's voice rang out.

'Yes, sir?' The butler was there in an instant.

'Send for the doctor!'

Umpelby, clearly distressed, undertook to do so, and Robert carried his uncle upstairs to his chamber, accompanied by a procession of women—first his wife, then Mrs Kendal, and finally Jane herself.

With the assistance of her grandfather's valet, they got him partly undressed and into the bed, where he lay looking frail, old, and strangely small. It was as though the stroke had taken some of his spirit. He had not woken up since it had happened.

'I shall stay here with him until the doctor comes,' announced Mrs Millthorpe. 'No!' she held up a hand against offers of assistance. 'This is my place. Please go and finish your meal. He needs quiet.' She looked at her husband and her face softened. 'You old fool…'

Her voice cracked with emotion, bringing a sting of sympathy to Jane's eyes.

Reluctantly, they left. Not a word was spoken as they descended, Jane flanked by Robert and his mother. They returned to the dining room, where they each picked at their food, straining their ears for any sound that might indicate the arrival of the doctor.

Robert was pale, stiff and grim. Despite his caring respect for his uncle, Jane could tell their relationship had not always been easy. She wasn't sure she would have liked to grow up under her grandfather's eye… She glanced again at Robert, seeing the pain behind the shock in his eyes. There was real affection there.

The doctor arrived within the hour, and after he had examined the patient told them to prepare for the worst.

Mrs Millthorpe was stoical in her response, though Jane could see she was hiding real distress.

Leaving Mrs Kendal to comfort her aunt, Jane followed Robert and the doctor downstairs and into the small front parlour.

'The next two days will be telling,' the doctor said sadly. 'He may start to recover, or another seizure may follow.'

'What is your prediction?' asked Robert.

'The fact he has been insensible all this time is not a good sign.'

'I see.'

There was a muscle working in Robert's cheek. Jane had to suppress an impulse to touch him.

'Thank you, Doctor.'

Once the doctor had taken his leave, after prescribing nothing more than watching and waiting, Jane and Robert were left alone.

'How do you, Jane?'

That is the first time he has said my name.

'Are you truly asking about *me*? When it is you who have been close to him for most of your life?'

'I…'

His voice tailed away, and Jane could clearly read the agony in his eyes.

'He has been a father to me. Not a warm, sentimental father, like my own papa, but a father nevertheless.'

His voice faltered, and before she knew what she was doing she found that she had put her arms about him.

He responded instantly, wrapping his own strong arms around her and pressing her to his chest. She could feel the deep thudding of his heartbeat reverberating through her. She turned her head sideways and rested her cheek against the hollow of his shoulder. It fitted as though she belonged there. His hands were now stroking her back with light caresses that left a trail of fire across her skin through the amber silk.

What had begun as a spontaneous offer of comfort had become something entirely different.

Robert's breathing sounded ragged, and the noise triggered a further increase in Jane's already tumultuous pulse.

'Jane…'

It was almost a groan, and she knew exactly what he wanted. She wanted it too.

She lifted her head to receive his kiss.

This time, unlike in the rumbling carriage, there were no errors. Her lips found his unerringly, and almost instantly she opened her mouth to allow their tongues to meet in a hot, fiery dance. Passion rose within her—burning, fierce and undeniable—and she was lost in it.

They kissed and kissed and kissed once more. Sometimes the kisses were soft and gentle, but mostly they were intensely passionate.

Eventually they stopped, foreheads touching, both breathing loudly.

'Oh, Jane… Jane…' he groaned.

The sound sent another wave of desire through her and she gloried in it. He took a deep breath, slid his hands to her upper arms, then stood back from her. Her body ached at the loss of contact—they had been pressed together from chest to hip.

'Tell me—do my kisses offend you?' he asked.

For a moment she was at a loss to respond. Then, 'Of course not! How can you suggest such a thing?'

His lips tightened. 'Because of what happened to you.

The thing that made you faint in the market—that made you run from Marmaduke Haw.' He took a breath. '"Master Henry, please, no!", you said. At the market.'

A shudder went through her. 'Yes...'

Briefly, she closed her eyes. When she opened them again he was gazing steadily at her, his expression filled with compassion.

Tell him.

So she did. Seated beside him on a satin-covered settee, she told him the whole revolting tale.

He listened with patience, with anger, and with understanding. She finished by reassuring him that he did not remind her in any way of the foul Henry.

'I like your kisses,' she concluded simply.

There was only one reasonable response to that. He reached for her and with feather-light tenderness kissed her gently.

She tolerated this for just a few moments, before burying her hands in his dark hair, pulling him closer, and demanding access to his mouth with her questing tongue. Passion rose again, and once more it was he who put a stop to it, sliding backwards on the settee so they were no longer touching. Both were breathing raggedly.

Their eyes met and a slow smile grew on his face.

Her answering smile signalled the deep contentment within her.

Slowly reality intruded. Her grandfather was in bed upstairs after suffering a severe apoplexy. And here they were dallying.

She could sense the frown appearing on her own face.

He saw it too.

'No, Jane, you will not feel guilty about this. If I am not mistaken, my uncle would think it excessively diverting, the old devil.'

She had to laugh. 'Do you know, I believe you are right?'

'Of course I am.' His eyes were laughing.

I am in heaven.

There was a sound in the corridor outside, then a scratching at the door.

With a rueful grimace Robert stood, stepping away from Jane and moving towards the fireplace. 'Enter!'

'Sir.' It was the butler. His eyes flicked briefly to Jane, but his visage remained impassive.

'Yes, Umpelby?'

'Henby has desired your presence, sir. She strongly believes Mrs Millthorpe should not sit all night with the master.'

Robert frowned. 'I agree with her. Very well, I shall come.'

He bowed to Jane, a hint of warmth in his eyes, then left.

Chapter Twenty-Five

For three days they kept a vigil by her grandfather's bedside. His valet and Robert shared the nights, while Jane, Mrs Kendal and Mrs Millthorpe took turns to sit with him during the day.

Her grandfather opened his eyes from time to time, which gave them all encouragement, but he seemed incapable of speech. Now and then he would take sips of wine, but grimaced when presented with food.

By Wednesday, he refused even wine.

Jane had written to her mama to explain that her return home would be delayed. Her focus was on assisting as best she could in nursing her grandfather, and in truth her former life at Ledbury House seemed far, far away.

Mama was there, and Miss Marianne, and her real life. But Jane had a purpose here. And people who were important to her.

The thought left her feeling torn, so she avoided it.

Mrs Millthorpe, despite continuing to complain, was assiduous in taking her share of the burden. Jane's opinion of her increased by the hour as she devoted her attention to her ailing husband. Only strong persuasion made her allow others to take her place.

On Wednesday evening Jane was sitting with her grandfather, quietly reading, when Robert called in to his uncle's chamber. They had had little time together since Sunday evening's encounter, and had, on the surface, settled back into their familiar warm friendliness. Inside, though, Jane could not see him as anything other than the passionate, handsome man who had kissed her so thoroughly.

Her heart leapt, as it always did on seeing him. 'Oh,

Robert, but you are too early. I can do two or three hours more before you begin your night-time vigil.'

'I know. I just wanted to make sure you have all you need.' His smile was warm.

Was he remembering what she was remembering?

'That is kind of you.'

There was a sound from the bed.

'Grandfather?' Jane hurried to his side, Robert following behind her. Her grandfather's eyes were open, and he looked first at her, then Robert.

Lifting his good hand, he sought hers. She gave it, her heart sinking at how weak his grip had become.

And this is his good side.

The other half of his body had lain useless since the stroke had robbed him of his speech and his independence.

Taking her hand, he deliberately placed it on the counterpane. Then he reached out again, this time towards Robert, at the same time making noises signifying urgency.

Jane twisted to look at him. 'He wants your hand, I think.'

Robert gave his hand and Jane glanced down at the counterpane, noting the contrast in the two—the old and the young. Robert's hand so young and strong, smooth of skin and whole in muscle and sinew. Her grandfather's claw-like, emaciated and weak.

Still, her grandfather's spirit was strong. He placed Robert's hand square on top of Jane's, making a sound of satisfaction at the back of his throat. Jane looked from him to Robert's hand and back again. Her grandfather nodded, then closed his eyes.

Jane and Robert stood like that for quite some time, Jane feeling safe and reassured by the warmth of Robert's hand on hers and his chest at her back.

I must remember this moment.

Eventually, guilt stirred her into action. 'You should go, Robert. You have a long night ahead.'

Gently, she withdrew her hand and turned to face him. He was standing very, very close.

'Make the most of these few hours to read and rest. I have all I need here.'

This produced a slight smile in response. 'Very well.' He took a breath, then stood back from her. 'I shall return at midnight.'

Jane nodded. Still he did not go. They both knew it was sensible for him to leave, yet Jane was loath to see him go.

He wishes to stay. Her heart warmed at the thought. *I wish he would.*

Then came the realisation. Her grandfather was dying. She could not be distracted by other matters. Everything else must wait.

Robert must have read the changing moods on her face, for abruptly he spun on his heel and left.

Once he had gone she sank into her chair and put her head in her hands, feeling bereft.

Caring for her grandfather was in a sense easy, for he just lay there. But it was also the hardest thing she had ever done. There was the constant worry of fearing he would die, that there was something she should be doing, that after he was gone her last link to Papa would die with him...

And then there was Robert. *Robert.* When had he become so necessary to her happiness? The thought of leaving here, never to see him again, was crushing.

I must be strong about this. I simply must.

In the end, she knew, events would propel her away whether she wanted to go or not. Her real life was waiting at or near Ledbury House.

Go well, my Jane, and never forget who you are.

Mama's written words were ever there, at the back of her mind.

I am a lady's maid on a short visit.

But the words no longer rang true in her heart.

I am Papa's daughter. I am part of the Beechmount Hall family.

No. I am Mama's daughter. I am a proud servant.

No. I am a former servant.

Her head felt as though it might explode, like a firework.

I do not know who I am. Mama, I do not know!

At Ledbury House they would have had her latest letter by now, explaining that she could not yet leave Yorkshire. It would be something of a shock, she knew. No one had expected her grandfather to become so dangerously ill during her visit. Robert had made it clear to them that, although he was old, his uncle had been in reasonably good health.

Both Lady Kingswood and Mama had replied to her previous letters in their own way, showing interest in the happenings in Yorkshire while also wishing her home soon.

Home. Where is my home?

Papa, Grandfather, Eleanor—they were all here, in Beechmount Hall. Their presence lurked in every room, laughed and played and lived in every part of the house and the garden and the lake and the hill.

They are part of this place. As am I.

Never had she felt such affinity for a place before. She loved Ledbury House, and had been happy there until a few short weeks ago. But she had never felt this sense of connection.

It feels like home. And it isn't just Beechmount Hall and the family. It is Robert, too.

She sat back in the armchair, gazing into the flames.

Robert...

Finally she allowed herself to look into her own heart. Where before it had contained only a very few people—Mama, Miss Marianne, and a degree of affection for Lord Kingswood and some of the other Ledbury House servants—now it was filled to the brim with Grandfather, with Mrs Kendal, with Mrs Millthorpe and Nancy, even with Miss Dodsworth.

Mostly, though, it was filled by one person.

Robert Kendal.

Surely the most handsome men she had ever encountered. Handsome face. Strong body. Generous heart. Lively mind.

His soul called to hers like a beacon in the dark.

I love him.

Her heart swelled.

I love him. Well, of course I do!

Closing her eyes, she savoured the knowledge, considering his face, his form and character in great detail.

I love him.

After a time her thoughts naturally returned to herself.

He likes me. He likes me exceedingly well...

Her heart fluttered as she allowed herself to dwell on wishes and hopes so long denied. Their friendship was strong, and they had an affinity of mind she had never before encountered.

He wants me, too.

Desire flooded through her as she relived the dizzying kisses they had shared downstairs. To share his bed would be heaven, and she had no doubt of it being an intensely agreeable and pleasant experience, were it to happen.

I know I could overcome my fears with him. I just know it!

But gradually, doubts began to creep in.

Can I think of marrying him?

She was an honest, respectable woman, but she was also a former servant. Could he possibly marry her? She shook her head. It just would not do. Why, it had been at the root of the divide between Papa and Grandfather. A gentleman should not—not ever—marry a servant.

She groaned aloud at the lowering thought, and her grandfather stirred in the bed. Hurrying to his side, she took his hand. It had not moved since he had used it to join Robert's hand with hers earlier. He seemed to be asleep, his chest rising and falling with low breaths.

'Grandfather,' she whispered. 'I love him. I love Robert.'

His eyes remained closed, but she was surprised by him briefly squeezing her hand.

He hears me!

She stayed with him for a while longer—until her grandfather's valet arrived just before midnight to see to him and change him. Knowing it would be immodest to stay, she nevertheless wished she could, for she would have liked to see Robert one last time before retiring.

Instead she kissed her grandfather's forehead, wished him a good night's rest, and promised to see him again early in the morning.

This time there was no response.

As she climbed into her own soft bed, grateful as ever for Nancy's thoughtfulness in building up the fire and warming the bed, she thought of Robert, beginning another long night in her grandfather's chamber. She could picture him there, book in hand, seated in the very armchair she had not long vacated.

'Robert…' she murmured as sleep claimed her.

'Miss Bailey! Wake up, miss!'

'Uh…?' Jane gradually understood that Nancy was there, holding a candle.

She looks upset.

'Grandfather!' Her heart ran cold.

Nancy made haste to reassure her. 'He's still alive, miss, but he's bad. The young master has said all the ladies should come.'

Jane was already rising. 'Oh! My slippers! What shall I wear?'

'Here, miss.' Nancy held out a diaphanous dressing

gown. 'Mrs Kendal says to take it, as she knows you don't have one.'

Jane had never had occasion to leave her bedroom undressed before.

'Thank you.' Jane slipped her arms into the lace confection, part of her mind recognising the beauty and workmanship in the fine garment. The rest of her mind was filled with pain.

Nancy lit a full branch of candles, and Jane carried it to her grandfather's chamber. The other two ladies were already there—Mrs Kendal crying softly in her son's arms, while Mrs Millthorpe had claimed her place by her husband's side and was even now gently speaking to him.

Jane approached. Her grandfather looked just as he had earlier—his face relaxed in sleep and his body and face calm.

Why have they called us? she wondered.

Then she noticed his breathing. Unlike the natural, steady breaths she had noticed earlier, her grandfather's breathing had now changed to a rapid succession of quick breaths, accompanied by the bubbling stridor of phlegm at the back of his throat.

The death rattle.

Abruptly the noise stopped, and Jane counted to five inside her head before Grandfather breathed again.

He is dying. She glanced at the others. *And they know it.*

Robert, maintaining one arm around his mother, reached out to Jane with the other, and she gladly accepted the comfort of his embrace. Instinctively she reached out to Mrs Kendal with her other arm. The three of them stood like that for quite a few minutes, before separating wordlessly.

Her grandfather's valet appeared with an extra chair, two sleepy footmen following him in with dining chairs.

Most of the household is awake, then.

Once seated, there was nothing for them to do but wait, and watch, and wait again…

* * *

For the rest of his life Robert knew he would remember this night. His uncle was spent, his body finally relinquishing the powerful spirit that had dominated most of Robert's life to date. As well as the inevitable sadness, he felt also relief that his uncle would no longer have to battle with a body that simply would not behave the way he wished.

Following the stroke on Sunday, Robert's unspoken dread had been that his uncle would be forced to live on, trapped inside a broken cage which allowed no speech and limited movement. At least this way, hard as it was, gave him freedom.

For many hours Robert simply sat with the three women and his uncle's devoted valet—who, unsurprisingly, could not be persuaded to seek his bed. There was a calmness in the air that was entirely unexpected. Each of the ladies shed tears at times, but their collective acceptance of the inevitable led to a certain harmony and serenity that was unanticipated yet entirely welcome.

At times his attention wandered, and he found himself plagued by flashes of memory. Jane had arrived in his uncle's chamber wearing a thin nightgown, covered only by his mother's old lace dressing gown, and with her long dark hair unbound. He had never seen anything more beautiful.

The fact that she was clearly unaware of how her clothing so imperfectly concealed her form was a matter of both great interest and frustration to him. On several occasions he had to remind himself sternly that carnal thoughts were not appropriate in this present situation. Still, he saved the memories for a more appropriate time.

Jane and his mama took turns to doze in the armchair, and eventually he allowed himself to be persuaded to take his own rest there. He slept for only a short time, yet surprisingly deeply, and when he woke Jane was looking directly at him. Seeing his eyes open, she flushed slightly and looked away.

Robert glanced at the small clock. A quarter-hour before six. He rose, stretched, and made his way back to his uncle's bedside. As he did so his uncle's breathing paused again. In the way they had been doing all night, they all listened intently for him to breathe again. After what seemed like an age his uncle took another breath, and there was an audible sigh from Aunt Eugenia.

His mama tried to persuade her aunt to take a turn in the armchair, but she steadfastly refused. 'I shall lay my head here, at the edge of the bed,' she agreed.

'An excellent notion!' Mama pulled her chair closer to her aunt's. 'I shall join you.'

The two ladies rested their heads on the counterpane, and before long their breathing steadied and deepened.

Robert took his place by Jane's side and lifted her hand. She squeezed his and let hers rest there. Eventually she, too, slept, her dark head resting on the side of his uncle's bed. Robert stayed awake, holding his beloved's hand and keeping vigil over his uncle.

They remained like that until just before seven, when the change happened.

The pause between breaths became almost a full minute.

Is this it?

Robert stood up. 'Uncle?'

The ladies lifted their heads, looking confused and sleepy-eyed. Then his uncle breathed again, and Robert sank down.

It was not the end, but it was nearly so.

At ten minutes to eight, on a cold morning in early March, he breathed his last.

Chapter Twenty-Six

Preparations for the funeral began almost immediately. The bells were rung in the chapel, the undertaker was called for, the bees were informed in the correct manner and the hatchment went up above the door.

After the long, slow pace of the past three days Beechmount Hall became a hive of activity. The servants donned black ribbons, armbands and gloves, according to their role and duties, and the ladies were given mourning caps with black ribbons sewn on.

Mrs Millthorpe—now wearing severe black bombazine—held long meetings with the cook and the housekeeper, while Robert focused on the steward and Umpelby.

Once the coffin arrived, her grandfather was placed in state in the front parlour, after the room had been draped entirely in black baize, the windows covered, and branches of candles placed at intervals on side tables.

His widow, along with Jane and Mrs Kendal, would keep vigil over him there until the day of the funeral.

Nancy had hastily dyed one of Jane's grey dresses a sombre black, and Jane was now wearing it. Along with the other ladies she'd spent long hours creating the funeral gifts—sprigs of rosemary, for remembrance, tied with black silk ribbon. She was fatigued from lack of sleep. They all were.

On the day before the funeral she received a letter from her mama.

'Oh!' she said aloud.

Mrs Kendal looked up.

'My mother is coming to Yorkshire! Indeed, she is already on her way. This is sent from Grantham.'

'She is? But how delightful for you!' Although Mrs Kendal's smile faded as she realised Jane's mother, a servant, would soon be among them.

'There is no need to be concerned,' Jane assured her. 'Mama means to put up in an inn in Harrogate and will call on me once she has settled there.'

'I am sure my aunt would make her welcome…'

Mrs Kendal's tone belied her words. Nothing was sure in this situation. Mrs Millthorpe had barely accepted Jane—and that was with the benefit of a decent education and Millthorpe blood.

It would create a dilemma for the family if they were forced to offer hospitality to Mrs Bailey. Jane was a legitimate granddaughter, whereas her mama had been a servant all her life. She would be the first to say she should not be a guest here. But then, Jane had believed that when she had first come to Beechmount…

This reminder of Jane's status came with something of a jolt. Halfway between servant and lady, unsure of her place and her future. Her grandfather had died before he could make a settlement upon her. Perhaps there would be no cottage…no allowance after all. Although, she reflected, Robert was honourable. He would surely see her looked after.

Abruptly she felt a wave of longing for her old life. Despite the hard work and her insecurities there had been a rhythm to her days, a pattern to her future. Now all was uncertain.

I have become too comfortable here. It is long past the time when I should have gone home. But home? Where is home?

All too easily she had settled into Beechmount Hall. Her grandfather's illness and death had been a fatiguing, intense, almost feverish process that, she believed, had changed her in some way. When Papa had died, she had naturally been distressed, but she had not lost anyone close to her since then.

Getting to know her grandfather had been a precious adventure. Through him she had come to know something of her grandmother, and their life here when Papa was a child. She hugged the knowledge to her.

No matter what, I am glad I came here.

Inevitably the thought immediately led to one person: Robert. With Mama coming for her there would be no need for Robert to accompany her on the journey back home. The realisation hit her like a blow. The thought of five full days in his company had been sustaining her through the notion of the goodbyes that would come at each end of that journey—first saying farewell to Beechmount Hall and its residents, and then—heartbreakingly—bidding adieu to Robert himself.

Now all her imaginings were worthless.

Days spent alone with him in the carriage…

Intimate evenings dining in inns…

All lost.

Mrs Millthorpe returned then, giving Mrs Kendal the chance to dash upstairs for a short nap. They had all been sleeping like cats since Sunday—short naps in chairs and an occasional longer spell in bed. Even Jane, who had become accustomed to early starts and late nights as a lady's maid, was finding it a trial. How much more difficult must it be for the others, who were used to sleeping late any time they needed to?

Mrs Millthorpe looked pale and weary, and Jane's heart filled with compassion for her. She ordered tea, and made her hostess comfortable before picking up her work again. They sat in companionable silence for a time, before Mrs Millthorpe spoke directly to Jane—something that had become increasingly common since her grandfather's illness.

'Miss Bailey… Jane.'

Jane looked up.

'I am glad you are here. Glad my husband was able to meet you before he died.'

There was a lump in Jane's throat. 'Thank you. I shall be gone soon, for my mother is already on her way to fetch me. But I, too, am glad I came.'

'Oh, but—' Mrs Millthorpe stopped abruptly. 'Never mind.'

She would say no more, and they both returned to their tasks.

Mr Edward Hubert Millthorpe was laid to rest on a blustery Sunday in March. He had a gratifying turn-out for his funeral, and the ladies stood on the steps in silence, watching the cortège leave Beechmount Hall for his final journey.

The carriages were pulled by perfectly matched Belgian Blacks, each horse wearing a nodding headdress of ostrich plumes provided by the Featherman. The bearers and pages all wore matching black cloaks, gloves and hatbands, with the pages each carrying the customary wand.

No expense had been spared, and Robert had been busy with the funeral furnisher, arranging payments to everyone from the bell-ringers to the coffin-maker and the upholder.

Grandfather would have been proud.

Robert led the funeral procession and every gentleman from the district was in attendance—and some ladies. Dressed all in black, save for his snowy-white shirt and cravat, Robert looked fine and handsome. He had handled the business well, and Jane knew how much Mrs Millthorpe had relied on him.

He will make an excellent master for Beechmount Hall.

Jane's eyes clung to the line of carriages until they were out of view. A robin chirped from a nearby branch, his song the only relief amid the unbearable sadness of goodbye. Was that the same robin she had seen through the window the day she had first conversed with her grandfather? She liked the thought, and held to it with quiet composure.

Finally, there was nothing more to see, and the three ladies turned and stepped inside.

After all the busyness of the past days the house seemed eerily silent. Jane would feel unsettled, she knew, until Robert returned. Part of her was seeking her grandfather still, her mind suggesting he was simply having a rest upstairs. She had to remind herself often that he was truly gone.

Many of the mourners would return to Beechmount Hall later for the funeral meal—food, drink and an exchange of memories of its old master. But, knowing there was nothing for them to do at present, the ladies slowly climbed the stairs to their chambers.

Strangely, Jane could not rest. She had barely seen Robert these past days, had not once been alone with him, and the absence of him was an ache in her heart.

How shall I manage when I return to Ledbury House?

She shed a tear, and then another, but was unsure why she was crying. Was it at the impending loss of Robert, grief at losing grandfather, or self-pity for herself? In truth, everything was jumbled together in a single monstrous cannonball of pain inside her.

After turning restlessly in her bed for two hours, she admitted defeat and went downstairs. She found sanctuary in the Blue Parlour. Curling up in her grandmother's armchair, she finally closed her eyes.

'Jane, you are needed in the library,' said Mrs Kendal, bustling into the room.

Jane had taken to reading in the Blue Parlour in the afternoons, desperate to engrave the room and its portrait into her memory during these final days.

It had been two days since the funeral, and by Jane's calculations her mama would arrive on the morrow. Jane had not written to her since receiving her last letter, as any further letters would not reach her. Jane was spending most of her time trying to avoid the thought of being separated from Robert for ever.

'Yes, of course,' she replied, rising. 'What is amiss?'

'My uncle's lawyer is here, with his clerk. They want all of us—including you. The lawyer is to read my uncle's will.'

'Me?'

Why me?

It was all rather bewildering.

She followed Mrs Kendal to her grandfather's library. Her eyes instinctively went to his favourite chair by the fireplace. It was empty, of course.

Grandfather is gone.

Blinking away the sudden stinging in her eyes, she quickly surveyed the room. Mrs Millthorpe was there, looking tired but calm. And two men who must be the lawyer and his clerk—one an elderly gentleman, the other in his thirties—sat together on hard chairs, a small table between them containing a stack of papers.

On the yellow satin settee near the window Robert sat, long legs outstretched. Her eyes drank in every detail of his appearance, from his dark hair—*I have touched that with my own two hands*—his unsmiling, handsome features—*I remember the feeling of his lips on mine*—to his broad shoulders encased in a jacket of dark grey superfine...

'Miss Jane Bailey?' The older man, presumably the lawyer, was addressing her.

'I beg your pardon? Oh, yes, I am Jane Bailey.'

He nodded, and made a note on the paper in front of him. Mrs Kendal sat next to her aunt in a pair of twin armchairs, and Jane chose the straw-coloured settee near the lawyer. Her grandfather's chair remained empty.

In the silence that followed Jane was aware of a curious sense of apprehension in the air. On the mantel, the clock began to strike the hour.

The lawyer, his features expressionless, picked up a parchment from the table. 'We are gathered today for the reading of Mr Millthorpe's last will and testament. He specifically requested that all of you be present. Ah... I should inform you he made a new will just days before he died.'

Jane sat up straighter. *A new will?*

'The will was properly made and witnessed, and its contents were discussed with Mrs Millthorpe at the time, I believe.'

Mrs Millthorpe inclined her head. 'That is correct.'

The lawyer began. Following the preamble there were gifts and legacies to Mrs Kendal, and to various servants and tenants—including his valet. Some of these were surprisingly liberal. Despite his quarrelsome mask, her grandfather had shown true generosity.

The lawyer paused before beginning the next part. '"I give unto my wife…"'

Mrs Millthorpe was to receive a generous sum, including an annuity, as well as the freedom to 'take up residence with her sister in Knaresborough, should she so wish'.

'Oh, Eugenia!' Mrs Kendal could not hold back. 'I am so delighted for you!'

'Thank you, my dear. It was one of many items we discussed. Of course as a widow I am free to live where I wish, but it is gratifying that his blessing has been included in the will.' She addressed the lawyer. 'Pray continue.'

The lawyer cleared his throat. '"The remainder of my estate, including the property known as Beechmount Hall, its estates, farms and income, as well as…"'

He continued, listing the entirety of Mr Millthorpe's fortune, which was significant.

This, then, would be Robert's part, thought Jane. Beechmount Hall had impressed her, but she'd had no idea her grandfather had been such a wealthy man.

The lawyer had reached the end of the list of assets.

'"All of this I give jointly unto my granddaughter, Miss Jane Bailey, and my wife's great-nephew, Mr Robert Kendal—"'

Mrs Kendal gasped.

Jane was speechless.

What? What did he just say? He couldn't possibly have said—

'Jointly!' Mrs Kendal looked as shocked as Jane felt.

'I have not yet finished.' The lawyer spoke quietly, drawing all eyes to him. 'There is a condition.'

He found his place in the document again.

'"…jointly unto my granddaughter, Miss Jane Bailey, and my wife's great-nephew, Mr Robert Kendal, on the condition that they be married to each other within two months of the date of my death."'

Robert leapt to his feet. 'Outrageous!'

'Sit down, Robert.' His mother spoke calmly, a considering expression on her face. She turned to her aunt. 'He discussed this with you?'

Mrs Millthorpe nodded. 'He did. I think it will serve very well. It is time Robert settled down, and who better for him than my husband's only remaining blood relative? I had concerns at first, but Jane has shown herself to be both pretty-behaved and accomplished. An unexceptional match, I think.'

'What happens if we do not marry according to my uncle's edict?' Robert, with a face like thunder, bit out the words. He had *not* sat down.

The lawyer consulted the document. 'There is a provision for a situation in which one or both of you is already married to someone else, but that is not relevant here… Ah! Here we are!' He adopted a formal tone. '"In the circumstance in which the marriage between Mr Kendal and Miss Bailey fails to take place by the required date, I give the previously detailed assets unto my wife."'

'I do not want them,' confirmed Mrs Millthorpe.

Jane, lost in complete bewilderment, had been watching Robert. His shoulders were stiff, his face pale, and a muscle was working in his cheek. She had sensed his shock and anger at the first revelation, and knew he was barely containing it.

Robert ran a hand through his hair. 'My uncle is attempting to force his will upon me and upon Miss Bailey!'

Although Robert was speaking of her, he was not looking in her direction.

'Even from the grave,' Robert continued, 'he plays with us like a cat with mice.'

Reality was beginning to dawn on Jane. Why had her grandfather done such a thing? She could not be mistress of Beechmount Hall! And he should not have included that condition.

Her hands were trembling, and the world seemed to be spinning slightly. Dazedly, she raised a trembling hand to her head.

Robert finally glanced at her. He made a strangled sound in his throat. 'Hell, damn and blast it!'

'Robert! Such language!'

His mother's rebuke fell on empty air. He was already striding to the door, clearly believing he could not stay without disgracing himself.

The door shut loudly behind him.

He was gone.

Chapter Twenty-Seven

The next hour passed in something of a haze. The lawyer completed the reading of the will, which included a message for Mrs Kendal. It contained the strong indication that her role was to encourage and support her son.

'He means me to assist in making this marriage happen…' Mrs Kendal said aloud what was clear to them all.

'He held you in high regard.' Mrs Millthorpe patted her niece's hand comfortingly. 'I hope you understand that?'

'Oh, I do!' Mrs Kendal rubbed a thoughtful finger along her jaw. 'But he should know Robert is more easily led than commanded.'

Mrs Millthorpe chuckled. 'They are—*were*—alike in many ways. My husband's preferred tactic was to command. You know that.'

'Indeed. But my son cannot be coerced. Despite his outwardly placid nature he is made of steel.' She joined Jane on the settee. 'How do you, Jane?'

'I…' Words failed her. She tried again. 'I hope you understand I never sought this? I—'

Mrs Kendal took her hand. Her eyes flicked to the lawyer, then back again. 'We shall discuss it later.'

Outside, the sound of hooves on gravel indicated that Robert had already changed his clothes and was off on his stallion. Jane could not resist looking towards the window. How striking he was! How proud! And how angry…

He disappeared from view and Jane discovered Mrs Kendal was eyeing her keenly. Then that lady nodded decisively and murmured to herself, 'Mishandled completely, of course… But my uncle was not known for delicacy in such matters. Still, I think I can contrive very well…'

The lawyer and his clerk eventually took their leave, promising to visit again when everything became 'rather clearer'.

As soon as she could, Jane made her excuses and left for the safety of her chamber, to rest before dinner. As she walked she could sense the heightened interest and curious looks of the servants. Only Umpelby, when she passed him in the hall, remained inscrutable.

Oh, they all know something is occurring! Jane thought, with a hint of bitterness.

How many times had she herself been curious about a visitor, or anxious about something to do with her mistress? Oh, never purely for gossip—unlike some of her colleagues. For her the curiosity had always been imbued with loyalty and concern. Never before had *she* been the subject of such scrutiny.

Unsurprisingly, Nancy followed her to her chamber soon afterwards. The other servants would have told her that Miss Bailey had gone upstairs. When she arrived, Jane braced herself for some indirect or artful questioning, but Nancy remained her useful cheerful self, settling Jane for a lie-down and promising to freshen and press the black dress while she was resting.

There was little likelihood of her sleeping. Despite this anxious to be alone, Jane complied, lying down on top of the bed in her shift, with a soft blanket over her. Nancy had already pulled the curtains and lit the fire.

As the door closed behind her Jane expected a hundred thoughts to come flying through her mind, yet only one did.

I wonder when Robert will return home?

She closed her eyes.

Robert pushed Blacklock as hard as he had ever done. Thankfully, the stallion was equal to it. And as they soared through the countryside Robert felt the tension in his shoul ders begin to ease, the black rage begin to dissipate, and finally he began to think clearly.

He had spent the first part of his ride cursing aloud in the strongest and most offensive terms possible. His dear departed uncle had come in for particular criticism, along with his aunt and the entire profession of lawyers. Mostly, though, he was angry with himself.

Damnation! I saw the possibility of this type of complication on the horizon, yet I failed to act.

He slowed Blacklock to a trot, curving around the edge of the field.

Robert had thought his uncle would bequeath everything to Jane. Or possibly everything to Robert, with a requirement to look after Jane. He had never anticipated *this* outrageous nonsense. To force a marriage on his own granddaughter! Why, it was positively medieval!

He shook his head. He was guilty of arrogance, of blindness, and of extraordinary folly. Of course his aunt would have pleaded with him not to cut Robert out. Yet his uncle, having seen Jane's true value, had had to act in her interests. He began to appreciate his uncle's dilemma.

But, dash it all! Why did he not speak to me about it?

There would be a hundred compromises in terms of splitting the estate. He frowned, thinking it through. The estate generated a decent income precisely because of its scale. To disentangle one part from another would potentially compromise the whole.

Very well, then, he continued silently, *you could have left me the house and lands and made Jane a considerable heiress by giving her your fortune.*

But there were two problems with this. First, the savings in the bank were a safety fund against possible hard times, and second, what would a young serving maid and her widowed mother, a housekeeper, know of such matters?

Robert understood Mrs Bailey to be a woman of sense, but she could not have had any experience of the world that

Jane would be thrust into as an heiress in extremely comfortable circumstances.

Fortune-hunters.

His next thought would also have been in his uncle's consideration. As a lady's maid, Jane might eventually marry a footman, a groom, or a valet… His gut twisted at the very notion. As a wealthy and beautiful young lady of quality she would instantly be besieged by the worst rakes, bloods and gazetted fortune-hunters.

Including me, perhaps?

Ah, but I am different! I truly love her.

His own thoughts sounded hollow.

How is she ever to know that?

Besides, he acknowledged to his unseen uncle in a more subdued tone, *you want her to make Beechmount Hall her home, don't you?*

He recalled his uncle's pleasure on that day when he had shared the keepsakes from his first wife and his son. That was the day Robert had asked Jane about the possibility of living apart from her mother. Jane had been adamant it was out of the question. Might that now change?

He shook his head. He had absolutely no notion.

Finally, he allowed himself to remember her pale, bewildered face after the will had been read. Jane had really had no idea.

No matter what, her days as a lady's maid were at an end. Did she understand that? While part of him was delighted that she would never more scrub clothing or wait on someone else, he could not yet see a way through this muddle of his uncle's creating.

The irony, of course, was that marrying Jane was his greatest wish. His heart's desire. And yet if marriage was forced on her it would surely break the fragile connection that had been building between them.

The entire situation was a complete disaster.

And he had not the least idea how to mend it.

* * *

Nancy had been as good as her word. Jane's black dress had been freshened and pressed. It now clung to her form perfectly, and there was not a speck of mud on the hem, nor any imperfection elsewhere.

It makes me look pale, she noted, seeing her own reflection as Nancy dressed her hair. *Paler than I feel.*

In truth, she was feeling curiously calm, given the momentous events of the afternoon. Naturally she was gratified that her grandfather had included her in his will. It meant the connection she had felt with him had been present on his part, too. But an altogether different connection was currently occupying her mind.

Robert.

At a stroke, her grandfather had removed the remaining distance in their stations. As an heiress she would be accepted everywhere. Money opened doors that character could not.

She knew enough of Robert to see that he already respected her. Indeed, she had had to remind him on numerous occasions that she was a servant. He had never treated her as inferior to him.

Yet it was one thing to treat a guest with respect and quite another to marry her! Particularly in a forced marriage that, judging by his heated reaction, was abhorrent to him.

Her grandfather had probably believed it was for the best.

Gratitude, affection and annoyance at his high-handedness battled within her. To cut Robert out in such a way! How could he do such a thing? Until a few short weeks ago Robert had had the expectation of being sole heir. How it must grate to lose his place to a near-stranger—and a servant at that!

Much as her heart danced at the very notion of marrying him, it was impossible to think of him being *compelled* into doing so. She only wished to marry him if he genuinely wished to marry *her*.

Distantly, she heard the dinner gong sound.

'I am late!'

She allowed Nancy to place one final pin in her coiffure, then descended in some haste.

The others had already entered the dining room. Breathless, she took her usual seat beside Robert, without looking at him directly. Murmuring a general greeting, she devoted her attention to her food and took a minimal part in the conversation. There was simply too much going on in her mind, and she felt intensely uncomfortable being seated next to the man she had wronged through her very existence.

If only I could speak to him properly!

The evening ritual continued. After the meal—which Jane had barely tasted—the ladies retired to the salon, leaving Robert alone with his port. As they rose Jane saw Mrs Millthorpe glance briefly at her grandfather's empty chair, her eyes suspiciously bright.

The will was not referred to by any of the ladies, which strengthened the air of unreality about the situation that was now taking hold of Jane's mind.

Had it really happened?

Perhaps the whole thing had been driven by her imaginings!

But Mrs Millthorpe's next comment brought her sharply back to reality.

'I shall travel to Knaresborough on the morrow, to discuss my move there. My sister wishes to buy new furniture and re-do the hangings in what will be my chamber, and she has invited a number of merchants to call the day after.'

The other two ladies then engaged in a comprehensive discussion about closets, curtains, beds and wall-hangings, to which Jane contributed only occasionally.

Mrs Millthorpe was truly leaving! It would be the end of an epoch here at Beechmount Hall. Although in truth, she realised, with her grandfather's death that had already come to pass. A new age was about to begin.

She could sense anxiety among the servants. Were they worried that some of them would be let go under the new master or mistress? Henby and Eliza were to accompany Mrs Millthorpe to live in Knaresborough, but the others—particularly the junior house servants—were awaiting news.

So many lives depend upon what Robert and I do next.

For a moment she allowed herself the indulgence of imagining herself as Robert's wife—a wife he loved. Her heart skipped as hopeful memories persuaded her to believe that he felt something for her. Their kisses... The way he looked at her sometimes... The friendship they had forged in the carriage during the journey that now seemed a life-time ago...

With a sense of shock she reminded herself that it had been just a few short weeks since they had met. Surely she knew enough of the world to understand that young men often indulged in warm flirtations with no thought of love?

He joined them then, and their eyes met briefly when he entered the salon. His blazed with some unknown emotion before he glanced away, leaving her feeling both deflated and anxious.

Mrs Millthorpe and Mrs Kendal also shared some unspoken communication, before Mrs Kendal said brightly, 'Do draw up a chair near the fire, Robert, for it is particularly cold tonight!'

Her grandfather's chair had been moved to the wall. Without commenting, Robert lifted a different armchair into the space where her grandfather's usually stood and sat in it. Jane nodded. There was a sense of *rightness* about it.

How could her grandfather allow anyone to supplant Robert as the rightful master of Beechmount Hall? It did not bear thinking about.

That night, sleep would not come easily, she knew.

Tomorrow... Tomorrow I shall speak with him and discover whether our fate is entwined or not.

Chapter Twenty-Eight

Having lain awake for an age, ruminating on the seemingly unsolvable riddle facing her, Jane had eventually fallen into a fitful sleep. It did her no good, though, and it was almost a relief when Nancy arrived to bring her morning tea and reset the fire.

Jane was no closer to knowing what she might say to Robert, but her stomach was already churning with the knowledge that the conversation would likely happen this very morning.

When Nancy pulled back the curtains and opened the shutters Jane discovered the day was bright and clear, with pale March sunlight arrowing its way into her chamber. It reminded her of that similar day last month—the day Robert had arrived at Ledbury House.

How much has occurred since then! And how much I have been altered by it all.

As she descended the stairs she felt a strange sense of familiarity, of completeness—as if that day was somehow the mirror of this one.

Mr Kendal had been out riding, Nancy had informed her, but was now returned.

Carefully calculating the likely amount of time it would take him to wash and change, she waited in the Blue Parlour. He knew it was her habit to read there in the mornings. Surely he must seek her out? They did, after all, have important topics to discuss.

A book was in her lap, open, but she could not take in one word. Inside, her heart was racing, her pulse tumultuous, and her mouth was dry.

The next hour may well decide the course of my life.

And so, when a scratching came on the door, she sat up straight, took a breath and said, in a reassuringly clear voice, 'Enter!'

It was the second footman.

'Visitors for you, miss,' he said, before announcing, 'Lady Kingswood and Mrs Bailey.'

Mama! And Miss Marianne!

In all the drama she had temporarily forgotten that Mama would be here today. She rose, a glad smile breaking over her face. A moment later she was enveloped in Mama's warm embrace. And Miss Marianne also gave her a spontaneous hug.

They both looked wonderful. Miss Marianne was wearing her warm brown pelisse over the green silk day dress, while Mama was attired in her customary dark grey, her lace cap firmly in place.

They exclaimed, and greeted her, and kissed her, gave their condolences on the death of Mr Millthorpe, and then admired Jane's new side curls.

She patted them with more than a little embarrassment. 'My—my grandfather insisted I accompany the family to a soirée at one of the neighbouring houses...'

'Oh, how delightful!' Miss Marianne was all smiles at this news. 'Did you wear the amber silk? Although it is, perhaps, a little plain for such an evening.'

Just like Miss Marianne—straight to the point.

'No. We—two of the other servants and I—made a dress. Or we remade an old dress that used to belong to my grandmother. The one in that painting, in fact.'

Mama was frowning. What did she *truly* think about the Millthorpes? About being here at all?

'I was pleased to learn a little of Papa's history while I was here,' she offered tentatively.

'It is strange being here in Beechmount Hall,' Mama mused. 'Your papa was raised a gentleman, and he might have inherited all of this if he had not married me.'

How do I explain about the will?

'It was not something I fully understood when I was young and he was courting me,' Mama went on, looking pensive. 'He under-spoke, I think, when he talked of his home and his family. I had not expected anything so grand.'

No one mentioned money, but it was clear to all of them that there was wealth here.

'Later,' Mama continued, 'I felt guilty about the break with his family, but he always reassured me.'

She glanced around, taking in the Aubusson rug, the paintings, the exquisite furniture and the air of care and cleanliness about the room.

She looked again at the portrait. 'So that is my Ned as a child? I can see the likeness.'

'It is. Apparently he spent many hours in this room during his childhood. It was his mother's favourite parlour.'

They sat together on the long settee, talking for a while about Papa, and the discoveries Jane had made about his life here.

'I can see exactly how the estrangement happened,' she concluded. 'My grandfather was extremely strong-willed, and tended to state his opinions in animated terms. I believe,' she reflected, 'he had regrets about what happened.'

Mama sorted. 'Regrets are all very well. Where was he when your papa was dying? When you were being raised a servant?'

Jane knew better than to try to persuade her. 'I know. It seems he did not know that Papa had changed his name. And at least he brought me here before he died.'

'I am sorry, Jane.' Miss Marianne patted her hand. 'I know you only knew him for a short time, but in a sense he was part of you.'

'Yes. Yes, he was.' Jane sent an anxious glance towards Mama. 'But it does not make me any less your daughter, Mama.'

'Of course not!' Mama hugged her. 'I saw the hurt your

papa carried with him always. I think he would be pleased you came here and that the enmity was put to an end.'

'Your letters were most informative, Jane,' said Lady Kingswood, sharing an intent look with Mama.

What?

'Indeed they were,' Mama echoed. 'We feel we know so much about your life here. Your letters were full of your grandfather and his second wife, and Mr Kendal and his mother. Your sorrow at Mr Millthorpe's death came through very clearly, too, along with…with other things. Tell me, are the family at home?'

'Mrs Millthorpe has left for Knaresborough, to visit her sister. The others are here, though.'

'Good.' Again, they exchanged a glance. 'Tell me truly, daughter, were you welcomed here? Did anyone treat you badly because you were raised a servant?'

Memories flashed through her mind.

Mrs Millthorpe speaking French and commenting on my hands.

Eliza refusing to serve me.

Marmaduke Haw and his treatment of me.

Then came other recollections.

Mrs Millthorpe later.

Nancy's kindness.

Umpelby's welcome.

Miss Dodsworth.

Grandfather.

Mrs Kendal.

Robert.

'I have been made most welcome and treated with warm kindness.'

They were watching her closely. 'I am glad of it,' said Mama simply.

Jane smiled. 'But what has made you travel all the way here? When I got your letter I was astounded.' She addressed Lady Kingswood. 'And I did not know you were also coming!'

'I have never before visited the north,' said Miss Marianne. 'I aim to see some notable places and scenic beauty while I am here. I thought it a good opportunity to travel with Mrs Bailey now spring is coming.'

This seemed unlikely, but Jane had no choice but to accept Miss Marianne's statement. At least they would not be in a hurry to return to Ledbury House.

'I simply wanted to see you,' said Mama. 'In your last letter you talked of your grandfather's illness. Such conditions might last for years, and I wanted to be here when you decided for how long you were going to stay—or indeed whether you would return at all.'

Jane gasped. So the possibility was already in her mind! Could she then tell her that she dearly wished to stay without hurting her feelings?

She opened her mouth to speak, then closed it again.

Nothing is settled with Robert. He may or may not want this marriage. No, I cannot yet speak about this.

Instead she said simply, 'Yes, but my grandfather survived only a few days after the stroke. He would not have wished to live as an invalid, I think.'

'No, indeed. From what I know of him, he was a proud man.'

'He was.'

Wistfully, Jane remembered her grandfather's eyes—always assessing, judging, watching, occasionally revealing the quick thoughts flying through his animated mind.

'He had a good death, if such a thing is possible.'

'It is—and I am glad.'

Jane smiled gratefully and on they sat, exchanging news of Ledbury House and the latest doings of the family, as well as tales of their journey north. It was so good to see them both again.

But she still needed to speak to Robert.

Chapter Twenty-Nine

Robert had ordered a bath after his ride. Although he was desperate to speak to Jane, part of him was focused on delaying, in case an inspiring form of words should come to him. He dressed with care, feeling nervous and unaccustomedly unsure. He had never made an offer of marriage before. Any man would be nervous on such an occasion. And, thanks to his uncle's meddling, he could not be sure of her feelings on the matter.

If it were as simple as a man and a woman deciding whether to marry then he would, he knew, be much more assured. The connection between them was undeniable. He felt it deep within his bones. It was a heady mix of desire, admiration and deep friendship—in his view the perfect recipe for a good marriage. Even if she did not yet love him.

No, it was worldly matters that threatened to separate them. Her previous status as a servant and the way she continually referred to it. Her potential separation from her mother, her home at Ledbury House and her much-loved employer. The compulsion that his uncle had laid upon them both.

But none of these things was insurmountable, he believed, and he was determined to persuade her on each of them as needed.

Still rehearsing arguments in his head, he descended to the ground floor—where he was informed of Miss Bailey's visitors. This halted his progress immediately.

He stood in the hallway, rubbing a thoughtful finger along his jaw. 'I see… Yes. Thank you, Umpelby…'

The butler coughed discreetly.

'Yes, Umpelby?'

'Might Lady Kingswood enjoy refreshments in the salon with Miss Bailey and possibly Mrs Kendal?'

Robert looked at him blankly, then realised what Umpelby meant. 'An excellent notion! Can you inform my mother?' He grinned. 'Now to manage the rest of it!'

Umpelby bowed, a hint of a twinkle in his eye. 'I have every confidence in you, sir.'

'Hrrmph!' Robert marched on towards the Blue Parlour with renewed vigour.

Yes, this could work very well.

There was a knock on the door. This time it *was* Robert. In a swift appraisal Jane drank in every inch of his appearance—long muscular legs, flat stomach, broad shoulders, handsome face and damp hair. Today he was wearing buckskin breeches, a silver-grey waistcoat, and a superfine clawhammer jacket in charcoal-grey. He looked, to her eyes, like a Greek god.

'Lady Kingswood! And Mrs Bailey! What a pleasure to see you both!'

His face creased in a welcoming smile, he bowed to the ladies. Then, sitting with them in seeming ease, he accepted their condolences, asked about their health, and questioned them a little regarding their journey north.

There was a pause.

'Mrs Bailey,' he said with a casual air, 'there is something I particularly wish to speak to you about. I know my mother is now going to the salon, where she will be serving refreshments. Might I suggest that you, Miss Bailey, accompany Lady Kingswood there and we shall follow you shortly?'

'Of course.'

Jane's mind was immediately flooded with possibilities. *Will he speak to Mama of the will? Of Papa or Grandfather? Does he actually intend to make me an offer?*

This last thought was so disturbing it threatened to quite

overcome her. She barely heard Lady Kingswood's enthusiastic assent, so focused was she on trying to decipher his intent. But Mama looked perfectly comfortable with the notion of speaking to him.

She led Miss Marianne to the salon, where Mrs Kendal was indeed there to greet them. Tea was served, and cake, and again Jane was reminded of that first day she had met Robert, when she had spilled pastries all over Miss Marianne's carpet.

The ladies talked, and Jane contributed occasionally, but her mind was in the Blue Parlour, where her mama and the man she loved were discussing matters unknown.

Finally, the door opened to admit Mama.

'Jane, might I speak with you for a moment?'

Jane agreed with alacrity, and followed Mama out to the corridor. Umpelby was there, standing back at a suitable distance. He must have led Mama to the salon.

But where was Robert?

Mama took both her hands. 'I have been told about the will. Tell me, daughter, do you want this marriage?'

Jane did not hesitate. 'With all my heart. But not if Robert is compelled into it against his will.'

'I think you may be easy on that score,' Mama replied wryly. 'We shall speak more later. Go now. He is waiting for you in the room with the portrait.'

Jane could not go without asking the question burning on her lips. 'When I left Ledbury House you gave me a note. It said—'

'*Never forget who you are.* Yes.'

'So how can I possibly go from lady's maid to mistress of—' she gestured '—a place like this?'

Mama shook her head. 'Because neither of those things are who you truly are. They are only what you *do*, how the world names you. What I wish is for you to be true to who you are. The essential Jane. In that sense it matters not whether we are servants, royals, or anything in between.

You have every right to be your papa's daughter and at the same time to be proud of your achievements when you were a servant. Do you understand?'

'I think so.' Jane's view of her mother became blurred with sudden tears. 'Oh, Mama, why are you so *wise*?'

They hugged, and Mama wiped her tears away.

'Go, child. You have my blessing.'

Jane's heart was pounding as she reached the Blue Parlour. Entirely conscious that momentous events were occurring, she took a deep breath, then entered.

There he is!

Her heart skipped as it always did on seeing him. He was not seated, but rather pacing up and down in some agitation.

'Jane!' He came straight to her, taking both her hands. 'I have spoken to your mother about the situation we find ourselves in.'

This was not particularly promising.

'Yes…?'

'We have agreed that it is a damnab— a dashed inconvenience that my uncle's will says what it says.'

Inconvenience?

'In what way?' Her voice sounded remarkably even.

'Dash it all! I knew I might make a mull of it!' He took a breath. 'Before my uncle's illness I already knew he might make you his heiress, and I was at peace with it. All of this should have come to your father. It was never mine.'

'But you said yourself that no one ever talked of Papa. And you are known as the Young Master by all the servants. Surely you had expectations?'

His expression turned rueful. 'It is true that everyone— including my uncle—made lazy assumptions about my taking over after his death. But then his Runner found you, and that changed everything. I have seen the Runner's report, you know. It was among the papers I am going through with the lawyer. In it you are described as "unmarried, virtuous and handsome".' He grimaced. 'Would my uncle have sent for you otherwise?'

Jane was surprised into laughter. 'I suspect not!'

'Indeed. Now, why do you think he insisted I must travel all the way to Bedfordshire to fetch you myself?'

Her eyes widened. 'He wished for us to spend time together! Why, the sly old—' She broke off, unwilling to speak ill of the dead.

'Precisely. I think he had this in mind from the start. And when he saw how superior you are it remained only to test you in public.'

'The soirée?' she said.

Robert thinks me superior. That is a good thing.

'Yes. Deliberately he did not assist you. He did not offer money for a gown, nor lessons in correct behaviour. He simply waited to see how you would do.'

'I was so nervous.'

'And yet you were more than capable. In fact, you were a success. But I shall tell you something now. When you sang, I think he knew he loved you.'

'He did?' She tried to recall. Remembered her grandfather's tears. 'I reminded him of his first wife...'

He nodded, swallowing hard. 'I know my uncle dictated his new will only a few days afterwards. His intention, clearly, was that we should marry and share Beechmount Hall and everything else.'

Here it is...

'I cannot cut you out of the inheritance that should rightly be yours.' She lifted her chin, determined to do the right thing.

'And I shall say exactly the same to you.'

They looked at each other.

'So we are at an impasse,' he said.

'Is there no other way? Some clause? Some option...? I do not like to see you forced into a marriage that you do not want.'

'Again, I shall mirror that back to you.'

That is true!

'So what can we do?'

'Well, we have two options, it seems.' He led her to the settee and sat beside her. 'We can ignore the will and walk away, or…' He lifted her hand. 'We can marry.'

'You would marry a former servant girl?'

'Your father did, and seems not to have regretted it.' His smile faded. 'Of *course* I would marry you, Jane. Why, it has always been you who has kept reminding me of your status. From the start I have thought of you as my equal.'

She nodded. 'But will they cut you if you marry me?'

'Who?'

'Your neighbours. Your friends. Society. Some of them do not yet know that I am—or was—a servant.'

'You saw the response at the soirée. Some were surprised, but you soon won them over with your gracious manners and your song. I do not anticipate any difficulty.'

She gave him a sceptical look.

'Truly! I think perhaps you overestimate my own status. I am nothing more than a country gentleman in the north of England. I have no title, and no desire to move among the *haut ton* of London. Who is to say whom I should marry?'

Strangely, this made sense.

'Now,' he continued, 'there is one objection that I myself must make, and it is an important one.'

Her heart sank. *What objection?*

'I have seen first-hand the close affection between you and your mother, and indeed between you and Lady Kingswood. I know you and your mother have never before been apart, and you told me yourself in this very room that you saw your place as being with her. It seems to me that in deciding what we must do we must give strong consideration to this.'

'Oh, but—' She stopped.

She had been about to say, *But I will leave behind m*

home, my employer, and even my mother, if only we can have a marriage of love.

'I therefore took the opportunity for a discussion with your mother just now.'

'You did?' Shock made her voice quiver a little.

'Apparently she and Lady Kingswood had discussed this very possibility during their journey north. They seem to have the impression that you and I had forged a firm friendship.'

'Oh!' She felt her cheeks turn a fiery red.

I did not realise my letters had been so revealing.

'Lady Kingswood has already resigned herself to losing both her maid *and* her housekeeper.'

'She—she has?'

He nodded. 'Your mother has declared that she will leave Ledbury House and move to Yorkshire, should you desire it.'

It was too much. Sudden tears started in her eyes.

That Mama would do such a thing for me!

'She made it very plain,' he continued, 'that you must be content to choose this marriage without compulsion.'

Jane nodded. 'Very well. I am content.' Her tone was brisk, businesslike.

This is not how I thought I would be agreeing to marry.

'Capital!' He matched her tone. 'I shall see to it that all the arrangements are made.'

'Thank you.'

There was an awkward silence.

'Right. Let us go to the salon and share our news.'

He offered his arm.

She took it, conscious of an air of unreality.

Am I truly going to marry him? My heart's desire? And yet all I want to do is cry...

Chapter Thirty

They were married a month later, in the chapel at Arkendale. There had been a flurry of interest in the district when the banns had first been read, and Jane and Robert had endured visits from almost every notable family in the area.

Emma Dodsworth had been delighted, the Haws politely cynical, and Mr John Foster teasing.

'I knew it!' he declared. 'I sensed it that night at our soirée!'

Robert had growled some noncommittal response, but Jane had taken some encouragement from Robert's friend's assessment.

I did think that night that Robert was developing warm feelings for me. Oh, please let it be so!

As she repeated her vows in the chapel, wearing a modest black silk dress, Jane was struck by the same air of unreality that had smitten her on the day they had agreed to wed.

Who is he? And who am I to be marrying him?

He placed a ring on her trembling finger and gave her a reassuring half-smile. She simply looked at him, incapable of responding. She was lost between hope, anxiety, and somewhere deep inside a glow of happiness that she was marrying the man she truly loved.

Many marriages begin as a family arrangement, she reminded herself. *Particularly among the quality. Often they work out just fine.*

In truth, her sense of who she was felt distant, unclear. At times she felt as though she was leaving herself behind. As if Jane the serving maid was no more.

At a stroke, she was taking on an entirely new life. Mistress of Beechmount Hall. Wife to the man she loved.

Someone who gave instructions rather than followed them. Someone with responsibilities for an entire house and its staff.

From now on she would share Robert's bed and work on winning his heart. Perhaps they would even have children...

She focused again on the immediate challenge—that of the bed. Tonight she would lie with him.

What if the terror comes upon me? What if I cannot easily fulfil my responsibilities as a wife?

Mama had had no advice for her beyond bidding her enjoy her marital duties.

Ah, but yours was a love-match, Mama. And you had not previously been terrorised by a man.

After trying and failing to reassure herself that all would be well, Jane decided simply to avoid thoughts of what lay ahead tonight.

Robert had been unexpectedly distant with her during the short weeks of their betrothal. He was busy, he'd said, with estate matters—and indeed there was seemingly much to be addressed. But even in the evenings he had remained merely unfailingly civil towards her. Kisses had been limited to salutations on her hand or her cheek. He had made no attempt to share with her any of those passionate, intimate kisses she craved, and which might have reassured her about the mating that was to come.

So now she smiled at the wedding breakfast, and said all that was proper, and hid from the world her quaking anxiety about what lay ahead.

Finally, the wedding night was upon her.

She retired after supper, feeling decidedly awkward and more than a little anxious. Nancy helped her prepare for bed in her new chamber—the one that had been Mrs Millthorpe's. The adjoining chamber, which she still thought of as belonging to her grandfather, was now occupied by Robert.

With Nancy gone, Jane lay alone in the huge bed, the

covers pulled up to her chin, and tried to be calm. It was, of course, impossible.

By the time Robert scratched on the door connecting their chambers, she was trembling from head to toe.

'Come in!' she managed.

The door opened.

He stood framed in the doorway, taking in the scene. He had removed his boots, jacket and waistcoat, and his cravat was hanging loosely on his chest. Despite her fears, Jane felt a thrill of excitement on seeing his handsome face and strong shape.

My husband!

In his hands he held a bottle of wine and two glasses. 'Come,' he said, indicating the chairs by the fire. 'Have a drink with me.'

Yes. I can do that.

Turning back the covers, she slid out of bed and padded closer to the fire. She felt both vulnerable and positively indecent in her thin nightgown.

'Thank you.'

Her voice was husky as she accepted a full glass from him. They drank, eyes meeting eyes over the top of their wine glasses. With his free hand, Robert slowly and gently trailed one long finger down her cheek, in an echo of that long-ago caress in the carriage. She felt the same thrill she had that day, yet somehow could not move, could not show him she liked it.

Then Robert took her hand and drew her down beside him on to the carpet in front of the fire. There they sat drinking wine and quietly talking. They discussed the wedding, and who had been there, and the wedding breakfast—a muted affair, considering the household was still in mourning—and the demeanour of the lawyer, who had officiously wished them well and congratulated them both.

Gradually, inevitably, Jane began to relax.

This is Robert! she reminded herself. *My Robert! I have nothing to fear from him.*

The cravat had been abandoned, and she found herself gazing hungrily at the line of his throat and that part of his strong chest now visible at the neck of his shirt.

He noticed, and she blushed.

'Jane,' he said softly. 'All will be well.'

Lifting her hand, he kissed the knuckles, then turned it over to kiss the palm. Jane gasped as desire instantly and unexpectedly flooded through her. He pressed her hand against his cheek.

Tentatively, and then with increasing confidence, she explored his beloved features—those high, arched brows, the strong cheekbones, the angle of his jaw—then moved her hand downwards. Her fingers gently traced the line of his neck all the way to his breastbone, where she delighted in the feel of the dark hair she had noticed earlier. He seemed to be holding his breath, but at this touch he inhaled raggedly, catching her hand and removing it, before setting down his glass and lifting both his hands to trace her face as she had traced his.

'Jane,' he murmured, 'you are so beautiful.'

Her heart hammered in her chest as his strong hands swept across her face and brow, gently stroking. His gaze dropped to her mouth and instinctively she leaned forward to meet him and claim the kiss she had been waiting for.

The kiss began softly, gently. Time stood still as she lost herself in him, in the flick of his tongue and his hands in her hair and his chest against hers… Now his hands were on her back, gently stroking, driving her to madness. She reciprocated, thrilling to the sensation of his firm back through the thin fabric of his shirt. His scent was all around her—a heady mix of shaving soap and Robert-ness.

She remained nervous, yet knew in her heart that Robert was not Henry.

They paused, both breathing raggedly.

'Jane,' he said, 'there is something I wish to ask you.'

He shuffled across to rest his back on one of the arm-chairs, keeping her cuddled within the arc of his left arm.

'I wish to tell you,' he murmured, 'that we do not need to consummate this marriage tonight. Given what you suffered when you were seventeen, I am determined to be slow and careful with you.'

A wave of emotion flooded through her.

'What a wife you have been saddled with! To prepare for disappointment on your wedding night? Outrageous!'

He sat up straight and tilted her chin so she had to look at him. 'I promise you I am very well satisfied, with both my wife and my wedding night. Why, just look at me! I am seated in comfort before an open fire, with a beautiful woman in my arms and all our lives ahead of us. We have no need to hurry these things.'

'Then—then it need not be tonight?' Abruptly, her last remaining nerves vanished, drowned in a wave of disappointment.

But I want this!

'It *will* not be tonight. This I promise you. Tonight we shall share yon bed and lie in each other's arms. I shall wear my shirt, you your nightgown, and we shall sleep like that for as many nights as is required for your fears to quieten.'

'Truly?' Her heart was soaring at his generosity, even as her mind was given over to thwarting his plan for restraint. 'But—but I was always given to believe that a man's needs could not be denied…particularly when—when temptation is present.'

'Ah. Well, as to that… My "needs", as you describe them, are strong indeed. You are the most bewitching woman I have ever beheld. But—' He took her hand. 'I am no animal. I must and shall practise self-discipline. To do otherwise would be to force you against your will, and that must never happen.' He grimaced. 'It will be a just punishment for the many misdeeds in my life.'

She shook her head in wonder. *What a husband I have!*

'And what if I were to tell you that I very much want this to happen tonight?' she asked.

'I should be delighted—if sceptical.' He eyed her keenly. 'It would require restraint from me, and honesty from you. Will you give me honesty?'

She nodded. 'Yes.' Her throat closed with emotion. 'Thank you.'

He smiled, and kissed her.

It took just two hours for the marriage between Robert Kendal and Jane Bailey to be consummated. Two delicious, sensuous, thrilling hours.

The groom had combined all his self-restraint with every seduction method in his arsenal, and the bride, when it finally happened, was entirely caught up in desire.

The monster inside her memory, it seemed, had made an exception for Robert.

'Perhaps it has gone completely,' Jane wondered aloud.

They had just come together for the third time in this long, wonderful night, and Jane was both pleasantly sore and in awe of the capabilities of the human body—male and female.

She rolled onto her front and propped herself on her elbow, her spare hand tracing his body from shoulder to chest to navel and back again.

He is so beautiful!

'In all honesty, tonight I care not! It matters only that it does not overtake you in this bed. *Our* bed.' His eyes devoured her firelit curves. 'This night was worth waiting for. All my life I have wished for a connection such as this. I have finally found it with you, my Jane, my wife.'

Jane stilled.

What is he saying? Can he love me a little already? Have courage. Ask him.

She opened her mouth to speak, but found a direct ques-

tion too much. Instead she murmured, 'Your wife, yes…
But a wife you were compelled to wed.'

His eyes narrowed. 'As I highlighted on the day you
agreed to marry me, we were both equally compelled.'

There was a sudden air of expectancy between them.

Jane looked directly into his eyes.

*I know he loves me. I feel it in his touch, see it in his
care of me. In the patient seduction he practised tonight.
The way he is looking at me this very instant. He tells me
with his eyes. With his body. But it is my responsibility to
make us both say the words. He has given me so much. This
I can give to him…*

Chapter Thirty-One

She took a breath, considering which approach to take. 'So, if we were both compelled, how can we ever know if we wished to marry regardless?'

This startled him, and then he laughed. 'Ah, Jane, your courage never fails to astound me. Here we both are, dancing around the edges, and then you take us both directly to the heart of the matter.'

His smile faded.

'I have sensed,' he began carefully, 'a certain affinity between us, which for me began the day you threw cake and tea all over me.'

'I did not!' she retorted hotly, sitting up. 'Not one drop nor one crumb came near you!'

He was laughing, and raised himself up to smack a quick kiss on her lips. 'Yet I could not fail to notice you. I remember hoping that if the mysterious Miss Bailey brought a maid to accompany her on the journey, that maid would be you.'

She smiled, recognising the sincerity in his eyes.

'And throughout the five days of our journey north I came to know you in a way I have never known anyone else. My uncle's strategy was a clever one.'

She arched a brow. 'But would that not have happened with any young woman you spent time with?'

'Well, no. I am an odd creature—as I am sure you have divined. Generally I prefer my own company, or spending time here with the family. For you not to irritate me even *once* during five long days was something of a miracle!'

His smile indicated that he was half jesting.

'For me to argue with landlords and drive farm carts

was, however, quite another matter. And when you were overcome in the market—forgive me if the memory distresses you—I was beside myself with worry and outrage. I must always, I believe, aid those in need of assistance, but that day I was driven by something much deeper, much more personal—although at that point I was not ready to look it in the eye.'

He sighed.

'Our idyll ended when we got here,' he continued. 'And yet I recall being anxious that you should love this place, and that the people here should love you. And this was *before* I knew you were a legitimate granddaughter.'

He frowned.

'My aunt was, I'm afraid, rather cold towards you at first. It made my blood boil to see it, but I admired your calm equanimity in the face of her rudeness. It spoke of good breeding, and strength of character—further reasons, if I needed any, to deepen my high regard for you.'

His eyes pinned hers.

'Your demeanour as I have been speaking gives me hope and encouragement, so I shall tell you the last. The evening of the soirée, when I saw you in your finery, I thought you had never looked more beautiful. Yet I had already seen beauty in the rosy cheeks of a serving maid and the courage of a woman determined to deliver a farmer safely home. But it was when you sang that I finally realised I was head over heels in love with you.'

In the silence that followed Jane thought her heart might explode, so great was her happiness. 'You did…? You are…?'

How stupid I must sound.

He nodded, a slight frown appearing as he awaited her response.

She smiled—a smile that built deep in her soul and then radiated out of every part of her.

Never has anyone experienced such perfect happiness.

He returned the smile, his containing relief as well as joy. 'So you love me?'

She nodded furiously, momentarily unable to speak.

'Then I shall ask you formally—something I did not do last month. Miss Jane Bailey, will you be my wife? Not because we must, but because I love you.'

She found her voice. 'Yes! Yes! And not because I must, but because I love you too.'

The kiss that followed was one that neither of them would ever forget.

And outside, on a perfect day, dawn was breaking. In the early-morning light a robin flew past, a twig in its beak. Spring was here and there was much to be done...

Epilogue

Mr and Mrs Kendal were, it was widely agreed, the most delightful young couple in the district. Following many years during which their house had been closed to parties and balls and picnics, local society was delighted to discover that the doors of Beechmount Hall had been opened once more.

Once the year of mourning for her grandfather was properly observed, young Mrs Kendal became the most engaging, the most welcoming, and the warmest hostess in the West Riding. She and her adoring husband were welcomed everywhere, and even after their children came along—first little Edward and then, two years later, his sister Marianne—the Kendals maintained their habit of warm hospitality.

Their musical nights, in particular, became well established in the local calendar, as Mrs Kendal—who was learning to play the piano—had the most delightful singing voice. Mr Kendal, it was noted, seemed happy and contented, and less serious than he had been as a younger man. He laughed often, adored his children, and was continuing to do an excellent job as master of Beechmount Hall.

The couple treated their servants and their tenants with great generosity, and were open about the fact that Mrs Kendal had herself spent some years in service, due to an estrangement in the family. Her mother, a retired housekeeper, lived in the east wing of Beechmount Hall, and had forged a firm friendship with Mr Kendal's mother.

Their friends Lord and Lady Kingswood, along with their children, came to visit at least once a year, and the

Kendals frequently returned the favour, visiting Ledbury House as often as they could manage.

On one such visit, well after midnight, Jane and Robert were lying in their dishevelled bed, satisfyingly tired after their recent exertions, when Jane was moved to comment on how strange it was.

'What do you mean?' asked Robert, idly caressing her shoulder, trailing his fingers gently down her arm and back again.

'Every time I come here I remember my life as a maid and how I would worry about my life.'

His forehead furrowed. 'What worries, my love?'

She gave a half-smile. 'At the heart of it I lacked constancy. I lost my papa, and my home, and then I was without a home again when we left Miss Marianne's so abruptly. I felt like—like a tree trying to root itself in quicksand.'

'How things have changed,' he murmured, leaning forward to kiss her softly. 'Beechmount Hall is rooted in granite, not sand.'

He trailed kisses along her cheek towards her ear, but she forestalled him by turning her head and capturing his mouth.

They kissed long and lingeringly, until she broke off to add, 'That is not what I have learned, though. It is not Beechmount Hall that has quieted my worries. It is you. And us. And the children. Yes, the place is important. But it is the thing between us that makes it home.'

'Love?' he said gently.

She nodded. 'Love.'

* * * * *

If you enjoyed this book, why not check out
these other great reads by
Catherine Tinley

The Earl's Runaway Governess

And be sure to read
The Chadcombe Marriage series

Waltzing with the Earl
The Captain's Disgraced Lady
The Makings of a Lady